CONTENTS

Foreword
Preface
Ghosts of a Coven Past   4
Limited Bibliography   217
Musical Suggestions: 219
Afterword   222
About The Author   224
Books By This Author   226
READ ON FOR AN INTRODUCTION TO THE GHOST   232
HUNTER SERIES

FOREWORD

I hope you like this book. A combination of real-life events inspired the story and the character. Visit my website to read about them at:
https://peterjwhite.weebly.com/the-hollow-men.html

If you liked the book, please leave a reivew on Amazon. We indies rely on people like you to get the word out. Thank you!

Sign up for the Ghost Hunter Newsletter at
https://peterjwhite.weebly.com/news.html
to get the second book in the Ghost Hunter series: *Slouching Towards Tenancingo* for **FREE.** (And to be apprised of approaching publication dates, character info, interesting links and stories related to the series as well as free short stories and other bonuses. It's a win-win situation here. And how often do those come along? Go for it!)

To learn more about the five books in the Ghost Hunter series (number six is in progress) and other titles by the author, go to PeterJWhite.Weebly.com.

Other Books in the Ghost Hunter Series:

Ghost Hunter: The Hollow Men

Ghost Hunter: Slouching Toward Tenancingo

Ghost Hunter: Bangkok Redemption

Ghost Hunter: The Bad Beginning (prequel)

Ghost Hunter: What Lies Beneath

Horror

Ghosts of a Coven Past: A Tale of Witchcraft, Spirits, Satanism, and Possession

PREFACE

I originally wrote this book as a housewarming gift. The quote attributed to Roger Nimanator inspired both the creation and the content. My apologies for a failure to include a mycelial network. Next time...

It's one of my favorite pieces. I'd say great art is inspired by great friendship, but that'd be calling this great art...

Ghosts of a Coven Past:

A Tale of Witchcraft, Spirits, Satanism, and Possession

By Peter J White

To Ryan C Niman, the second kind of friend

The second kind of friend...helps us to do and become what we want to, according to your own assessment of our possibilities. They refrain from projecting their own desires onto us, instead choosing to play an important (and often more difficult) supporting role.

—

Martin Heidegger (1962). *Being and Time.* Translated by John Macquarrie & Edward Robinson. London: SCM Press.

"So this Friday we're meeting to discuss Squid Game. Err, Lovecraft Country. And anything else gothic/Halloween-y that you may have read/watched. And I can tell you about the 1885 townhouse we are buying which, if the books we've been reading recently are any guide, is probably haunted, infested by paranormal mycelium, has some sort of undead body in the basement, or was the site of a secret society ritual gone wrong. Or some combination thereof. Perhaps tomorrow's inspection will tell us which."
—Roger Nimanator

"You unlock this door with the key of imagination. Beyond it is another dimension: a dimension of sound, a dimension of sight, a dimension of mind. You're moving into a land of both shadow and substance, of things and ideas. You've just crossed over into... the Twilight Zone."
—Rod Serling

GHOSTS OF A COVEN PAST

Roger Nimanator was a thoughtful, studious man with a mind uncluttered by dogma, an open door to a lot of things: ideas, suggestion, debate, investigation, research, cultures.

Life.

The other side.

That's where the trouble started. As Rod Serling alluded, there is a doorway to the other side, and it's there for anyone to access. It just takes a certain level of…openness.

The Nimanators were a globetrotting family with a habit of settling in old neighborhoods.

In Asia—and Israel—that meant places populated for thousands of years. Not centuries, but millennia. Populated centers with millions of people. For millennia.

That adds up to a lot of people.

A lot of people who died.

Odds are, given those kinds of numbers, a lot of those people died unexpectedly. Unprepared.

They are the ones that get stuck. The ones that don't make it over, glued to a hinterland between this world and the next.

It was in Korea the spirits found the door Serling alludes to and came tumbling in.

Not in a way Roger noticed at first, though.

Life in Seoul was pleasant, if mildly boring. Plenty of history, but the twins were young and active enough to make it brutal to watch over them for any length of time. Exhausting.

Holly, his wife, had fled part-time back into academia, on loan from the FBI to The University of Seoul in an exchange program. This led to a certain low-level of paranoia; after all, South Korea is adjacent to one of the craziest anti-American governments on the planet. A Fed—at a university, no less—raised more than a few eyebrows. Surveillance was not a question mark.

So the adults in the family walked with an extra bit of self-awareness at all times.

Which was exhausting, too.

What little time Roger did have, he busied himself in his academic interests. He dug into the history of the area a bit, then waxed philosophical, going through a long period of Karl Popper and then a touch of Heidegger's take on Nietzsche, with his long, windy passages that went on for pages. And pages. And pages.

Roger skimmed through it. He liked what Heidegger had to say, but often thought each four-six page lecture could've been boiled down to its title.

As he was reading through Heidegger's view of Nietzsche's take on nihilism, his eyes started to bother him. Little black flickerings off to the periphery.

He reached up for the lamp and adjusted it to better hit the page.

The text jumped up at him, clear as could be for a thirty-year-old paperback.

But still, the flitting, just off the edge of his peripheral vision.

Not getting enough sleep. The twins.

A warm smile filled his being as he thought of them.

Frick and Frack, he thought. Those are some busy little boys.

The boys, just a nudge over two, had somehow conspired to cook that morning. They'd discovered the flour, and when Holly stumbled into the kitchen, bleary-eyed and sleep-deprived at 5:30 AM to fumble around for the coffee she'd preprogrammed to steep the night before, she was greeted with a blurry blare of white, all the lights in the kitchen blazing, flour everywhere, even caked up on the top of the twin's hairy little heads.

Especially on those furry little brows.

Her screams had brought Roger running from the bedroom.

He smiled at the memory—far enough away now that the initial trauma had faded to amusement.

A wave of cold ran through the room, and Roger frowned.

Usually too hot in here. What the hell? Did the twins get a window open?

The thought had him out of his chair and into the twin's room within the space of a half-dozen rapidly increasing heartbeats.

They were in their room, a bed against the wall on each side, both snarled into tight little balls of sheets and covers.

The little animals, Roger thought. *A bitch making those beds in the morning.*

A wave of love ran through him and carried him into the middle of the room where his head drifted from side to side, looking from one to the other.

He folded his legs underneath him and sat in the middle of the room, a familiar posture. He reached out a hand to each side and rested each on a hot little back, the rhythm of the twins' breathing deeply satisfying.

He glanced up at the window.

Impossible for them to open, the latch at the top way out of reach, and taped down with duct tape.

Thoughts of shadowy figures flitting at the edges of his vision passed, as did the memory of the sudden, unnatural cold that had propelled him from his chair.

He unfolded his legs, got to his feet, then stooped over each little body, kissed the sheet in a place as close to a furry little head as he could figure, then left the room and closed the door behind him.

His open volume of Heidegger called, but the bed called louder, and he switched off the reading lamp and made his way through the darkened apartment to his bedroom.

Holly was a sound sleeper, but he knew better than to turn on a light, so he used his phone, the latest phone Apple had made, preordered and immediately screen protected with quality glass, to light the way to his side of the bed.

He was asleep before he'd even fully got the covers over him.

The next morning he'd forgotten all about the peripheral phantoms and puzzlingly disturbing blast of cold air.

And he had never noticed the pocket of cold that had gathered by the side of his bed—icy, translucent waves shimmering in the dim light, gathering into something vaguely human-shaped.

Korea passed in a fog of fatigue and joy. The twins grew, acquired speech and voracious appetites for learning, and Roger was hard-pressed to keep up. Holly's term came to an end, and the bureau decided a little town north of Jerusalem was the next place for her to be. Another exchange. In yet another country with extraordinary levels of surveillance and political complications.

So much for dropping the now-unconscious level of vigilance.

Which, Roger figured later, likely had something to do with the trouble.

An ever-vigilant mind must be controlled, after all, or it'll take over, begin to color things the way the intrinsically paranoid mindset was inclined.

Sleep deprivation didn't help, either.

The twins demanded an astonishingly intense level of attention, and each had discovered the magic of alone time by rising when the other slept for a few hours of frolic and adventure. Roger was tired. Holly was exhausted. The twins thrived.

On a rare night with both kids snoozing at the same time, Roger sat in his reading chair with a volume of Karl Popper, *The Open Society and Its Enemies,* in his lap. Popper's thought on open societies, tolerance and intolerance seemed apropos for the times. The past week had seen thousands of missiles launched by the Hamas into Israel, and the family had taken shelter one day for hours in the bathroom, the high screech of missiles overhead, the thunder of the missiles exploding harmlessly in the sky as the Israeli defense system shot them down. Or most of them.

Enough had found their way in that the Israeli population was stirred up, crowds running riot, hunting down scapegoats in their communities, breaking into Palestinian apartments and dragging people out to beat senseless.

Roger's head dipped as fatigue had its way with him. He caught himself, sat straight in his chair and tried to focus.

Popper was putting him to sleep. Again.

He sighed, closed the book, and lay it on the table next to him to join the stack he was working his way through.

He leaned back, sleep drifting up to almost claim him, and in that middle ground between sleep and wakefulness his mind cracked open.

And the spirits found their way in.

Roger barely registered their flitting on his periphery anymore. Back in Korea, he had finally sought out an ophthalmologist who'd diagnosed ocular migraines. The doc's prescription had been more sleep and less screen time.

Both impossible. The twins conspired to leave him maybe four hours of sleep a night, and the side job he'd picked up, editing for a variety of publications put out in support of the Palestinians made for lots of screen time.

And so, he had learned to put up with the shadowy beings that lurked just out of sight.

A small part of him rebelled against the diagnosis: these things that danced around just out of sight had a presence. They were more than fatigued synapses flaring, more than tired rods and cones misfiring, more than tiny electrical storms of the occipital lobe.

And while Roger believed it was possible, theoretically, for spirits to exist, his solid, pragmatic nature demanded something more solid than myth and folklore for evidence. The idea that these flittings were spirits caught between this world and the next never occurred to him.

Not on a conscious level, anyway.

As his mind disengaged from the physical world, a

shimmering off to one side of the room coalesced. Roger watched it out of the corner of a half-closed eye, in a sleepy, dreamy state where critical thought fell away and observation replaced it.

The shape darkened, took form.

A pocket of intense cold wafted through the room and settled on him. The paralysis of rapidly approaching sleep prevented him from pulling the blanket on his lap up, and he shivered, mind idly taking in the cold, while something deep in his soul sounded a faint alarm.

The cold felt personal. Malevolent.

He shivered again and reached to pull up the blanket, but his limbs refused the command.

The shape tightened, the outline distinctly human now, female. A glowing trail of mist stretched from the woman's core to the knot of cold surrounding him. Fingers of mist reached for his chest, penetrated, scrabbled for his core.

Something scraped across the tissues of his heart, a cold scratching that hurt in a way Roger had never experienced.

Panic exploded through his system, set his heart racing, pulse pounding in his temples and Roger found himself in a death struggle with an entity determined to worm its way into his soul, icy fingers grasping for the essence of his being.

Roger fought it as best he could. It was like awakening to find oneself in the depths of an ocean, the surface barely visible far above, the faintest glimmer of light reaching through the murky waters promising air and light.

Roger fought for the light, chest heaving, sense of suffocation and claustrophobia debilitating. The harder he fought, limbs thrashing, the farther the surface seemed. The cold fingers now had a grip on his heart, and he knew the cold was about to take him, drag him to the other side...

Other side of what?

Roger came to, chest heaving, and found himself in the middle of the room, blanket a puddle at the foot of his reading chair, reading light casting a golden glow across the room.

Holy crap. What the hell was that?

His rational mind seized on the events, ticking off the symptoms of a somnambulant state.

Just a dream.

But holy hell. That felt so real.

His heart was pounding against his ribs hard enough to hurt, and Roger took a few shaky breaths and got control. Slowed his heart.

He shook his head, bemused at himself.

Something about the unrest, maybe. The spirit of malevolence working its way through the land. Somehow, my mind gave it shape. Brought it into my home.

Satisfied with his explanation for the event, Roger padded over to his reading chair, picked up the blanket, folded it, set it on his chair, flicked off the reading light, and found his way into his bedroom.

He collapsed into bed, sleep rushing up to take him.

Yet a part of him, a kernel at the center of his soul, still pulsed with alarm—an atavistic awareness of a breach between this world and the next, an understanding of the peril to his soul he had barely escaped.

His dreams were troubled, suffused with a sense of suffocation and cold, and he awoke the next day exhausted, the events of the night before dim and insubstantial, but the small knot of panic deep within still there, a strong sense that the world as he knew it was about to change in ways that he'd rather it didn't.

The foreboding never completely left him, and it fueled the family decision to leave Israel and return to the States. The twins were in kindergarten now, and Roger was dissatisfied with the education they were receiving, the boys so far ahead of the others that their boredom drove them to a series of pranks and outright disobedience that made for more parent-teacher meetings than Roger thought possible.

Holly's tenure at the university was coming to an end, and she was ready for a change. And she was worried about Roger.

Roger had put away Popper after that night, developed an interest in the mystical, working his way through *The Golden Bough*, Huxley's *Doors of Perception*, and some of the more recondite writings of T. S. Eliot. He picked up the Bible and read it cover to cover.

He also read a lot of ghost stories. Lovecraft and Poe at first, then a long foray into the murky depths of the internet: ghost hunters, "true" ghost stories, and the like. He discovered all the streaming services had series on the paranormal: Netflix, Prime, Hulu all with offerings targeted to the credulous.

Roger was far from credulous, but he was open. With a driving curiosity fueled by the weird things happening inside his own head.

And something else.

Each story added fuel to the small knot of panic that throbbed deep within. The flittings on the periphery of his vision came and went, as did the cold, and each time the cold reached for him, his sense of impending doom deepened. He found himself distracted, a part of him vigilant, unresting, scanning for...

What?

That was the problem. The threat was inchoate, and so silly that he refused to even to try to articulate it.

But the more he avoided it, the stronger the feeling grew, and Roger began to worry about his sanity.

The twins were his center of joy, but he found himself snapping at them more frequently. At times, the boys watched him with eyes wide, little foreheads furrowed with worry. They sensed something awry, but like Roger, had no words for it.

The sense of foreboding grew, and sudden noises startled Roger into a low-level panic. He began biting his nails, his fingertips taking on a reddened, chewed look. His eyes no longer reflected the inner calm that was his natural state, but darted from corner to corner, the feeling of a building threat just out of sight never leaving him.

He took up running again, leaving the house for hours at a

time, jogging down the streets and overpasses, putting in miles and miles, and always with a sense of something just at his heels, coming for him. As his body strengthened and thrived, his nerves never settled. When sleep came, it brought with it the cold and suffocation, and he awoke each day more tired than the last.

Finally, Holly had had enough.

They'd put away enough money living overseas, rent and daily expenses taken care of by the Bureau, that Holly could take a couple of years off. If she wanted. They sold the house they'd been renting out in Seattle for an astonishing sum, the housing market there in the midst of another bubble.

Holly had family in Pennsylvania, and she liked the idea of moving closer to them. Someone to help with the twins. Give Roger a break.

Because Roger was breaking.

They bought a brownstone in Allentown, all the touring and arrangements done over the internet. Another old neighborhood. A beautiful home filled with gleaming hardwood. Four bedrooms, two baths, an oriel jutting out over the street. A park nearby for the twins to play in. Less than a hundred miles from New York City.

Roger busied himself with the move. Under duress from Holly, he'd visited a shrink—an M.D., of course—and the doc had prescribed a round of Lorazepam for his nerves. Roger wasn't convinced his troubles were physical, but found the Lorazepam soothing, if soporific. His startle response lessened, and he stopped snapping at the twins.

Worth it.

Probably.

And yet, a tiny voice at the center of his soul protested. The drug hadn't done away with the niggle of panic at his center, just layered it over with a fog that dampened its noise.

There was something dangerous in that, and Roger found himself gazing at the little white pill he took three times each day, inner debate raging. Trading calm for vigilance. Blinding him to the dangers he felt sure were out there, looming.

But he took the pills.

The Nimanators found Allentown an upscale family friendly city, where, according to the U.S. News & World Report, "A quiet architectural renaissance has blossomed in Pennsylvania's third-largest metro area."

They placed the twins in a gifted program, a co-op that demanded a fair amount of parental involvement, and the twins' pranks and disregard of authority lessened.

There were still a lot of parent-teacher meetings.

With the twins in school, and Roger busy with his own academic interests, Holly grew bored and applied for a position with the nearest field office the bureau had: Pittsburgh, just over an hour away. Her expertise lay in human trafficking, and there was plenty of that along the eastern seaboard. The Bureau welcomed her back.

Roger found himself with more alone time than he'd had since the twins came along.

He slept better.

Living back in the States, the need for vigilance should have lessened, but Roger's part-time work in Israel had drawn attention: he'd been the editor for a Palestinian organization that put out a newsletter and published in academia. The Israelis had placed the organization on their list of terrorist organizations, and so Roger's name had entered the system.

Mostly, Roger found that amusing.

Holly did not. She'd argued they needed to challenge this, point out the benevolent nature of the organization, but Roger had convinced her to let sleeping dogs lie.

After all, they were back in the States now. Where no one cared about the Palestinians, or the Israelis, or the whole mess in the Middle East.

He put the situation out of mind, but when he was working online and there'd be a jitter, a stutter of the flow of data, part of his mind wondered if someone, somewhere, was monitoring his internet traffic.

The house itself was a joy. Built in 1885, it'd been thoroughly modernized and remodeled with a gleaming kitchen filled with the latest gadgets and stainless steel appliances, more electrical outlets than you could shake a stick at, and high-speed internet. All of the hardwood had been refinished and polished until it gleamed.

Roger loved the house.

The basement though…

Nearly a hundred and fifty years of progress hadn't made much of a dent. The old coal furnace sat rusting in a corner, the brand new gas one on the other side of the room. The cinderblock walls were black with age and soot, the floor a set of uneven cement blocks set into the dirt, the ground underneath pushing the blocks into a treacherous series of little edges just high enough to catch an unwary toe and send one sprawling.

None of that bothered Roger, particularly.

The cold did.

The unfinished basement was a pool of musty, cold air with an edge that stood the hair up on the back of Roger's neck.

The cold had a presence. One that the dim, unconscious part of his mind connected to the phenomena that had plagued him in Korea and Israel.

He pushed it out of mind, mostly, and avoided the basement. The twins were forbidden access and he installed a solid hasp and padlock on the door to be sure they stayed away.

Pounding. Something shaking the foundations of the house, the whole house reverberating: windows and doors rattling, chinaware tinkling, silverware clattering.

Roger drifted just below consciousness, the sound waves running through him, informing the shadowy visions of a dream.

Underwater. Surface far above. A barely discernable light.
Suffocating.

Something down here with me.

An icy cold penetrated his being, fingers of ice scratching at the fibers of his soul.

Pounding. Like a giant fist hammering at the gate of a huge door.

Roger's nose twitched.

Smoke. Wood smoke mixed with something foul, rotten.

A clamoring. No, chants. A mix of voices, something ritualistic in the tones and cadence, rising and falling in volume and pitch.

A long, drawn-out scream that penetrated Roger's temples, drove an icy pick into his brain.

Roger thrashed in his bed, arms flailing as he swam for the surface, the icy thing down there with him a translucent blue-green, reaching for him…

He reached the surface, burst through, gasping for air.

And found himself sitting upright in bed, Holly asleep at his side, mouth open, a tiny trail of drool edging its way down her cheek. A gentle snore.

The room was frigid: Roger's breath filled it with clouds of vapor.

The still, quiet at the center of his soul contracted, a panic building.

The presence. Something here…

Roger blinked, heart hammering his ribs. The cold penetrated to the marrow of his bones, reached for his heart.

Roger swung his legs over the side of the bed and stopped, suddenly loathe to let the bare skin of his feet touch the cold wooden floor.

The floor glistened.

Frost?

His slippers sat lined up neatly by the bed, and he stretched a foot out, snagged them with his toes and slid them close enough to slip into.

Something wrong with the furnace. That was the pounding. Gas heated water running through the pipes. Cooling. The pounding the stress on the plumbing from the changing temperatures…worked its way into my dreams, that's all.

He stood and made his way to the door.

He reached for the door handle, then stopped, some inner part of him sounding the alarm.

Don't open the door. Someone there, standing on the other side.

The hair stood up on the back of his neck and he shivered, raised a hand and tried to smooth down the hairs.

Don't be ridiculous. You've been reading too much of this ghost shit. It's gotten into your head, that's all.

His hand found the knob and a shock of cold ran up his arm, made a beeline for his heart.

He wrenched the door open, the cold so intense it lit the marrow of the bones of his hand and arm with a shockingly intense burst of fiery pain.

A frosty mist like smoke drifted up the stairs from below, obscuring the steps and stairwell.

Roger reached for his bathrobe on a hook on the back of the door, shrugged into it and stepped into the hallway, shivering.

What the actual hell?

He took a step forward and stopped.

Don't go down.

Someone there.

No. Something there. Something ancient. Malevolent.

He shook his head to clear it, but the mist and the cold and the sense of doom only deepened.

Roger forced himself into the hallway and began descending the steps.

The wooden steps were slick with frost, and he reached a steadying hand to the banister.

Another shock of cold ran through him, raced for his heart, and he snatched his hand away, teetered, and nearly fell.

The furnace. That's all. Pilot light must've blown out.

He descended into the frosty mist, cold deepening with every step. He belted the robe around him, but the cold was more than physical.

That presence. Again. The cold an actual entity. Aware. Seeking. Hungry.

He shook the thought away, and step by painful step, made his way to the kitchen on the ground floor.

He stopped at the threshold in shock.

The door to the basement stood open, a black mouth oozing mist into the house.

What? How?

The padlock lay open on the floor.

Roger forced himself into the kitchen, fumbled for the cabinet to one side of the sink, and pulled down the big black flashlight there: four double-D batteries gave the flashlight a heft that was comforting.

He flicked it on and shone it into the gaping mouth of the door.

The light stopped at the door, failed to penetrate the misty gloom rolling in from the basement.

Just normal cold, Roger told himself. *The pilot blew out. Basement subterranean. Frost and cold normal for this time of year.*

He fought against the clamoring niggle of panic at the center of his soul and stepped toward the gaping door, made his way to the head of the stairs.

Don't go down there.

He shook his head, irritated.

Nonsense. Your imagination playing tricks. Just go down there, get the fucking pilot light lit, get some heat flowing. The twins will freeze in their beds if you don't do something.

He stepped across the threshold.

The old wooden stairs were slick as ice, a gleaming layer of frost covering them, the cold reaching through his slippers to travel up the bone marrow, an icy pain that startled him with its intensity.

Get moving.

He fought his way down the stairs, each step an effort, like wading into the ocean against an oncoming tide.

Each step brought him deeper into the icy mist, the cold a living fire.

His nose twitched: *smoke. Something foul burning.*

Shapes appeared in the mist, shadowy figures below in a circle swimming through the fog emanating from the cold concrete floor and walls.

Nonsense. Just your mind playing tricks with the shadows and mist.

Just below the level of consciousness, the chanting. Again.

Is that Latin?

He shook his head.

The flashlight trembled in his hand, the bulb dimmed.

No.

His feet found the cold stone floor and he felt his way across the basement, the dim light of the flashlight only serving to carve edges out of the fog, to delineate the shadowy forms... *dancing?*

OK. Furnace in the corner. Just to one side of the stairs.

But that means turning my back...

Everything in him fought to race back up the stairs, grab Holly and the twins and get the fuck out.

Something is really, really wrong here. Something very bad.

He turned his back on the capering shapes in the fog and found the furnace.

He squatted down and reached for the tall narrow box of fireplace matches he kept to one side of the furnace.

He set the flashlight down on a concrete paver, its dim light barely reaching the wall beaded with moisture rapidly icing up two feet away.

Something behind me...

He spun around and the mist closed in on him, ice reaching all the way in.

A face appeared, oblong and distorted, mouth stretched vertically in a long narrow slit, eyes like stretched eggs, a malevolent yellow-red glow in their center.

Almost on me...

His hands found a match and he yanked the long stick of wood out of the box, struck the sulphurous tip against the grain of the charcoal bottom and the match flared, impossibly bright, blinding him.

He cried out as the face grew an arm, reached for him, then snatched its hand away as the flame of the match flared.

The fog retreated, solidifying into a knot of figures in a circle at the center of the room.

Light the pilot. Drive the cold away.

The match had burned down halfway, and Roger fumbled and turned the knob to the gas partway, depressed it, counted a slow one-two-three, then set the match to the little nozzle for the pilot light.

The pilot took and the furnace came to life with a roar that drove Roger back on his butt.

The flashlight brightened, fully lit now, its glare reflecting off the frosty surface of the walls.

As Roger watched, the frost melted, water ran down the walls in trickles and formed puddles at the edges of the wall.

Roger closed the door to the furnace and turned.

The mist was gone. The shadowy figure melted away with the frost.

But most importantly, the presence had fled.

What the holy hell was that?

Roger took a shaky breath and climbed to his feet. His heart calmed as the cold receded.

The furnace creaked and rattled as the heat of the flames expanded the metal and Roger heard the pipes throughout the house knocking as heated water flowed through them.

Pilot blew out. That's all. It happens. Pennsylvania is cold at this time of year.

But the still, quiet part of his soul protested, the niggle of panic there no longer a niggle, but a throbbing knot threatening to overwhelm him.

Roger took a couple of long, slow breaths to calm himself, willed his pounding heart to settle.

Whatever the hell that was, it's gone now.

He looked down at the tall narrow cardboard box of matches in his hand.

Mother Mary's face smiled up at him, and he startled.

Her eyes alight with consciousness.

Her lips turned up in a smile.

Roger set the box hastily back in place, retrieved the flashlight from the floor and shone it around the basement.

Just a basement, edges of the uneven concrete pavers catching the light.

Frost all melted away now.

Roger sniffed.

Just the faintest hint of smoke. Something foul. Like a dead rat putrefying and set on fire.

Roger made his way to the steps and climbed out of the basement and into the kitchen.

The flashlight gleamed off the ridged silver of the padlock, and Roger stooped to pick it up off the floor.

House reverberating from the furnace, must've somehow rattled the lock out of the hasp. Must've left it open.

He turned and shut the door to the basement, set the lock back into place and clicked it closed.

He pulled on it, hard, testing it.

That's not going to come loose again.

He started at the lock a long moment, the faint niggle of panic at his center tickling his nerves, then turned, put the flashlight back in place and climbed the stairs to go back to bed.

Just a dream.

Nothing more.

Roger woke the next morning with a single, driving thought: *There's something here.*

The cold niggle of panic at his center had taken over a substantial portion of mental hardware and its support system, and he recognized he wasn't thinking entirely straight, but he was done brushing away the warnings.

It was time to get this shit figured out.

Up to now, his foray into the paranormal and the world of spirits had been desultory: dipping here and there without aim, intellectual window-shopping, really.

But he had picked up some common threads. About openings between this world and the next. Theories of cause and effect, from the conspiratorially-minded to the pseudo-scientists that rule the underside of the internet.

One thing all sides agreed on: history was important. These spirits had to come from somewhere, after all.

Just a question of doing the research. Historical records, police records, newspapers, building permits and city and county records.

Could do this sleepwalking from my den.

When he hit the kitchen, Holly had already left, and the kitchen had the freshly-wiped down scent touched with just a trace of her perfume.

Just missed her. Dammit.

She'd never awakened last night, so far as he could tell, nor had the kids. His little adventure the previous evening had been a private one, apparently.

The twins were up, fighting in the bathroom.

"Give me the good towel!"

"I got it first!"

The sound of a water glass tinkling over and dancing across the counter had Roger in the room in time to catch it before it rolled off the counter and hit the tile floor.

"What's the problem here?"

"Timmy took the good towel, but it's mine!"

"It's not yours! And I got to it first."

Tommy got a hand on the towel and yanked, but Timmy was ready for it, and used the momentum of the yank to slam his chest into Tommy's and then snatch the towel back when Tommy stumbled back.

Roger shot out a hand to catch Tommy and glared at Timmy.

"Hey! That was uncalled for!"

Good move though, the kid's got solid instincts.

"You apologize to your brother. And just for that give him the fucking towel!"

The twins' eyes widened.

"You dropped the F-bomb!" Timmy shrieked.

The two collapsed into laughter, literally rolling on the floor.

The spark of rage that had briefly gotten a hold of him fled at the sound of the laughter bouncing off the bathroom walls.

"All, right. God damn it, you two. Stop laughing."

"G-g-g-goddammitttt...." Timmy giggled.

The two howled again and Roger sighed and bent down to pick up the towel.

"All right, you two clowns. Get dressed. We're leaving in ten minutes."

He left the boys snickering to one another as they climbed to their feet and headed for their room.

There was space for the boys to each have his own room, but they'd been firm: not interested.

Holly had argued with Roger that the healthiest thing to do was to force them into separate rooms. They were becoming too interdependent, she thought. It was time for them to individuate. Develop personal identities.

"They're six years old," he had said. "Give them time," he'd sighed. "After all, the school system ought to beat that out of them soon enough."

There'd been some heated discussion re. educational philosophy, but Holly let it lie this time. And she allowed them to share a room.

Just until second grade, though, she'd said.

For now, the Co-Op would do. At least they got a first-hand look at curriculum. And were able to supplement as best they could.

Outside, the cold, crisp air shaped clouds out of their breath as they tromped down the sidewalk together.

The sidewalk was a double-wide: two squares of cement set side by side with enough trim to fill to the curb. About every six concrete blocks or so, ground had been ceded for a tree, and the trees, shorn of all signs of life, marched up the street on both sides, in both directions, spindly arms reaching for the gray sky and to the sides of the buildings that lined the street.

Steel grates at sidewalk level on each rowhouse covered basement windows, and Roger shivered and pulled his jacket tighter around himself.

"What's with you Bags?" Timmy said. He'd recently taken to calling Roger that, had a habit of creating nicknames for people.

Roger shook his head, looked both ways, then led the twins across the sidewalk, a lane of red bricks set between long narrow borders of concrete set into the asphalt.

Such a picturesque little neighborhood, Roger thought, *but with two hundred years of inhabitation, lots of opportunity for murder and mayhem. Ghost-making stuff. Spirits.*

He shook his head again, irritated.

Are you really entertaining this, Roger? Seriously? Should we check vampire lore as well? Werewolves? Witches?

Well, witches, yes, actually. That chanting was in Latin—I think.

Oops, that means check into Satanists, as well.

Holy fuck.

"Dad!" Timmy tugged on his hand. "We're here!"

Roger looked up, startled.

Walked six blocks and didn't notice a thing. Damn.

Tommy stood halfway up the walk to the school, thumbs hooked under the straps of his backpack, watching. Impassive, with just a slight twist of concern to his lips.

Roger waved at him and smiled.

"Have a good day, Tommy!"

Tommy nodded, turned, and headed for the building.

"I better catch up," Timmy said.

He looked up into Roger's eyes.

"Are you really OK, dad?" he said.

Roger hugged him tight.

"You bet, buddy. Just tired, that's all. Didn't sleep much last night."

He released the boy and gave him a pat.

"Better catch up with your brother," he said.

Timmy glanced at his dad, concern still there, but then smiled and turned and dashed after his brother, taking the six long, low concrete steps in two bounds to hit the platform and dart through the right-side steel and glass door of the twin doors leading into the building.

Roger watched the steel mouth of the door close behind him and looked up at the two-story brick and concrete building. The long, low building stretched along an enormous block and faced, across a median with trees that had to be a hundred years old, also dead-looking, a neighborhood of long, low ramblers. A residential neighborhood. Of course.

So little history, really, when you think about it, Roger thought. *Nothing like Israel. Still, that school was built in 1920. It's a hundred years old.*

He shrugged to himself and turned around, headed for home.

Then again, who's to say? How many natives passed through this land, over the millennia?

He filed that one away for future research, then turned his attention to the search ahead.

Start with newspapers. Everything I can get that's online. Go back as far as I can with that. Make a list of incidents, groups, gossip, etc. anything suggesting an event that might lead to...

An image of the stretched-out face with its molten yellow eyes flashed in his mind and Roger startled.

He glanced around to make sure no one had noticed, then put his head down and focused on the walk.

I'm getting to the bottom of this. And putting it to rest.
Somehow.

Two hours later, he sat at his command console in the den. Beautiful, mahogany shelves inset into the walls housed his collection of books, filling three walls of the den. He had bought a mahogany desk, a behemoth of a thing, with an eye to matching the wood of the shelves.

It was perfect. Almost. The desk a slightly darker shade than the shelves, but Roger felt the color paired nicely.

He gazed up at the books, mind ticking over what he had uncovered.

House built in 1885. But I knew that when we bought it.

The town itself had been established by William Allen, a Chief Justice of Colonial Pennsylvania's Supreme Court. Allen, also a former Mayor of Philadelphia and successful businessman, hoped to create a commercial center, and planned the town to lie along the Lehigh River. The low water level most of the year, however, made river trade impractical. And so Allentown had remained a quiet little village of Pennsylvania Dutch farmers until the 1830s with the arrival of the Lehigh Canal and then the railroad. By the 1850s the iron industry had taken hold and the expansion of the railroad provided a steady market for the iron. By the end of the Civil War, the town had grown under the influx of a German and Irish workers to a major city.

Until the collapse of the railroad boom and the ensuing Panic of 1873 had sent the economy into a tailspin that lasted nearly a decade. Iron furnaces closed shop and that was the end of iron in Allentown. Eventually, the town recovered, finding itself with a flurry of local industry: silk mills, furniture factories, breweries and cigar manufacturers, among other things.

Yeah, yeah. So what.

More interesting, had been his research into the supernatural.

As it turned out, Pennsylvania had been a hotbed of activity from the beginning. Folk magic and witchcraft were woven throughout the history of the state. Only the prudent management of William Penn himself had prevented a tragedy on the scale of the Salem Witch Trials.

But the witches were here.
Are here?
Interesting. But how is that helpful? Witches? Really?
Roger leaned back in his chair and rubbed his face.
Exhausted. Chasing rabbits down holes. Witchcraft. Shit.
He closed his eyes.
But the chanting. The fog. The cold. And that face…
What else could it be?
He snorted.
Your imagination? Hello?

But the cold niggle of panic at his center refused to accept that. The rational part of his mind, still dominant, could yammer all it wanted, raise a thousand objections, mold an iron-clad case, but that still small center at his soul would not be swayed.

It knew.

Whatever happened here happened a long time ago. Even if witchcraft is somehow involved in whatever the fuck happened down there, now it's more of a haunting.

He shook his head.

Listen to yourself.

But what about Korea? Israel? All that shit flitting at the edges of your vision? The woman in Israel scrabbling for my heart? What explains that?

Ocular migraines combined with a somnambulant state. The random firing of synapses enlivened by imagery from my reading. All that Gothic shit. Lovecraft. Shirley Jackson. Walpole. Blackwood. Mary Shelley. Colored my mind.

Doesn't explain the fog. Or the cold.

How about a pilot light gone out? Subterranean basement in the cold of a Pennsylvania winter?

What about the hasp? The open padlock?

Vibration. Pipes were clanging with temperature change. The whole house shook, remember?

The face?

The flare of the match reflecting off the fog in the basement.

Wait. Didn't the face appear before you struck the match?

He couldn't remember now. The events of the evening before had taken on a dreamlike cast and the ongoing argument between his rational self and that still small center now overloaded with a low-level electric panic that muddled the memory.

Something happened, goddamn it.

Mother Mary on the box—the matches left over from a previous resident. Meant for lighting votive candles. Catholic.

Roger opened his eyes stood up.

Enough of this nonsense for now.

His computer monitor, a 32" curved HD screen, filled with the face from the night before: stretched vertically into a slit of a face with narrow gaping mouth and yellow eyes, a frosty nimbus of gray hair filling the screen.

Roger startled, bolting to his feet and sending his chair scooting across the room on its little wheels to crash into the doorjamb.

He glanced at the chair, then back at the screen.

Just the open windows of his research: a Wikipedia page on witchcraft, another on the history of Allentown, email.

What the actual hell?

He glanced at his watch.

Shit. Haven't eaten today and it's noon. Just hungry, that's all. Imagination playing tricks.

Go get something to eat.

But he was loathe to turn his back on the screen, that still small center in his soul on full alert, insisting there was danger there.

Don't be an idiot. Go get some lunch.

He pushed the yammering panic away, turned his back on the screen, and made for the door. As he stepped over the threshold, a cackle issued from the speakers on either side of the monitor, filling the room with an unearthly, evil glee.

Roger spun around, hands up, heart hammering his chest.

The monitor sat placidly on the desk, the same three windows open.

Roger backed out of the room into the hallway and made for the stairs. The muscles in his back clenched as if expecting a blow.

Nonsense. Nothing there. Just hungry.

But the still small center of his soul would not let go, and he carried a sense of unease down the stairs and into the kitchen.

Roger sat at the kitchen table, mug of coffee cradled in his hands, aromatic steam rising into his face.

The twins gamboled around the house, the sound of their footsteps and voices carrying down the stairwell.

Gray light from the overcast sky entered through the wood-framed windows to each side of the range and the skylight above. Roger eyed the brick wall idly, his mind tracing the one-hundred-and-fifty-year-old mortar at the end of the kitchen. The exposed plumbing that led to the wide porcelain kitchen sink had been covered with a brick-orange wall hanging.

The plumbing angled down the wall to the sink, giving the room a slightly off-kilter feel that kept drawing his eye as he sat sleepily at the table.

The smell of the coffee, the feel of the warm thick mug between his hands, and the sound of the twin's footfalls, shrieks and tussles above comforted him, quieted the battle raging within. On the one hand, his rational self refused to give credence to his nocturnal experience or the flash of *that face* on the monitor, or the cackle that'd issued from his speakers, or the visions of Israel and Korea.

Nonsense.

He'd turned up an article in a 2003 edition of "Folklore" that seemed relevant: "Nightmare Experience, Sleep Paralysis, and Witchcraft Accusations," by a guy named Owen Davies.

You don't toddle downstairs and relight a pilot light while undergoing sleep paralysis.

Yeah, but faces don't just appear out of anywhere, either.

The face haunted him: elongated, stretched out, yellow eyes filled with an awareness that felt personal, intimate in way that sent a shiver of dread up his spine.

A wave of cold washed over him and he gripped the mug, lifted it to his lips with both hands, and sipped.

He glanced at the door leading down to the basement. The padlock gleamed silver in the afternoon light and Roger's eyes traveled down to the thin gap at the bottom of the door.

Gray mist seeped into the room, a ghostly trail that pooled across the floor and reached for the stairs.

Fucking basement.

Insulate that bastard, maybe.

He cocked his head as he realized the twins had grown quiet. He set the coffee mug down on the table and listened.

Silence.

Not good.

He stood, wooden chair scraping across the polished hardwood floor and headed for the stairs.

"Timmy? Tommy?"

Nothing.

Roger put a hand on the balustrade and climbed the stairs, peering around the corners of the landing and down the hallway, eyes searching for the twins.

The door to the bathroom stood open, a clammy gray-white light seeping into the hallway.

Mist pooled on the floor.

What the actual hell?

"Timmy?"

He reached the landing and paused, a feeling of dread overtaking him.

It's her. The one with the face. The witch.

Don't be such a fucking idiot.

"Timmy?"

Nothing.

"Tommy?"

A gurgling sound came from the bathroom and Roger sprinted down the hallway.

Both boys stood in a pool of mist, hands at their throats, eyes bulging, staring into the mirror in front of them blankly. A column of mist rose from the floor behind them, its shape vaguely human. Trails of mist reached out from the column and encircled each twin's throat in spiraling tendrils that looked like ghostly vines.

Dread rooted Roger to the spot for what seemed an eternity, and then he was at the boys' side, wresting their hands from their thin little necks.

The cold entered through his chest and he gasped in pain as

an icy hand gripped his heart. He looked up for a second, startled by the intensity of the pain—*heart attack?*—and found himself looking straight into the rheumy yellow eyes of *that face*: an old woman with a long hooked nose and a wart the size of a dime under her right eye. Moles dotted both cheeks, a wisp of hair sprouted from her chin, and her bushy eyebrows pulled down in a frown of rage at his interruption. She opened her mouth, revealing yellowed and blackened teeth, gaps here and there where a tooth was missing, and a foul stench filled the room with a revolting odor so powerful Roger gagged.

A screech of rage and then a sound, very much like that of a bubble popping, and the room cleared.

The twins blinked, eyes watery and looked around.

"Dad?" Timmy said. "Where did you come from?"

He looked around bemusedly.

"What happened?"

Tommy was rubbing at his throat, one eyebrow pulled down in an expression Roger knew meant his mind was ticking over the data, trying to make sense of what had happened.

A faint remnant of the foul smell had all three noses in the room twitching.

Timmy shoved Tommy.

"Nice fart, butt-face."

Tommy took a few steps in order to keep his balance, but offered no protest.

Timmy turned and darted out of the bathroom.

Tommy turned a serious face to Roger.

"Dad? What happened?"

Roger opened his mouth, closed it.

Cold dread seized him.

It's after my kids. It wants my kids.

He pulled Tommy to him and wrapped his arms around him, the warm little body comforting. Uncharacteristically, Tommy let him hold him for a long moment before pushing away.

"Something was here, Dad," Tommy said. "Something bad."

He looked into Roger's eyes for understanding. Confirmation.

Roger glanced away.

What do I tell him? That malicious ghosts are haunting this place? Some sort of supernatural force?

Tommy poked him in the belly.

"What was it, Dad?"

Roger shook his head and offered up his honest appraisal:

"I don't know, Tommy. I don't know."

He knelt down to get to Tommy's eye level.

"What did you see?"

Tommy blinked. He cocked his head, eyes going up and to the right as they always did when he was searching his memory.

"I can't remember, exactly," he said. "Timmy and I were playing tag, and he chased me here, and then…"

He shook his head.

"Something cold. And then you were here, but so was someone else."

"Who?"

Tommy's eyes looked into Roger's.

"A woman. A really old woman."

He shuddered.

"She's not nice, Dad. She's mean. She wants to hurt us, I can feel it."

His eyes went up again as he retraced his way through the memory.

"Was that real? Dad?"

Roger shook his head and repeated himself.

"I don't know, champ."

"It already feels like a dream. But a weird one. Are there such things as waking dreams, Dad? Do people…is that what a daydream is, Dad? Was it a daydream? Can people share a dream? A daydream? That seems weird. Impossible."

Tommy shook his head, puzzling it out.

Roger studied him. The boy was inquisitive, but not anxious. Not afraid. Curious.

A niggle of concern raised itself.

Not showing appropriate affect.

Then again, neither was Timmy. For him, it was instantly dismissed—like it never happened.

And already, the concrete details of the experience were fading: the icy shock of something reaching into his chest, the clear vision of the old woman in the mirror, the sense of her rage, the misty tendrils reaching out from the column sprouting out of the pool of mist on the floor...

Fading. Less and less real with every moment...

Like a dream...

Tommy blinked, then shrugged.

"Timmy and I have a massive game of Risk going, Dad."

He grinned.

"I'm slaughtering him."

And he was gone. Out the door, down the hallway, and into the twins' bedroom.

Roger heard some indistinct chatter, then the sound of dice on cardboard and the whoop of victory: "Spain is mine!"

He stood for a long moment in front of the mirror.

Something in his head felt ruptured, torn. The face in the mirror was strange, unfamiliar. A sense of out-of-placeness overwhelmed him.

Get a grip.

This time, you can't deny it. That was no sleep paralysis. Never heard of a group sleep paralysis.

But there are such things as mass delusions.

Don't you dare...

Come on, ghosts? Spirits?

Yes. Ghosts. Spirits. And they're not only coming for you now: they want your boys.

The icy sense of inner panic at his core climbed up his throat and for a split second panic came near to taking control, pushing him over the edge.

He fought it back down.

Got to get this figured out.

Could something in the house be affecting us? Like ergotism? Some kind of mold causing us to hallucinate?

Don't be a fucking idiot. Occam's razor: there are spirits here.

Occam's razor doesn't apply if your simplest explanation involves magic. If it did, everything would be explained like that.

But...

Roger expelled a frustrated breath and turned his back on the mirror.

But he couldn't leave the question behind. The one that followed him down the stairs, back to his seat at the kitchen table, cold coffee sitting in front of him.

What do you do about a ghost? One that's after your boys?

He sipped the coffee absently, grimaced, got up and walked over to the microwave.

Really, though?

Who do you call?

The Ghostbusters theme echoed in the back of his mind and he had to laugh at himself.

Fucking Ghost Busters. Right.

His inner core sighed at the thought.

Wouldn't that be nice, though?

He pictured Bill Murray and the gang going through the house with those guns of theirs, sucking the ectoplasmic spirits out of the air, containing them, cleansing the place. Sanctifying it.

Sanctify.

Mother Mary's face on the box of matches.

The microwave beeped, and Roger pushed away the image of Mother Mary.

More religious claptrap.

Nonsense.

But the still small voice within wouldn't let it go.

Roger sighed, raised the mug to his lips, gave the brew a taste test for warmth, nodded to himself and returned to the table, his eyes once again going to the mortar and the angled line of the plumbing.

Got to do something, though.

Shit.

Violetta Dunphy clutched her stomach as her gut spasmed and the pain dropped her to her knees. The woods swam around her, spinning, tilting, the world akilter. Sweat rolled down her brow, trickled under her arms and between her swelling breasts.

Sounds of pursuit echoed through the trees: snapping branches, heavy footfalls, hoots of the pursuers sounding like demented owls.

Get up, she urged herself. *Keep going.*

She'd been locked up in the old woman's shack for six months, watched over by members of the coven. As the child grew in her belly, so did her dread.

It'd been fun, in the beginning. Sneaking out at night, making her way through the woods by the light of the moon to the clearing where the coven gathered, the ceremonies with their chanting and dancing and drinking by the light of the bonfire sending thrills through her body.

Until the night it changed.

She'd noticed something off about the hard cider, a bitter taste, but hadn't thought anything of it until the woods glowed phosphorescent around her, shapes gathering at the periphery of the light of the fire.

A huge creature, seven-foot tall at least, had edged its way through the circle to stand by the fire. The creature had the body of a man: muscular, broad shoulders jutted out over a tapered waist, abdomen rippling with muscle, thick arms the size of small trees bulging, huge hands with long, spidery fingers ending with fingernails long and sharp as knives.

And the head of a goat.

Huge, black horns jutted from the creature's brow, and his eyes glowed red, orange fire reflecting in their depths.

Four members had broken away from the circle and dragged Violetta to the stone altar at the base of the fire. They'd lifted her and set her down on the hot stone amidst the disemboweled remains of the evening's sacrifice, blood still warm.

The circle closed around them as the coven members rejoined

hands and renewed the chant.

Violetta tried to resist, but whatever they had given her separated her from her body. Try as she might, her body would not obey her commands.

The four held her in place by her arms and legs. The two at the foot of the altar spread her legs and stepped to the side, holding her legs wide.

The creature laughed, a thick, guttural sound like a choking bear.

It grabbed its penis, a huge, curved thing with the tip like that of a dog's and stepped between her legs.

The chanting grew in volume as the creature placed its hands on Violetta's hips and thrust himself into her.

His penis burned like fire and despite the pain and the paralysis, Violetta cried out.

This excited the coven and the chant redoubled, echoing through the clearing and off the trees.

The pain grew, a burning inside her that felt like it reached up to her throat.

Violetta tried to fight, but again, her body refused.

The pain grew to a point where she thought she would die, a dim part of her mind horrified at the damage the thing inside her must be doing to her.

The pain peaked, and she felt the creature stiffen, then redouble its efforts and its seed spilled into her like pellets of molten lava.

The clearing darkened around her, her last vision of the full moon directly above, and she passed out.

To awaken in the old woman's shack, tied down to a bed in the corner, a huge black cast iron pot in the center of the shack over a fire, bubbling with some foul-smelling concoction, the old woman puttering around, muttering, occasionally casting something into the kettle.

She ignored Violetta, for the most part. Fed her. Emptied her bedpan.

Once a month, on the night of the full moon, the coven

gathered at the shack. The men held her as the old woman poured a foul-tasting brew down her throat. The walls of the cabin took on a phosphorescent glow, glistening a ghostly yellow-green, and the paralysis would spread through her and the men would pick her up and carry her to the clearing for the ceremony.

By the third month, Violetta felt the child in her belly growing, a little knot of fire that burned. Each move sent shivers of agony through her, sweat pouring from her pores.

As the seventh full moon approached, Violetta lay with her swollen belly in agony, watching the old woman through a film of pain and despair.

The old woman was tossing things into the kettle: a live frog, ash, the head of a pig. She uncorked a vial, and a putrid smell filled the tiny cabin.

The old woman stiffened, and the vial fell from her gnarled fingers into the kettle. Her eyes went wide, and she clutched at her chest and fell with a thump to the dirt floor.

Dead.

For the first time since the beginning of the ordeal, Violetta was alone. She tugged at the strip of herb-soaked cloth that bound her right wrist to the corner post of the bed.

It stretched.

She tugged harder and angled herself on the bed, reaching for the cloth with her teeth.

Pain shot through her as the child in her belly kicked and squirmed, seeming to understand she was trying to free herself, doing what it could to stop her.

She grimaced, relaxed, then pulled hard and angled her chin.

Her teeth found the edge of the cloth strip and she seized it and twisted.

It tore loose.

She managed to loose herself from the restraints, all the while the child in her belly protesting, each movement red-hot agony.

Violetta pushed the pain from her mind and sat up.

The child spasmed and the room grayed around her.

She staggered to her feet, walls spinning, and made her way to the door.

She pulled the rickety wooden door open and stepped onto the path leading into the woods, headed for the clearing.

The moon above was nearly full and lit her way with a silvery glow, sparkling off the dew that lined the grass and trees.

She'd not gotten far when she heard a cry behind, from the old woman's cabin.

She stepped off the path, into the woods, aiming for what she thought was the river. The river would lead her to town.

Freedom.

The cry from the cabin came again, and another voice echoed through the trees. Soon, there was a bevy of cries and the sounds of pursuit drew near.

Desperate, Violetta crashed through the trees and brush, the child within kicking and thrashing. Red-hot agony nearly took her breath away, but she fought through it, step after grueling step.

The child flailed inside again and the pain dropped her to her knees.

She looked up, hands on her belly and froze.

The old woman stood in front of her.

Ghostly green, with yellow eyes that gleamed, the trees just visible through her.

The old woman cackled and approached, reaching out long, spectral hands for her.

Violetta felt the old woman's hands pushing in, and realized with dawning horror that the spirit of the old woman was entering her, taking her over.

The child squirmed in her womb with delight and the agony tearing her guts apart grew to a level she felt her mind splintering under its assault.

Hoots like owls neared, heavy footsteps close. A branch snapped behind her and then strong hands gripped her shoulders. Figures swarmed around her and she cried out and tried to stand, but they were upon her.

The coven dragged her back to the old woman's cabin and installed a new master: a gnarled but muscular old man whose eyes traveled over Violetta as she lay strapped to the bed in a way that had her turning her head away in disgust and revulsion.

Something had broken inside her, the night of her flight: something deep and central. The child still kicked and squirmed, sending jolts of agony through her, but she felt an ineffable lessening in its power.

But the old woman's spirit more than made up for this.

The old witch had somehow wormed her way into Violetta's soul, and most of Violetta's waking and sleeping energies were devoted to preventing that bitch from gaining the upper hand.

In her agony and despair, Violetta turned to the faith that had never taken root: a faith that her family had suffered for—in her opinion, needlessly.

The Roman Catholic Church.

Mother Mary.

Pennsylvania was a haven from the persecution most of the colonies offered the Catholics, but only a relative one. The Church suffered from the prejudice of the majority of the population and this manifested itself in open bouts of violence and a general shunning of the Catholic people.

This needless suffering, in Violetta's opinion, had been one of the many bones of contention between her and her parents—a long-suffering couple who lived on the outskirts of the little village on the Lehigh River, just off the prime land bordering Jordan Creek. The couple worked their little plot of land and tried to live their lives with as little tumult as possible.

This self-enforced isolation further ostracized Violetta. The children at the village school never let her be: dipping her pigtails in inkwells, tripping her as she walked down the aisle of the one-room schoolhouse, whispering "witch" behind her back.

The witch thing because of her eyes, the genesis of her name. A radiant violet that on the rare occasions where she smiled lit with an inner light that brightened the room.

Their unusual tint, coupled with her status as the child of a Catholic couple, fueled the abuse that she had known for as long as she had memory.

The coven had been different.

They had also seen great significance in her eyes. Seen them as the mark of the chosen one.

And so, with no firm foundation of faith, no social support, ostracized and alone, she was easy prey.

And it had been such fun in the beginning: a wicked delight that sent shivers of pleasure coursing through her. Drinking the spiced mead and cider around the bonfire, learning the Latin chants, making her way down the silvery paths of the woods under the light of the full moon.

She'd given the coven's chants and spells about as much credence as she had her parents' faith, but the electric thrill of wickedness and secrecy added a spice to her life that had long been missing.Only to discover, in the end, that the coven's designs on her were far worse than anything Milton Blymire could have come up with back in the schoolhouse. To the coven, being chosen meant she was a brood mare. The vessel to usher in the anti-Christ: the devil himself.

A dim part of her mind had followed the logic born out of the understanding that the devil was real: if he was a real thing—as the child scouring her insides bore witness—then the rest of the cast of characters must have some basis in reality as well. Mother Mary. Christ. The Godhead.

It was Mother Mary that most comforted her. Something about her was the direct counterpart to the old woman. When the old woman's spirit grasped at the essence of Violetta's being, her mind leapt to the face that now lived with her constantly: Mother Mary's.

It worked.

Barely.

The gnarled old man was staring at her again, his hand dropping to rub and tug at his crotch.

No. No, no, no, please Mother Mary protect me.

The old woman's evil laugh cackled and reverberated through the back corridors of her mind as the old man's eyes dimmed and gleamed with a bovine lust, a thin trickle of drool running down the side of his mouth to wet his twisted and dirty black-gray beard.

Violetta turned her head away, the old man's gaze like a filthy cum-stained hand caressing her, leaving behind a sticky, disgusting residue that had her feeling dirty down to her very soul.

Roger lay in bed, Holly snoozing beside him.

Anxiety thrummed through him, his skin electric with it.

Something is in this house. Something happened here, long ago. There's a history. And somehow...I've awakened whatever it is that lives here. And now it's after my boys.

I've got to do something.

But what?

How about toning down the fantasy? Getting some real sleep? This is all the product of a sleep-deprived mind. Get some sleep, get some fucking insulation down in the basement, get the goddamn furnace serviced so the fucking pilot light stays lit...the furnace chimney perhaps? Maybe the cap has come loose, allowing the wind and rain in to douse the pilot?

But the yammering of his more rational mind was fast losing influence. The supernatural events of the past few days not only more and more concrete, but now shared: the twins....

The dreamlike nature of the visions troubled him, though. In the midst of an experience, the visions and spectres were as real as the mattress underneath him, but afterwards, the details faded away with an astonishing rapidity, leaving only a growing sense of panic that something was wrong.

The twins hadn't brought up the experience in the bathroom at all. To them, it was like it never happened.

Roger strained to remember: the mist traveling up the stairs, the column of it behind the boys, tendrils encircling their necks, their eyes bugged, that gagging sound...

Roger sat up in bed.

What was that?

He strained his ears, listening hard.

He'd left the door open, and that of the boys' room, telling Holly that Timmy had complained of nightmares and he wanted to be able to comfort him should they revisit.

She'd given him a look, but shrugged it off and fallen into bed and was asleep as soon as her head hit the pillow.

While she tried not to bring her work home, Roger knew the signs: a tightness to her face betraying the tension that ran through her. A temper held tightly under control, impatience with the twins and Roger seeping through. A heightened startle reflex. Eyes dimming as the boys and Roger recounted their day, a drawing inward as if to keep the details of her day from mixing with theirs.

She wasn't free to talk about it, but Roger knew the depth and breadth of the human trafficking going on in New England was deeply troubling her. He'd tried to quietly suggest that perhaps she withdraw from the task force, but that had sparked one of the few genuine bursts of anger he'd seen in their decade of marriage. So he'd backed off and let it alone.

Besides, the greater part of his own attention was captured by the battle going on within his own mind. And house.

And so the two of them drifted apart. Holly working 80-hour weeks, coming home to eat, collapse into bed, and then rise early and head back to work—often out of the house before Roger was up.

Something flitted across the floor in the hallway.

Roger's heartrate picked up.

He glanced down at Holly's sleeping face. She lay on her side, hand curled into a loose fist under her chin.

A cat appeared at the threshold of the doorway.

A cat? A black cat? Are you fucking kidding me? How cliché.

Roger moved to swing his legs over the side of the bed, only he didn't.

Body won't obey. What the fuck?

You're dreaming. Simple. Sleep paralysis. Told you.
This is no fucking sleep paralysis. This is happening.
Nonsense.

The cat arched its back and rubbed itself against the doorjamb in a way that sent a shiver of dread through Roger.

Sexual. Can feel the lust pouring off the thing...

The cat stretched, yawned lazily, the yellow slits of its eyes glaring in the dim light coming through the gauzy curtains covering the bedroom windows.

Those eyes...

The cat seemed to grin at him as if sensing his discomfort.

It walked lazily over to the side of the bed, coiled itself, then leapt up. It sat for a moment, staring at him, tail twitching, unblinking eyes staring into his, lips turned up to reveal its sharp little teeth.

Those eyes...reaching deep into me, reading my secrets, measuring the weight of my soul...

Nonsense.

The cat stood and put a paw on Roger's leg.

Cold shot through him and he would have gasped if his body had allowed him.

The cat grinned up at him, yellow eyes glittering, lips curled back, and took another step.

It walked up Roger's legs, the weight of the thing tremendous, out of proportion, the cold shock of its presence icy, penetrating to the soul.

Thing weighs as much as a grown woman...
How can that be?
Dreaming. That's how. Sleep paralysis.
Wake up!
No, this is real. The goddamn cat a familiar or whatever the fuck they call them.
Don't be an idiot. Wake up!

The cat seemed to relish the confusion and pain Roger was suffering, lingering with its paws on each of his thighs.

Then it lowered its head and butted his breastbone.

Pain shot through his chest and for a moment he was certain his heart had stopped.

The cat headbutted his sternum again and he found himself staring at the ceiling, unable to move, shadows from the streetlamp outside making ghostly shapes as the curtains swayed from the breeze coming through the cracked open window.

The shadows began to take shape: a ring of figures, dancing, flickering as if they were shadows cast by firelight. Trees in the background.

Smoke? Wood smoke and something else…flesh and hair and…

The scene suddenly so real Roger felt he'd been transported in place and time.

Nonsense. Wake up!

The cat walked up his belly to sit on his chest.

Weight tremendous. Can't. Breathe.

The cat stretched.

And kept stretching, growing impossibly tall, changing, morphing into…

An old woman, breasts stretched out tubes of flabby flesh hanging down to her soft, sagging stomach, swinging as she straddled Roger.

Those yellow eyes stared into his, and the creature's mouth opened, teeth a cross between a cat's and human, blackened, rotten, with sharp fangs intact.

A foul odor issued from her mouth and added to the sense of suffocation. Roger's mind began to fray under the onslaught, claustrophobia claiming him, panic rising.

The thing on top of him cackled again, sending a gout of foul breath into his face.

Roger tried to buck her off. To gag. To cry for help. To breathe.

Total paralysis.

Going to suffocate. Going to die any moment now.

The deep spot in his inner self was alive with panic, yammering at him:

Wake up! Wake up! Wake up!

The thing on top of him stiffened.

At first, Roger thought it was nearing an orgasm of some sort, but no...

Another presence had arrived...

A woman...

Flowers came to his mind, purple ones waving in a sunny field.

Violets? What the fuck?

The thing on him screeched.

The other presence was singing softly.

Some kind of hymn? What?

Roger remembered the stretched out face with yellow eyes closing on him in the basement, striking the match, the face exploding into mist, the face on the tall narrow box of matches...

Mother Mary...

The image of Mother Mary rose in his mind, and there was something so comforting there, so safe, that he clutched at it despite his deep-rooted agnosticism.

The thing on top of him contracted, the long, drawn-out howl of an enraged cat echoing off the walls of the room, the weight lifted off him, and Roger heard the thump of the cat landing on the wooden floor, its little feet racing across the threshold of his door, down the wooden steps, to the kitchen...

The basement?

Mother Mary stood there, head bowed, glowing softly incandescently white, the glow fading, fading, and...

Roger lay there, the icy cold gradually bleeding out of the marrow of his bones, through his core, dissipating, cold sweat on his chest and loins, breath shallow and quick, the shadows on the ceiling back to the normal castings of the gauzy curtain swinging in the cold breeze.

Holy fuck. What was that? Mother Mary? Really?

A sense of despair ran through him, and he would've given himself over to sobs, had he not worried about waking Holly.

How the fuck would I explain this to her?

Just a nightmare, that's all.

The Virgin Mary? What the actual hell?

Two presences...that old...thing...and something else. Someone else. Something new. Something that associated itself with Mother Mary.

Not Mother Mary itself.

No.

But closely linked.

Somehow.

The two together against that thing that rode me.

Witch. Go ahead. Say it.

Nightmare. Sleep paralysis.

What the fuck happened here? In this house?

Besides the tired imaginings of a man whose mind is unravelling, you mean?

I am not crazy.

How can you be so sure?

No. Something is here. Something happened. Is happening. And I have to stop it.

Yeah? How do you plan to do that?

Again, the despair threatened to undo him, but the innermost part of him flexed and he knew:

All real. And you will find a way...

How???

His mind went back and forth, exhausting him, and bit by bit, sleep crept into him, and all went dark. Blessed peace.

Mostly.

The old man's gnarled and twisted hand tugged more insistently at his crotch, his eyes dim slits of lust, the drool in his gray black beard glistening in the light of the fire.

Dread filled Violetta as the old man labored away, pants tenting under his rising member.

No, no, no. Not that. Mother Mary...

The old man shuffled across the floor, his thick shoes marking twin trails in the dirt.

Surprised the old goat can get it up.

He reached the foot of the bed, left hand tugging at himself, right hand stretching out to raise Violetta's nightgown above her knees, tracing her inner thigh with a crusty and blackened finger.

Violetta shivered in revulsion.

The child within kicked and writhed as well, sending rivulets of fiery agony racing along her nerves.

The old man poked at her sex with a thick finger, black crescent of dirt under his long and jagged nail.

A red spark leapt from Violetta's vagina to his prodding finger, and the old man's hand shot back. Violetta bucked, a shock of agony driving the breath from her.

The old man rubbed his arm, in apparent pain, and Violetta felt a small glow of satisfaction before the old man's eye gleamed anew.

"Can't touch yer cunt," he murmured. "the Dark Lord won't have it…"

He reached under her, calloused and dirty hand spreading her butt cheeks.

He grinned as his filthy finger found her sphincter.

"Ah, but yer ass is all mine, ya cunt. Praise Satan."

He moved to the side, fumbled at the straps holding her legs, loosening them, then to the head of the bed.

The baby kicked and writhed, seeming to do somersaults within and Violetta blacked out for a moment from the pain to find herself on hands and knees, swollen belly pushing into the bed.

A crusty hand lifted her nightgown above her waist, and she sensed the old man positioning himself between her legs.

The old man crooned, "Yer gonna take it up the ass, lassie. The ride of yer life."

Lust strained his voice.

Now, Violetta thought, *your only chance.*

She lashed out with a donkey kick that connected solidly with flesh.

Breath whooshed out of the old man and she heard him hit

the floor.

Violetta crawled off the bed and stood, hunched with pain as the child within continued its inner assault, the pain and fire within overwhelming her momentarily.

The old man fumbled around on the floor. His pants were around his ankles, hampering his attempts to rise, and Violetta hobbled over to him, raised a foot and brought it down on his throat.

He gagged, hands flapping like little birds in the dirt, and Violetta raised her foot and brought it down again.

The old man's eyes bugged out of his filthy face, filled with surprise and rage.

Choking, gagging, he attempted to turn, but Violetta's foot caught him on the side of the chin, the full force of her weight landing on him.

A cracking sound, and the old man went into spasms, making it hard for her to connect solidly as she brought her foot down again and again, each movement unbelievable agony.

But her revulsion and dawning understanding that this presented a new opportunity to escape the nightmare outweighed her pain and she stomped the old man until her strength failed her and she sat heavily on the bed.

The old man lay curled on his side, blood leaking from his mouth and nose black in the firelight.

His hands stretched and flexed like gigantic filthy spiders, then relaxed.

A long, bubbly breath issued from his mouth, ending with a guttural rattle, and he was quiet.

Dead. Thank the Lord on high. Thank you, blessed Mary, Mother of God.

The child within lay quiet for a moment and Violetta enjoyed a rare moment of respite and peace, then forced herself to her feet, found her thick wooden shoes, and slipped into them.

A cloak hung from a peg on the door and she shrugged herself into it, swollen belly pushing the thick and crusty fabric out. A cane sat propped in the corner by the door, and she reached for it.

Slowly, painfully, every moment agony, she eased the door open and exited the old woman's shack.

Free.

No, not free, she thought. *Not until you are far away from this place. These people.*

They will come looking.

She stood, head bowed, pain radiating through her system, the child within a devil, kicking her mercilessly, sapping her strength.

Get clear of this place, its strength will diminish, and you will be able to think.

She stuck the cane into the ground, leaned on it, took a step.

Then another.

And another.

The old woman bucked and writhed in rage.

More than two hundred years this cunt has defied me. Thwarted my every move. The Black Prince standing on the threshold, one foot in the world, the other in hell.

And now, a new family arrived, the man an open vessel, his life force there for the plucking.

She could feel herself strengthening with every attack on the man, his confusion and terror feeding her.

And still the cunt held the power to thwart her.

Perhaps…the twins the key.

One light, one dark, like the twins in the womb of that cunt.

Get the dark one to kill the light. Sway the balance of power. Allow us to banish the light, loose the dark into the world.

Or the man himself…no, open as he is, not open enough. Not for that.

It would take no less than total possession to get him to kill his son.

But the dark twin…

Perhaps.

I need more strength.

An ally.

The old woman could feel the stirrings of the old way in the county. Fresh blood: new acolytes arriving at the black altar.

For most of them, the old ways were a game. Like a round of the Ouija board. Parlor tricks and séances. Weak spells with little power.

I need a dedicated soul, one completely given over to the Dark Lord.

Perhaps, an acolyte...the sacrifice of a child...

Roger wandered through the deserted corridors of Trout Hall, the building housing the collections of the Lehigh County Historical Society.

The exhibits were reasonably well done, in a small-town sort of way, but promised Roger no respite from the battle in which he found himself embroiled: a history of the town with its various industries, a history of the local Native Americans, other exhibits given over to local figures.

What am I even looking for?

Something to explain what's going on.

Like what? A history of witchcraft in the area? Local warlocks?

Well, yeah. Exactly.

How about checking the listings for a competent psychiatrist? Get something stronger than Lorazepam?

Fuck you. I need...

A shrink.

A witch hunter. Some hint how I can send these...spirits packing.

Like anti-psychotic drugs, maybe?

Footsteps sounded on the wooden floor behind him.

Thump, swish, thump, swish, thump, swish.

Roger turned around to find an old woman working her way down the corridor toward him, her heavy cane thumping into the floor, feet dragging along behind it.

The hair stood up on the back of his neck.

It's her. The witch.

The old woman looked up at him, and Roger startled, expecting the yellow eyes, the stretched out face and hooked nose.

Instead, the old woman presented a sweet face wrinkled with laugh lines, lips turning up at the corners.

Roger relaxed.

Letting my imagination get away from me.

Duh. Understatement of the year.

"Hello?" Roger said.

The old woman paused, leaned heavily on her cane.

"Can you help me?" Roger said.

The old woman's head bowed as she rested, gray hair mostly held in place with a peaked black hat with wide brim, long black dress tenting on the floor.

She spoke without raising her head.

"No one can help you, young man," she said.

An icy finger traced its way up Roger's spine.

Ohmygod. It's her.

Don't be an idiot.

"Excuse me?" Roger said.

The old woman's shoulders began shaking, and Roger stepped forward.

A seizure of some kind...

Laughter bubbled out of the old woman.

Heard that before. Ohmygodohmygodohmygod.

"She's coming," the old woman said between cackles. "After more than two hundred years, she's finally found the vessel to bring her back."

The old woman raised a trembling old hand, knuckles thick with advanced arthritis and pointed a crooked finger at him.

"You."

The old woman's cackles echoed down the hallway.

This is a nightmare. You're back in your bed, sleep paralysis and imagination having its way with you.

"She will use you. You will usher the Dark Lord into this world."

Roger found his legs and backed away from the old woman.

"The twins!" the old woman called after him. "One dark, one light. They will free our Dark Lord. The dark one will..."

Roger found himself running down the hallway toward a door with a red "Exit" sign glowing above it.

He slammed into the panic bar, the door burst open, and he was outside, misty rain dimming the light, fog swelling from the ground, wreathing the winter trees in swirling fingers of mist.

His heart hammered his chest so hard it was difficult to breathe.

What the holy fuck was that?

He turned and looked back the way he had come.

The door flapped open in the breeze, giving him a clear shot down the length of the corridor.

Empty.

What the...

You're losing it. That's what. You're going to need something much stronger than Lorazepam.

No, no, no. That was real.

Already, the memory and the horror was dimming.

Roger raised his hands to his temples.

They were shaking.

This can't go on. I am losing it.

Lorazepam.

No, that's not it. Something has found me. The old woman.

With her Dark Lord? What next?

The old woman said something about the twins.

A bolt of fear shot through him, silencing the mental chatter.

My boys. Frick and Frack. Timmy and Tommy.

One dark and one light, she said.

Not the way I would've described them.

But it fits, in a way. Timmy bubbly and outgoing, loving, energetic. Tommy more taciturn, withdrawn. Thoughtful.

Dark?

He shoved the train of thought away.

Don't.

He turned in a circle, hands outstretched, face raised to the falling mist.

What do I do?

Trout Hall dwindled behind him as Roger trudged down the sidewalk, every step an effort.

The confrontation—*madness*—back at the Hall had exhausted him, and he wondered if he could find the energy to make it all the way home.

Should call an Uber.

A narrow stone stairwell descending into the basement of a building on his right drew his eye. A thick black wooden door with nine windowpanes sat at the bottom, sign above the door reading: Tarot. Palm Readings. Folk Medicine.

Why the fuck not?

Roger's feet found the stairs and he clattered down the stone steps and reached for the door.

Are you out of your fucking mind? Have you gone completely crazy?

Shut up. I need answers.

Next thing you know, you'll be cutting live chickens open, reading your future in their entrails.

Shut up!

He opened the door.

The interior of the shop had a pleasant odor of incense mixed with herbs and tea. Candles flickered on surfaces across the room, their flames dancing in reflection on the dark wooden shelves crammed with old leather-bound volumes.

A woman was seated at the head of a thick round table, its surface littered with books and cards, a single fat candle burning in the center.

She looked up as Roger entered, her face open and friendly.

Her eyes caught Roger and he froze, one foot over the threshold, the other still on the stones of the landing.

Those eyes. I've seen them somewhere…

The woman had arresting violet eyes, and she'd dyed the edges of her raven hair a purple shade to match.

Beautiful.

She raised an eyebrow at him, and one corner of her mouth

twitched up in a smile.

"You going to come all the way in?" she said.

Come all the way in. Odd thing to say.

The chatter in his head diminished.

Something about this woman, calming.

The woman's smile broadened.

"Come on in," she said. "I won't bite."

Roger felt the warm rush of blood to his cheeks.

"Sorry," he said.

He stepped across the threshold and closed the door behind him.

Back in the grave, entrapped with the bitch who had defied her, the one who had denied the coming of The Dark Lord with her cursed Mother Mary, the old woman raged.

So close. Again. This time, the bitch will not deny me.

She had fed well on the man in the bed upstairs. Ridden him like the beast of burden he was. She felt her strength renewing,

But it was not enough.

He was open, yes, she could taste him, the life force she had drained from him intoxicating, delicious, but just as she was cresting, riding him to the verge of orgasm, to the taking of his seed and the power within, the little bitch was back.

With her Mother Mary.

And open as he was, the fucking weak little worm of a man had seen the bitch, drawn sustenance from her and her holy Mother Mary, cast the old woman aside and broken the spell.

So close.

She screeched in frustration, the sound traveling up the old pipes of the house, singing through them, echoing from faucets in the kitchen and bathrooms.

I need an ally. Someone to strengthen me. Someone to weaken the bitch.

She composed herself. Pushed the rage down to a bubbling cauldron deep within.

Rage dampened and controlled, she tried to loose her spirit, to send it out to find...

Been so long. Trapped here with the bitch.

But the bitch has exhausted herself tonight, manifesting for the man upstairs.

And I have supped well.

She strained, the old incantations coming to mind easily, her strength renewed.

A thin tearing sound accompanied a wrenching within her soul, and the old woman's spirit broke free.

A thrill of exhilaration ran through her.

Strong enough for this!

She cackled in triumph.

More than two hundred years—bound to this bitch in the grave. Buried upright to prevent our escape.

Two hundred years, and finally, finally, a new page, a breaking of the stalemate.

Praise Satan.

Her spirit soared above the town, drifted through the ether dividing this world and the next, seeking, searching.

The new ones are out there. I've felt them stirring.

But where?

As she drifted on the ether above, the town below revealed little knots of darkness: souls open to the Dark Lord.

Dabblers. Children playing with toys. Casting spells without power, belief in them weak.

She circled above a decrepit block of apartments, a long line of rowhouses in disrepair.

Numerous corrupted souls there, minds blasted with drugs and filled with despair. Hatred. In the grip of the Dark Lord, but without any power. Spiraling down a path that led to the grave and a welcome into the dark kingdom.

Useless.

I need a soul that has dedicated itself to the Dark Lord.

With full understanding.

Open. Pliable. Willing. Strong. One whose desires align with my needs.

She drifted above the town, seeking the one.

So many lost souls.

And the hatred! Rich and full, the town literally glowing with it.

The Dark Lord has made great advances since my time.

Ultimately, though, the hatred and division in the population below, while it served Satan well and bolstered the old woman's hopes, was useless to her. Satan had claimed their thoughts and souls, but they had no knowledge of it—a peculiar sense of self-righteousness driving their division and hatred.

The flavor of these divisions and hatred so familiar...but how?

Understanding blossomed in the old woman's heart that filled her with delight and frustration at the same time.

Witch hunters. A witch hunt like none she'd experienced in her time, the population below divided evenly, both sides saturated with hate-filled self-righteousness.

And yet, useless. Blind to the reality that lay beneath their surface-level passion. Unaware of the Dark Lord's claim on them.

I need a soul who is aware of the Dark Lord and his grip. One...

She drifted near the edge of town, rowhouses giving way to single dwellings scattered in the fields on the outskirts of town.

Her progress slowed, and she felt the tug of the grave, pulling her back.

No!

But she had reached the edge of her power, her strength renewed, yes, but limited.

The bitch is stirring, beginning to realize I have sent my soul out...

Once fully awake...

No!

But the pull was relentless, the bitch with the violet eyes awakening, renewing the battle.

A black abyss opened below her, and she studied it:

An old house in the woods at the edge of town. Almost as old as me. Two stories, a portico, peaked roof, gables, boards over the windows, graffiti scouring its sides—praise Satan, a pentagram, hex signs, freshly painted.

She sniffed.

In blood...

A surge of power renewed her strength, and the pull of the grave lessened.

Praise the Dark and Unholy Lord—a true acolyte.

Cat's blood.

The blood of a child the most powerful, of course, but a cat's... serviceable. Whoever this new acolyte was, she—or he—open to the dark arts, willing to kill a cat.

This one knows the Dark Lord. Is attempting to harness his power.

With a little nudging...

The old woman's spirit circled the house. Its walls leaned inward, the roof sagged, cracks showed in the walls and foundation, but...

Someone in there.

Practicing the old ways.

Casting spells.

The old woman's spirit brightened.

A young woman, no, not a woman, a boy. No, not a boy.

Something in between.

Lovely.

A confused rage suffused the spirit of this young one. It was in pain and turmoil, filled with hatred.

The old woman sensed a lifetime of abuse and suffering. Children taunting, calling this young one names, tripping it. Beating it.

A dim and humid room. Some kind of tiles on the walls and floors, steel columns rising from the floor, spouting water from nozzles above, a place where children cleansed themselves after activity...

The young thing encircled, the other youths in the room around it, poking at it, punching it, and then...

The old woman's spirit pulsed with glee.

They raped it. One after another, thrusting into the poor thing's tortured body, taking turns, then the final indignity—a kick in the ass sending the young one sprawling, the final tormentor standing over it, loosing a long stream of urine to spatter on its back, then the delightfully monstrous boys filing out, one by one, to leave this one shuddering and sobbing in the dark, humid room of tile and water.

And this one had withdrawn. Hidden itself away.

Until it had found the dark arts, praise Satan.

Even now, it labored over its books, chanting, lighting candles, casting spells on its tormentors.

Filled with rage and hatred.

And hurt—deeply hurt, the pain reaching into the very center of its being.

The rage delicious, and growing, fueled by a cocktail of drugs.

Oh my, the old woman thought, *this one will do.*

All I need to do is plant the seed…

The old woman summoned all of her strength, reached into the young one's mind, all of her mental force bent on creating an image: a Ouija board.

The young one stopped its chanting, mouth falling open, eyes dimming.

Oh, yes, little one. Listen to me…

Get the board.

You and I have business.

And I will give you the power you dream of. Together, we will take care of those who have hurt you. I understand better than you will ever know.

The young one blinked, cast its eyes about the old house filled with centuries of dust and grime, broken furniture piled along one wall, a central altar with pentagram painted in cat's blood on the floor, candles guttering at each point, a lock of hair at the center.

Yes. Yes. You and I have business, little one.

The old woman's strength waned and she felt herself falling away, back to the grave, back to her combat with the bitch. The one who had defied her for centuries.

She allowed the tug of the grave to pull her back, satisfied.

It begins.

The Dark Lord shall finally have his day.

She allowed the bitch with violet eyes to pull her back.

Your day will come, sweetie. After more than two hundred years, a reckoning for your betrayal.

Back in the grave, she relaxed.

Wait. Drain more life force from the man.

The boys opening, soon accessible. Disturb their sleep to weaken their spirts, feed on the delicious nectar of a young soul—two young souls—use their life force to empower the young one in the house on the edge of the woods. Set it upon this family, teach it the proper spells, get it to step up its blood sacrifice...

Closer than we have been since that day so many years ago...

Roger sat across from the woman in the shop.

Alex Lancaster.

She held his left hand in hers, traced the lines in his palm with the index finger of her right hand.

Something about the woman quieted the battle in Roger's mind—a solidity about her, a confidence and belief that soothed his tortured soul.

Besides, her hand felt good.

"You are deeply troubled," Alex said. "A battle wages within your soul."

No shit, Roger thought.

"You have just moved to Allentown. An old rowhouse. In the West Park neighborhood."

A thrill ran through Roger.

Easy to guess I'm new here. But the neighborhood? How?

"There are forces in that neighborhood. Powerful ones."

Alex closed her eyes and took his hand in both of hers.

Roger seized the moment to look her over.

Beautiful. The purple highlighting of her hair suits her. Perfect skin. Young.

Alex's eyes blinked open.

"Focus, Roger. Bring to mind the events that brought you here."

Blood rushed to his face, and he looked away.

Alex's hands were warm around his. She tugged at him gently.

"Never mind that."

Roger looked into her eyes, then away.

So pretty. Violet. Never seen a shade like that. Contacts?

Of course. All part of the show.

Alex's grip tightened.

"Focus, Roger. Close your eyes. Bring to mind all that troubles you. Open the door and show me."

Roger tried to let go of the tension running through him.

"That's it, Roger. Close your eyes and focus."

Roger closed his eyes.

The face of the old woman as she loomed above him the night before flashed in his mind and he pushed it away with a surge of panic. He opened his eyes to find Alex's violet eyes fixed on his.

"Relax," Alex said. "I am with you. You are safe here."

Safe. Of course I am. Crazy, maybe, but safe. Once this is over, get to a shrink. Lorazepam. Or something. If it does not stop the madness, it will at least dampen it. Just being here shows how far I've unraveled.

"The spirits are very real, Mr. Nimanator," Alex said. "You've always known this, but you've pushed it away. Intellectualized it. Focus now. Stop the chatter in your mind. Drop the doubt—it only serves the dark powers that surround you."

Intellectualized. Maybe. Maybe not.

"Close your eyes. Bring her back."

Could she have seen? No. Impossible.

He closed his eyes, brought himself back to the memory of the night before.

The cat at the door. The paralysis.

Sleep paralysis, dumb fuck.

No. Something else. Something real.

"Quiet your mind, Roger," Alex said. "Relax. Open yourself. Let your doubt drop away."

The cat coiling itself beside the bed, leaping up, the touch of its paws icy, reaching into my core.

"Yes, that's it. Roger. Keep going. I am with you now."

The cat walking along my thighs, an icy coldness filling my soul. Head against my sternum. So cold. The shadows on the ceiling.

Alex's grip tightened.

"That's it. Show me."

The cat, stretching, rising, morphing into…

"Yes. Keep going Roger. We're almost there."

The old woman. Straddling me. Riding me. Long, flabby tits swinging. Those yellow eyes burrowing into my soul. Reaching deep. My secrets bare to her. Riding, bucking, energy flowing from me to her. Nearing a climax of sorts, about to…

And then…the other one suddenly there.

A flash of another presence.

Mother Mary?

Nonsense.

The old woman gone. The cat back. Scrambling for the door, claws scratching the floor, heading back down…

To the basement.

Mother Mary standing there, just out of the corner of my eye.

Gone the instant I tried to look at her.

Awake. Lying on the bed. Cold sweat pooled on my chest and loins.

He opened his eyes to find Alex looking at him, one eyebrow angled down, an expression of concern lining her beautiful face.

She let go of his hands and leaned back.

"You are an open door, Roger," Alex said. "The spirits can see that."

Korea and the flittings. Israel—the woman.

"You have placed yourself in a nexus. One that opens to the dark world. And the spirits there have found you."

Roger pulled his hand off the table into his lap. A sense of loneliness and isolation swept over him.

Don't be silly.

"Nexus?"

"A confluence of forces. A pooling of spirits. Two predominate those who orbit your presence, one light and one dark. They are in conflict."

Alex leaned back and her eyes looked up. As she tried to explain, her delicate hands made shapes in the air.

"These two spirits have been entwined for centuries. There is a history there. One I can't quite make out. The dark one is held in check by the light one. But the dark one's power is growing."

She brought her eyes down to meet his, rested her hands in her lap.

"You're feeling tired, lately. Drained."

Roger nodded.

"The dark one is feeding off of you, using your life force to overcome the light. Each has a powerful force behind it, supporting it. There is a depth to this that frightens me, honestly."

Wait. What? Frightens you?

"The dark one is attempting to open the door further, to allow the forces she worships ingress. An evil that surpasses anything I've seen. The light one also has a door open, and this has held the dark one in check. But…"

A shiver ran through Roger and he folded his arms over his chest.

"But?"

"The dark one is gaining power. If she gets the door open, she will overpower the light. Crush it. And then…"

Alex's brow wrinkled, and her face twisted.

"Then?"

She looked back into Roger's eyes.

The alarm in the depths of those violet eyes reawakened the panic deep within Roger.

"All hell will break loose, Mr. Nimanator."

"How…"

Roger's mouth dried up. He licked his lips and swallowed. Tried to work up enough saliva to speak.

"What… How can we stop this?"

Alex sighed.

"The first thing is to try to cut off the dark one's source of power. Deny her access to you."

Roger looked at her.

"I am going to have to do some work on this, Roger. It will take some time."

"But..."

Alex nodded at him.

"In the meantime, I'm going to give you something to try to keep the dark one away. I want you to wear it while you sleep. If we can keep the dark one from gaining power, perhaps we can buy some time. Time I can use to find a way to stop this. Close the door."

This is crazy.

The fear and panic within scratched at Roger's heart.

"Relax, Roger," Alex said. "The dark powers feed on your fear."

She leaned forward, and Roger caught a glimpse of her cleavage, her necklace disappearing between the curves of her breasts.

Beautiful. Skin so soft and silky.

"Give me your hand," she said.

Roger looked up.

Those violet eyes. Bewitching. Her presence so soothing. Comforting.

He put his hands on the table and Alex took them in hers.

The touch of her skin calmed him further.

"I'm going to give you a talisman. A shield. An amulet of black obsidian, moonstone and tourmaline. It will protect you, but it will also open you."

"I don't want to be open."

Her grip tightened.

"The dark forces work best in the shadows, Roger. They use your ignorance and denial against you. Your experiences take on a dreamlike cast, don't they?"

Roger nodded.

"The dark one wants you to forget. She wants you to doubt. Part of the spell she is weaving around you strengthens your doubts. To keep you off guard. If you are aware, you can defend."

"Defend? How?"

"Resist, Roger. Push her away when she comes. Call upon the power of light."

"That will work?"

Alex shrugged.

"It will help. How much depends on you."

"Me?"

"The depth of your belief."

Well, then. I'm fucked. This is mumbo-jumbo nonsense.

Alex's grip tightened further.

"Look into my eyes!" she said.

Her violet eyes flashed and Roger felt her gaze reaching into him.

"This is not nonsense, Roger. This is very real. You are in danger. Your family is in danger. The twins are in danger."

The twins? How the hell...

"Believe. Roger. That is the first step. Cast away your doubt. You don't want to turn your back on the forces gathering against you. You want to confront them."

She let go of his hands and stood.

She walked over to the jewelry case to one side of the shop and lifted the glass, reached in, and came out with an amulet on a black leather cord.

It was a pretty thing, luminous moonstone and tourmaline edged in gold, a shiny black obsidian crystal depending below the pearly sheen of the moonstone.

She shut the case and returned to the table.

She held the amulet to her lips, closed her eyes, and murmured a soft chant that Roger couldn't quite make out.

She reached for a white candle that was lying on the table, thrust its wick into the fire of a burning one, then passed the amulet through the flame of the white candle. Three times, her lips moving in a near silent chant. The flame sparked and brightened, rising a full six inches from the wick.

Alex set the candle in a holder, rounded the table, and stood behind Roger.

He turned his head to follow her, and she placed a warm hand on the crown of his head and swiveled it to face away.

Warmth spread from her hand down his spine to pool in his lower gut.

The panic within lessened.

She lowered the leather cord around his neck and tucked the amulet under his shirt, then adjusted the cord so that the amulet rested directly over his heart.

The warmth within increased, and—for the first time in a long while—Roger relaxed.

I knew I was wrapped pretty tight, but I hadn't realized how tight...

"That's it, Roger. Allow the pendant to gather the light within you, to bring the power of light to your soul."

The voice in his head, the one that had cast doubt on the entire sequence of events, the one that had steadfastly argued against the reality of the spirit world was quiet.

Could that have been what had me so tense? Doubt?

"The amulet helps to open you to the power within," Alex said.

She slid round the table and retook her seat across from him.

Roger noticed the way her dress accentuated the curve of her hips, her breasts.

She really is a beautiful woman.

"When the dark one comes for you, call on the light."

"The light?"

"Close your eyes, Roger."

Roger closed his eyes.

Calm. I feel...OK.

"Think back to last night. To the one who appeared and broke the dark one's spell on you."

Standing off to the side. A glimpse. Mother Mary? The Catholic Mary?

"The blessed Virgin is a very powerful spirit, Roger. For those who believe."

"But...I don't. It's just...myth. Stories. I..."

Alex leaned across the table, brought her face close to his.

Her perfume...lavender? Violets? Something flowery, with a hint of musk underneath.

"Do you believe in the dark one? The one who rode you last

night? The old woman?"

Roger considered it.

The face in the basement. The mist rising up the stairs.

The twins! In the bathroom, the column of mist rising behind them, taking shape...

The old woman on top of me, icy grip reaching inside, draining me...

A switch clicked inside and a cold certainty flowed through him.

"Yes." He nodded. "I do."

"There is a balance, Roger. Always a balance. Light and dark. If the dark ones exist, then so does the light. Do you see?"

Makes a certain kind of sense. I guess.

"I think so."

Alex nodded.

"Good. Accept that the spirit world is as real as the physical one in which we move and breathe. The forces there are beyond our ken, and so we color them with imagery more familiar to us. A woman. God in the form of man. A demon."

"I think I see what you mean."

"When the old woman was about to take you, and the other one intervened, she appeared to you as Mother Mary. The Blessed Virgin."

"But...I don't believe in that."

Alex smiled.

"Don't you? What happened when you saw her?"

"The old woman...became the cat. Fled the room."

"Such is the power of belief. Part of you believes, Roger. You need to strengthen that part. The amulet will help to open you further to this. Heighten your awareness. Already, you are open. A conduit. The spirits are swirling around you, hungry for the ingress to this world that you offer. They see you as their way in."

"Why? Why do they want in?"

"The dark seeks to destroy the light. It wishes only to kill. And destroy. It wishes to steal the life force away from you. The light seeks to give life. Abundant life. With enough belief, you can battle the dark, drive it away."

"That's all there is to it? If I believe, I can banish the dark? Send the old woman packing?"

Alex's brow furrowed.

"Perhaps. The dark one that seeks your soul is more powerful than any I've ever encountered. Ancient and wily. Practiced in the art of deception. There is a depth there beyond my ken. I need…"

A flicker of doubt rippled across her face.

The panic deep within Roger flared.

Her face cleared and she patted his hand.

"Relax, Roger. We can defeat her. But she is powerful. Her strength is growing. Our first step is to deny her the strength you have provided her. This will buy us time. I will consult with my colleagues. Learn what I can about this. Gather the forces of light to combat the darkness she represents."

"You're not sure though, are you?"

Alex shrugged, a crooked smile on her face.

"Nothing is certain, Mr. Nimanator. Not in this world. Or the next. The only thing I know for sure is that the power of the light can defeat the darkness. With enough faith."

The old pendulum clock on the wall chimed three times.

Roger startled and looked at his watch.

"Oh, shit. It's three o'clock. I've got to get the twins."

He stood and Alex rose with him.

"Wear the amulet. Sleep with it. When the dark one comes to you, call on the light. Look for Mother Mary."

Roger walked to the door, Alex in step with him.

"But what…"

"This is the best I can do for you now, Roger. Come back tomorrow. I will know more then."

Roger stopped at the door.

"Wait. What do I owe you for this?"

He reached for his wallet.

Alex waved him away.

"Nothing. The amulet and my services are a gift. I serve the light. I live to overcome the darkness. That is my fate."

She smiled at him.

Those eyes. So beautiful.

She waved him away.

"Go. Get your children. Dwell on the light. Focus on it. Believe, Mr. Nimanator. Believe."

Roger looked into her eyes for a long moment, then nodded.

"Thank you, Alex."

"Don't thank me yet. There is a long road ahead, I think. Now go."

She patted his shoulder.

Roger nodded again, then crossed the threshold and climbed the stone steps into the mist that still lingered on the street above.

Violetta pushed her way through the woods, occasionally using the thick and heavy cane to beat back bushes to clear a trail.

She was close now, the house near the banks of Jordan Creek less than a mile distant.

She broke through the treeline to the farmland at the edge of town. Mist curled from the turned up sod and blanketed the fields.

Home almost in sight.

Her body convulsed, the pain dropping her to her knees.

She held onto the cane, tip planted in the soil that reached to the treeline.

The contraction tightened, the pain unbelievable, and she found herself panting, short, fast breaths, desperate for air.

The contraction waned, and Violetta gathered herself to stand. She pushed heavily on the cane, driving it deeper into the earth and got halfway to her feet before another contraction buckled her knees and she thumped down to the dirt again.

This one lasted longer, an interminable period of pain driving away all other thought.

The child within burned like molten lead.

The contraction stopped, and she gasped for breath, on her hands and knees now, panting.

Father God, Mother Mary, help me.

The child within went wild.

Feels like a savage animal inside of me, clawing to get out.

Another contraction tightened her abdomen and a burst of warmth wet her legs as something inside broke.

Blood.

She fell to her side as the child scrabbled to get out.

She rolled onto her back, and dimly noticed the full moon cresting the trees, stars bright and twinkling above.

The contraction and scrabbling within intensified and Violetta cried out, her wail echoing across the misty field.

The contraction let go of her, but the child renewed its efforts.

Something inside tore further and warm fluid gushed from her, soaking the coarse material of her cloak.

She cried out again as another contraction gripped her, driving the breath from her.

The moon and the stars faded away in a sea of red as pain swept her vision away.

She came up, gasping for air, the moon and stars dim now, fading.

Voices sounded across the field.

No. No, no, no. They can't have found me.

Flickering lights moved across the field in her direction.

Torches.

No. Please, Father God. Mother Mary.

Another contraction seized her and the rip within tore further, more fluid gushing out to soak the ground beneath.

The child clawed its way out of her womb to land on the dirt between her legs, her dress now up to her waist, bare legs coated in blood and fluid open to the night sky.

The child screeched.

Like an angry cat.

Her body convulsed as another contraction took her.

She pushed, mindless now with pain and horror, weak, the

body taking over.

Another child landed in the dirt beside the first, its tiny mewls weak.

Twins?

The first child howled again, the sound raising the hair on the back of her neck.

Footsteps crunched across the frosty ground, the flickering light of the torches nearer now.

Voices.

Violetta's vision abandoned her as her womb contracted; more fluid and tissue gushed out of her.

So weak. So tired.

Thirsty.

Cold.

But the thing within me gone, now. The fire gone.

As her pain waned, the felt herself drifting away, spiraling down into the darkness.

By the time the villagers reached her, Violetta lay flat on the dirt, the twins between her legs covered in blood and afterbirth.

The villagers gathered around her, held the torches out to better illuminate the scene.

From the depths of the black pool that had claimed her, Violetta heard the voices raise in pitch and volume, outrage and fear pouring into the night sky.

Then darkness claimed her and the voices faded away.

Zoe blinked.

What was that?

She'd been in the middle of her latest attempt: the Spirit Commado Beside the Black Raven. The cat's blood she'd used to paint a pentagram still glistened, the black candles at its five points guttered and smoked in the drafty old wreck of the house, the lock of hair sat where she'd placed it, perfectly centered.

Tryan's hair.

Just the thought of him filled her with rage.

Tryan must die. Painfully. Slowly.

Zoe had read up on cancer of the penis, and it sounded like just the thing.

None of her books on the dark lore specifically mentioned cancer, but disease...that was a different story. There were plenty of curses to cause the chosen victim's spirit to waste away.

Her diligent study hinted at the possibility, though. She just needed to summon the right demon and set it upon Tyran. That, combined with the right spell...

Just as she was settling in to the proper incantations, the time right according to the Seventh Book of Moses, a veil had dropped over her vision.

The dust and grime of the room, the broken furniture had fallen away as the flames of the candles grew, smoke pouring out, blotting her sight with a thick black pall that carried her away.

A vision.

An old woman with yellow eyes.

Calling to me.

Did the spell work? Even before I'd completed it?

A thrill ran through her.

Something had appeared. Something ancient. Evil. Implacable. Powerful.

Zoe blinked again as her mind turned over the experience.

Already, though, the details were dimming, the vision translucent and impossible to grasp.

The face of that woman: stretched out, elongated, penetrating yellow eyes reaching deep into my soul.

A kindred spirit.

A demon? Conjured by the Spirit Commado?

And then: clear as if it were sitting in front of me: an old Ouija board. Solid wood, the planchette darkened with age, glass eye at its center dim, but shimmering with power: a window into the world beyond.

Cliché as fuck.

After all this time, all these useless incantations, Tyran is as strong and cocky as ever. Cruel eyes glowing with malice and sick humor as he bullies his way through school, growing more powerful, more of an asshole, more worthy of an excruciating and drawn out death.

After she'd recovered from the attack in the locker room, Zoe had sworn never to return.

Not until that bastard is dead. And his friends.

She'd imagined herself with a gun, entering the school, bursting into a classroom, shooting Tryan and all his evil little buddies dead.

But no. That was too good. Too easy.

And cliché. Bullied child gets daddy's gun and returns to school for vengeance.

No, no, no.

The one thing I will never be is cliché.

And Tryan must suffer. Horribly. For a long, drawn out period. And then, just before he dies, he must know that it was me. I did it.

Zoe had dived deep into the ancient lore that soaked the history of Allentown, discovered that hexmasters were on the rise again, the belief in the old ways resurging.

But most of these were "good" witches. Some even considered themselves Christians.

The fools.

No. Zoe would have none of that God. The God of Light.

Darkness.

That was the answer.

Evil powers.

An eye for an eye.

Blood for blood.

Tryan's penis would blacken and swell with cancer, the pain indescribable. Agony would accompany his every waking moment and haunt his dreams.

The old woman.

Demon?

She understood the situation, knew rage like this.

And she has the means to satisfy the most bloodthirsty visions.

The Ouija board flashed in her mind again.

And wants to partner with me.
Praise Satan.
Zoe gathered herself from her cross-legged stance and leaned forward to blow out the five candles.
The spell worked. I'm done here.
The old woman will give me everything I want.
A dim warning sounded in the depths of her soul.
But why? Why would she help me?
Zoe pushed away the errant thought and rose.
Because she is bound by my spell. Get the board.
As she made her way through the dim light that seeped through the gaps in the siding of the old house, following a trail she'd carved through the dust that lay thick throughout the house, a new vision appeared:
The Ouija board. On a shelf in one of the many antique stores in town: Ye Olde Mercantile.
The vision evaporated and the walls of the old house returned.
Excellent.
Zoe stepped across the threshold, wood creaking and complaining under her, pulled the door shut, and walked carefully across the floorboards of the portico, avoiding the ones so rotten they would not bear her weight.
As she traced her way up the path and through the gate to the dirt road that led into town, a rising sense of power filled her, stoked her rage, and she clenched a thin and delicate hand into a fist.
Tryan will die.
Painfully.
Praise Satan, the Dark Lord.
Her step was light as she made her way to town, her heart filled with rage and the joy of coming vengeance.
A dim pang of warning sounded in the depths of her heart, and she pushed it away easily, focused on the prize: a long, drawn out painful death for the bully of Allentown.

Holly straddled Roger, pinning him to the bed.

She leaned over him, interlaced her fingers with his and brought her face down for a kiss.

"Missed you, baby," she said. "It's been so long."

Roger kissed her back.

"You've been so busy. Fourteen-hour days. Hardly see you anymore."

"There's a lot going on. Big operation."

"The Russians?"

"Mmm-hmm."

"Do you really have to go? Five days seems like a long time."

Holly straightened up, her hands running down his chest.

"What's this?"

She hooked a finger around the leather thong on Roger's neck and pulled the amulet from underneath his shirt.

"Picked it up in an old shop downtown, near Trout Hall."

Holly held the amulet in her palm, studied it.

"Doesn't seem like your kind of thing," she said.

"I like it," Roger said. "The woman who gave it to me said it protects me."

"Protects you? From what?"

Roger looked away from Holly.

The old woman. The cat. The mist. The presence...

"From spirits," he said.

Holly stiffened.

"Spirits? Really, Roger?"

Roger met her eyes.

If I tell her, she'll think I've gone crazy. She'll worry the whole time she's away.

"I've, umm, been having some bad dreams," he said. "Really weird ones. An old woman in the house. Evil. The dreams are so real, Holly, and I..."

Holly dropped the amulet and it plopped back onto Roger's chest.

"Oh, Roger, again?"

A surge of anger ran through Roger and he twisted his hips to roll her off of him.

Shit. Now I really can't tell her.

Holly stretched out beside him, raised herself up on an elbow and stared at him.

"You're off the Lorazepam," she said. "Maybe, that was a mistake. If the dreams are back…"

Roger rolled to his side and propped himself up on an elbow to face her.

"I don't want to go back on that. It…dims me. Dulls the edges of my perception. And there's a tiny hangover after, like a little spike driven into my forehead."

He looked into her eyes.

Worry. Not to the level of alarm, but…

He sighed.

Holy crap. If I tell her what's really going on, she'll freak.

A sense of loneliness swept through him.

He fingered the amulet.

"Look, Holly," he said. "It's not a big deal. It's just an amulet. I like it."

"You said it protects you from spirits. That's getting out there, Roger."

Roger tucked the amulet back under his shirt.

"I'm not getting 'out there,' Holly. Relax. You're blowing this up."

Holly snorted.

"Magic amulets? To protect against bad dreams? That's out there in my book, Roger."

Yeah, well some things don't fit into your book, do they, Holly?

Holly watched him as he struggled to find a response that would pacify her. Get her off the subject. She reached out and placed her palm on his cheek.

"Are your dreams that bad?" she said.

Roger grunted and nodded.

"Tell me," she said.

Roger rolled onto his back and laced his fingers behind his

head, stared at the ceiling.

"They start with a mist floating up from the basement. It pools out from under the door in the kitchen, climbs the stairs, and rolls into our room."

"Mist?"

"Yeah. Like a thick fog. Only it feels…ominous. Dangerous."

"That's it?"

The cat. The old woman. The pillar behind the twins.

"When it crosses the threshold into our room, it morphs. Shifts into shapes: a black cat. An old woman with yellow eyes…"

Roger shuddered.

"Baby!" Holly said. "This is really bothering you!"

Roger glanced over at her. She pulled herself into a cross-legged seat next to him and put a hand on his chest.

"You don't think the Lorazepam would help?"

Roger shook his head.

"I told you. I don't like the way it dims my mind."

"Maybe you should see someone. Talk about it."

Alex Lancaster. With her violet eyes and highlighted hair.

"A shrink? I don't think so."

Holly patted his chest.

"If your little magic amulet doesn't work, then?"

"I'll think about it, OK?"

Holly looked at him for a long moment, hand on his chest, the amulet under her palm.

She leaned down and kissed him.

"You're worrying me, baby."

"Can't have that," Roger said.

He reached up and pulled her close to him, his lips going to her neck.

He nibbled.

Holly squirmed.

"Roger…"

Roger rolled her onto her back and began to work his way up her neck, took her earlobe into his mouth and nibbled some more.

Holly arched her back, and Roger worked his way back down her neck, hands on her now, stroking, caressing.

The familiar rhythms of their lovemaking took over and Roger gave himself over to the experience.

Roger was on his back, Holly riding him, their lovemaking approaching its peak.

She was panting now, murmuring his name softly.

The room was growing cold. Holly's breath was visible, mist puffing out of her mouth.

She doesn't notice the cold.

Roger looked over her shoulder to the door.

Mist was flowing under the door, pooling, taking shape.

No.

Holly arched, her head rolled back and she began to tremble.

"That's it, Roger. Ooh, baby…"

Can't let myself go. Not with that thing here…

What did Alex say? Call on the light. Mother Mary.

Ridiculous.

His hand went to the pendant.

The amulet was vibrating, buzzing.

The mist grew into a pillar.

The pillar moved to the foot of the bed, rising up above Holly's shoulders, taking shape.

Mother Mary, protect me!

The mist shimmered, began to break up.

Roger's orgasm neared and he forced himself to relax.

No. Not with that thing still here.

Mother Mary, please.

The pillar of mist lost its shape, fell to the floor, and withdrew under the door again.

Holly bucked and trembled, tiny cries coming from her, then collapsed onto his chest, her whole body vibrating.

Roger held her, to him, orgasm forgotten, his own heart slowing, relaxing.

"Mmm," Holly said. "That was a good one."

She rolled to her side and grabbed for a towel, tucked in between her legs, then scooted under the sheets and snuggled up against him.

Roger put an arm around her, and she nestled her head on his shoulder, her hand tracing designs on his chest.

She tapped the amulet.

"Whatever that thing's good for, it seemed to help with the sex."

She smiled and snuggled into his side.

Roger raised his head to look at the door.

Just a door.

No mist.

Mother Mary?

"Yeah," he said. "It did."

The old woman was back in the grave, bound to the hated one.
Again.

The energy pouring from the room upstairs had called to her. She'd managed to get to the foot of the bed, was close to manifesting, and then…

A sharp spike of pain. A bolt of light dissipating my energy. Forcing me to withdraw, just when I was so close to pulling the essence from him.

The man has found himself an ally. A little magic.

Child's play. Caught me off guard.

She focused her energy, managed to rise.

She could feel the hated one pulling at her, but she'd gathered enough energy to resist.

Up the stairs, under the door, into the kitchen.

A bolt of energy shot through her.

What?

The energy revitalized her. Her spirit rose above the house into the starry sky lit by a gibbous moon, vitality crackling through her.

The young one from the house on the edge of town.

Zoe.

Yes! That's it, little one. Call me.

This one has power. And it has opened itself to the Dark Lord. Fully.

Available. Ripe for the plucking.

A thread of silver mist curved through the night sky over town, twinkling in the moonlight.

The old woman followed it to a run-down wooden structure near the ninety-degree bend in the river that cradled the town.

Strong energy here...

A series of broken-down brick structures sat on a grassy knoll across from where it lived.

The old woman turned her attention to the crumbling buildings.

Much pain here.

The energy of the place filled her.

A confluence of spirits.

The old woman's inner being throbbed and tingled in resonance to the pain that filled the compound.

Dozens of them.

Each damaged in some way, the soul warped and bent. Confused.

The old woman sifted through the energies pulsing and flitting about the compound.

A hospital of some sort. For damaged minds—a place to house the insane.

A thrill ran through her.

How interesting! So many tortured souls, all gathered in one spot. Most of them like lost little puppies looking for their bitch...but...

A pocket of dark energy flared from the depths of one of the buildings just off from the main central one.

Basement. A dungeon of sorts. A place to house the dangerous.

Ahh, these souls had direction. Passion. Knew what it felt like to spill blood, the warm rush as it splattered, the thrill of watching the light in the eyes of a chosen victim dim and blink out.

Knew what it meant to steal souls...

The old woman felt her power grow as she sifted the energies flowing through the dark underground corridors and cells.

The aura of the place radiated outward, crept into the surrounding neighborhood, pooled where the young one sat now, in an attic room, the ceiling slanted down to create the point of a triangle where it met the warped and buckled wooden floorboards.

The young one sat cross-legged at the edge of a pentagram painted onto the boards with cat's blood.

This one has a thing about cats. Something about them representative of its inner turmoil. The act of killing them cathartic, the blood of the animal enriching, empowering.

Just wait, little one. You think a cat has power...

The young one's hands rested on the wooden planchette of an antique Ouija board, its lips moving.

Calling me.

Power surged through the old woman, the young one's spirit filling hers.

Ah. Nothing like a living spirit for power. The soul not yet reaped, ripe for the plucking.

And this one has so much rage. And pain. Such a tortured little thing.

Delicious.

The old woman drifted down from the night sky, following the trail of silver mist emanating from the attic room.

She studied the young one.

This one is different. Neither female nor male, some sort of indeterminate in-between.

Interesting.

More interesting was the warped spirit within.

Powerful. The hatred and rage within banked over the course of its young life filled with petty and large torments. A lifetime of abuse and suffering. An outcast.

The young one ceased its chanting and looked up, startled.

Ah. It feels my presence.

Perfect. Wide open to the spirits, its dark energy food for the soul. Its spirit malleable, a tool waiting to be used.

Begging for it.

Well, little one, you and I have much to do.
Praise Satan.

Zoe labored over the Ouija board, her old copy of the Sixth and Seventh Book of Moses open to the Spirit Commado Beside the Black Raven.

It worked before.
And I've done what it wanted.
The demon.
My demon.
Mine.

A thrill ran through her.

Tyran will pay.

She focused her thoughts on Tyran's penis, willing cancerous tumors to spread from within, blackening it, filling Tyran with an agony that brought him to madness.

Zoe centered the Ouija board in the circle of the darkening pentagram on the floor.

Blood drying. Soaking into the floorboards.

She reached for the planchette.

Where to start?
What to ask?
The name.
Step number one to controlling a demon: name it. In their name lies power.
My demon.

A shiver ran through her.

Cold up here. As always.

Her breath misted in front of her.

But not this cold.
Something…

Zoe startled and looked up.

Mist filled the room, a shapeless pooling on the floor. Roiling. A dark energy there.

It's here!

Zoe's skin prickled and an electric thrill ran through her.

My demon!
She spoke to it.
"What is your name?"
The planchette jumped and slid under her fingertips, centered over the D.

It jumped again: A.

M.

I.

A.

The planchette grew still.

"Damia?"

"Is that your name? Damia?"

The planchette jumped to the upper left, centered over "Yes."

Zoe's lips curled up in a feral smile.

Damia. Mine to command.

"Damia. Can you curse someone? Give them cancer?"

The planchette stirred, moved to the center top of the board, rested on the "Ouija."

Ouija? What?

Rage surged through Zoe.

"Damia! I asked you a question. Can you curse someone?"

The planchette leapt under her hands, yanking them to the left.

Yes.

The rage cooled. Slightly. A tingle of excitement raised goosebumps along Zoe's arms.

Her teeth showed as her smile returned.

"I command you, in the name of Satan, to curse Tyran Hollenbeck!"

No response.

"Damia! In the name of Satan, the Dark Lord of all, I command you to curse Tyran Hollenbeck!"

Nothing.

Zoe lifted her hands off the planchette in frustration, the bird bones of her hands coming together in fragile little fists.

She lifted her head, screeched at the warped planks of the

ceiling.

"God damn it! Answer me!"

Her breath puffed out in agitated clouds.

Cold as hell up here.

The candles at the five points of the pentagram guttered, thick black smoke rising from them. A foul stench filled the room.

Zoe gagged.

"Damia! What the fuck? What…"

The thick smoke from the candles filled the room. The walls fell away, and Zoe could no longer make out the grain of the floorboards in front of her. Her head swam and the room began to spin. Her stomach clenched and she tasted bile. She fought back the rising vomit, swallowing it, the acid burn hot all the way down.

A cackle echoed inside Zoe's head.

An old woman's laugh. Like a witch out of a cartoon.

An image of the witch from an old Bugs Bunny cartoon flashed in Zoe's mind.

The smoke roiled and tightened, forming a shape in the center of the pentagram.

Yellow eyes rimmed in red peered at her as the smoke formed itself into a woman, bent with age, hair like wire, long craggy nose bent, mouth a black cavern with the dim red glow of a bed of coals, the walls just visible through her.

"Child," the old woman crooned. "This grows tedious. Tell me. What do you want?"

Zoe blinked back tears from eyes that stung from the acrid smoke, the taste of bile in her mouth, her teeth coated with it.

"Tyran Hollenbeck must die. I want his cock to blacken and swell with cancer. I want pain to rule his every moment. I want him to die a long, lingering death. And I want him to know. Know that it was me. I want to laugh at him and spit in his face as he dies."

The old woman's cackle filled her head.

"That's it, child," she said. "Stoke your hatred. Fuel it."

The wispy, transparent nature of the old woman thickened as

she took form.

"Why should I curse this Tyran of yours, hmm?" the old woman crooned.

"Because you are mine! I conjured you! And I command..."

Pain exploded in Zoe's chest.

Like a hand of ice gripping my heart, tearing it.

She doubled over, forehead coming to rest on her knees.

The old woman was laughing, softly.

"Oh, child," she said. "You have no idea."

"Mine," Zoe gasped. "In the name of Satan, I..."

Ice spread from her heart up to her shoulders, down to her groin, the pain a burning, icy fire. Her lungs froze and she fought for breath even as her stomach heaved again and hot bile poured out of her mouth into her lap.

"Yes, child. The Dark Lord. Satan. Very good."

Zoe clenched her fists, focused on drawing a breath.

"You will obey me," she said, her voice thick, vomitus still in her throat.

"Oh, child," the old woman said. "You still don't understand?"

The icy fire spread through Zoe, climbed up her neck, invaded her brain. Her thoughts scrambled, every atom of her being throbbing in pain.

"You have opened a door, dear child."

The room was gone. Her thoughts scrambled into fragments.

Suffocating.

A flash of the witch from the Bugs Bunny cartoon.

Glistening crystals.

A fire circle in a clearing of the woods.

A very pregnant young woman, stretched out on a stone altar, hooded figures encircling her.

A huge figure at the edge of the fire circle.

Running through the woods, bursting into a field.

Torches bobbing at the edge of the field, approaching.

Pain a hot fire in the gut.

A tearing within, flesh ripping like rotten fabric.

Blood spilling out between a woman's—my?—legs.

A fiery ingot glowing red orange expelled from the womb—a baby...
Another ripping tear.
Agony.
A second child expelled from the womb to thump to the dirt clods of the field underneath.
Torches approaching, encircling, voices rising...

The floorboards snapped back into her vision, and Zoe felt the fabric of her jeans, sticky with vomit, against her forehead.

She drew in a gasping breath.

Air!

She panted, grateful to be able to breathe as never before.

She pushed herself upright with weak and trembling arms.

The attic room greeted her, the ceiling angling down, the candles burning steadily, the smoke, and the old woman...gone.

"What..." Zoe rasped, the taste of bile still thick in her mouth.

She spat into the center of the pentagram.

Roger blinked awake.

The house was quiet, just the soft tinkle of the fins of the baseboard heater as hot water flowed through the pipes, warming the room.

His hand went to the amulet on his chest.

He fingered it.

Peaceful. Quiet.

His mind traced its way through the house: out the door, down the hallway to the twin's room.

Silent. Nothing stirring.

He sighed.

This is crazy.

Holly snuffled beside him and rolled onto her back, an arm across her forehead.

Roger propped himself up on an elbow and looked at her.

Still beautiful. Angled cheekbones, strong jaw, body lithe and muscular yet feminine with curves in all the right places.

Holly's mouth dropped partly open and snored lightly.

Roger smiled.

My babe. Such a good woman. Strong. Driven.

He traced a finger down her side, a feeling of warm love running through him.

Wind buffeted the window.

Roger looked up.

What was that?

Another blast of wind and the light coming through the window cast moving shadows as the trees on the street swayed.

Something coming.

Roger sat up and swung his feet off the bed to rest on the floor.

The old rowhouse shook as another blast of wind hit its sides.

The bedroom darkened.

Streetlights out?

He glanced at the window.

The streetlight outside glowed, but it had dimmed, its light barely making it to the window.

Wind swirled outside and the temperature of the room dropped.

The presence. Back.

Roger's hand went to the amulet and Alex Lancaster's voice sounded in his head: "Call on the light, Roger…"

Just the breeze. Storm brewing.

"The forces of darkness want you to doubt…"

No. Not just the wind. The old woman.

Back.

Hand still on the amulet, Roger let himself open to the forces stirring anew in the house.

She's here. It was her absence that woke me.

But how? Where?

He shook his head.

Doesn't matter. She's here. Now.

He looked to the door and was startled to see mist pooling on the floor, masking the floorboards underneath.

Checking on me. Testing…

Roger closed his eyes.

"Call on the light..."

"Mother Mary," Roger whispered, "come to me."

He felt a shift in the energy in the room. The streetlight outside blinked and brightened.

The mist retreated back out the door, floorboards glistening in the light.

Ha. Take that, you bitch.

He watched the door, feeling empowered.

Got your number now. Mother Mary, thank you.

The room was completely free of the mist.

He felt for the presence of the old woman.

There. Outside the door. Retreating. Down the hallway...

Roger lifted his feet off the floor and snuggled back into the warm cocoon of the bed.

The still small voice of panic at his center quieted and he allowed himself to close his eyes and let go, drift back to sleep.

The old woman hovered in the hallway outside the door.

So. The man has found himself some magic. Thinks he has the upper hand now.

She smiled.

Let him think so. I have supped enough off him. And now...forces are moving. I'm free, for the first time in centuries. Found allies of my own: the young one wide open, mine for the taking. The spirits in the basement of the old hospital. Energy enough.

She drifted down the hallway, found the gap under the door of the room to one side of the bathroom and slid through.

Twin beds, one on each side of the room.

The twins.

She cackled.

The real prize here. Two young spirits, ripe for the plucking.

She felt for their spirits.

Pure light. Untouchable. No darkness at all.

Frustration pulsed through her.

She focused on the darker of the two—this one open just a crack.

Enough for a first attempt...
She summoned all her strength and reached for the sleeping boy.

He murmured in his sleep, tossed, wrapped the blankets more tightly around himself.

That's it, little one. I'm coming.
She reached for his mind, his spirit dormant, but stirring.
There!
The little one's chest rose and fell as his breathing shallowed and picked up.
I'm in.

Tommy tossed and turned in his bed.
Chasing Timmy down the hallway to the bathroom, something weird about the house, the floors angled, hard to run on, the feeling of slipping and sliding, the floor no longer solid.

In the bathroom, the mirror glowing silver white, an aura that lit the room with something like moonlight.

Timmy transfixed in front of the mirror, staring.
What?
He looked to the mirror and the silvery light darkened, the room faded and he found himself looking into eyes that stared out of the mirror at him.

Yellow eyes. Rimmed in red.
Tommy gasped and jerked awake.
He sat up in bed and looked about wildly.
Nothing. Just Timmy asleep in his bed, covers pulled up to his chin.

Tommy's breath was visible in the cold of the room, and he pulled the covers up to his chin.
Something was here.
Is here.
"Go away!" Tommy said.
Timmy stirred.
The cold seeped out of the room and Tommy relaxed.
He took a last look around the room.

Just the room. Timmy asleep.

Not so cold anymore.

He lay back down in bed and snugged the blanket tight.

Just a dream.

Nothing to worry about.

I'm a big boy now. I can handle this.

His eyes drooped, closed, and soon he was fast asleep.

The old woman stood just outside the door.

Progress. An in.

But the child has an awareness. And enough light in him to push me away.

She smiled.

For now...

The grave tugged at her, and the old woman gave in and let the hated one reel her back in.

Tired. Expended a lot of energy tonight.

But supped well.

Progress.

The villagers gathered around the woman sprawled on her back at the edge of the field.

John Lewis, a tall, burly man with a hat covering his balding crown held his torch over the tableau.

"Violetta Dunphy," he said. "The witch."

The child that squirmed in the dirt between her legs opened its mouth and screeched, a cry that sent shivers of horror running through him.

"Demon spawn!"

The child squalled and writhed, dirt stuck to its bloody little body, revealing a curled tail. The circle of villagers drew back.

"A devil child!"

"Satan's offspring!"

Fear moved through the villagers.

John Lewis held out a thick and callused hand.

"Give me a shovel," he said.

No one moved.

"I said, give me a shovel," John roared.

William Willard broke from the circle and held out a shovel.

"Hold my torch," John said.

He took the shovel, steeled himself as the child's cries echoed through the field, each cry sending a shiver of revulsion through him, and stepped forward and raised the shovel.

The child rolled its tiny eyes and centered on his.

The torchlight dimmed, a faint red-orange glow as the field and villagers faded.

The serving girl bent over the table in the lounge, skirts bunched up around her waist, his thick hands gripping her hips as he thrust into her. He slipped out, thrust blindly, and felt the tight grip of her anus as his thrust missed its mark and he sunk balls deep into her.

A thrill ran through him, heightening his pleasure as the serving girl cried out in pain...and delight.

Sodomy.

He bucked madly as orgasm overtook him, a whole body release that curled his toes.

Best orgasm of my life.

The little eyes cut through the mist of memory and John Lewis blinked.

A cry of rage erupted out of him and he brought the blade of the shovel down hard, the edge catching the child under the chin, driving through its tiny little neck, and sinking into the earth below.

"Demon spawn!" he roared.

The circle held still.

A breeze moved quietly through the field, the only sound the tiny gurgle as blood ran out of the child's decapitated body to the dirt below.

Something mewled.

The circle murmured in renewed horror.

"Another one!"

Violetta moaned.

"The witch lives! The bride of Satan!"

Horror gripped the crowd and a few of the men stepped forward, shovels in their hands.

Shovels thumped against flesh with dull thumps over the keening horror of the crowd.

Finally, it was done.

The men leaned against their shovels, panting, the women bunched together in horror, the flickering torchlight illuminating faces beaded with sweat and dirty clothing.

John Lewis found his breath.

"Dig a hole," he said.

The crowd looked at him.

"Ten feet, at least. We'll bury the devil's spawn deep in the earth. Upright. So their spirits cannot escape."

No one moved.

"I said dig!" John Lewis roared.

The spell broke.

Soon, the men were hard at work, the only sound the slice of metal into the gritty soil, the thump of shovelfuls of dirt and rock piled by the growing hole in the earth.

Tommy tossed in his bed, the dreams not willing to let go.

An old woman. Nasty. Yellow eyes.

Crouched by the bed. Whispering into my ears.

Strange words.

The old woman radiated a force that pounded in his head—a throbbing, angry pulse that drove away his thoughts, raised imagery of blood and violence.

Something thumped into his face, and Tommy jerked awake.

"Get up, lazy bones!" Timmy said, raising the pillow in his hands to bring it down again.

Red rage filled Tommy and he snatched the pillow from Timmy's hands and scrambled out of bed, intent on catching Timmy.

Tackle him. Get my knees on his chest, punch the shit out of him. Ground and pound.

The sheets bunched around Tommy's legs and he sprawled

full-length on the floor.

Timmy danced out of the way and sprinted out the door, giggling.

Kill him! Beat him until blood stains the floorboards...

Tommy blinked.

Wait. What? Kill him?

The rage seeped away, a cold pit taking its place in his stomach.

Kill him? What?

Tommy lay on the floor a long moment, his mind swirling.

Something is wrong.

Something in this house.

Got into me...

Cold dread filled his bones as he dragged himself from the floor.

I hate this house.

I hate this town.

Something's wrong.

Something's very wrong.

Alex Lancaster pulled her battered midnight blue Toyota Corolla up to the white picket fence at the little cottage at the edge of town.

A row of rose bushes lined the fence, their canes bare and brown against the fence, burlap wrapped around their bases.

The screen door creaked open in the cold as she stepped out of her car. An old woman stepped onto the porch. Her face lit up as she spotted Alex.

"Alex!" she said.

She stood on the porch, wrapping a heavy shawl around her shoulders as Alex lifted the latch on the gate and walked up the path to greet her.

The old woman's face wrinkled as Alex approached.

"What troubles you, child?"

Alex climbed the steps to the porch and wrapped the old woman in a hug. She kissed her on the cheek.

"Good to see you, Grandma," she said.

The old woman leaned back and looked into Alex's eyes.

"You're here on business," she said. "Let's go inside."

Grandma Nurse puttered about the little kitchen, a teapot on the stove warming. She walked over to the cupboard and opened it, scanned the glass jars neatly arranged on shelves, selected one, and pulled it down. She rummaged in a drawer for a pair of tea bails and carefully packed them with the leaves and stems from the jar.

"Dreamer's tea?" Alex said.

Grandma Nurse nodded.

"Mugwort, wormwood, and damiana, with mint to cut the bitterness," she said.

She set the tea bails into mugs, brought them to the table and put them down just as the teapot began to squeal.

She poured steaming water into each cup, set the teapot back on the stove and seated herself across the table.

The two women sat quietly for a moment, sipping tea.

The kitchen shone in the early morning sun coming through the multi-paned windows, countertops sparkling.

"So," Grandma Nurse said. "Tell me."

Alex told her. She spoke of the man who'd come into her shop the day before, the spirit strong upon him, the visions he'd revealed as they sat.

The old woman nodded along, saying little.

Alex finished.

"He's got twins, you say? Boys? Fraternal or identical?"

"Fraternal."

"One light and one dark..."

"They're too young to be either, really," Alex said.

"But they are open," the old woman replied. "And their father...a natural medium."

"Yes. But he's unschooled. Unaware. The visions impress themselves upon him like dreams."

"But there have been physical manifestations? Things moving?"

Alex shook her head.

"I don't think so, Grandma. Just visions. Physical sensations—cold. Mist."

"Don't discount the mist, child," Grandma Nurse said. "That is a physical manifestation."

Alex nodded.

"Yes, of course."

Grandma Nurse leaned back in her chair, her eyes moving up and left as she searched her memory.

"They've moved into an old rowhouse in the West Park neighborhood, you say?"

Alex sipped her tea and nodded.

"That used to be fields on the edge of town. Not far from the Witches Clearing," the old woman said. "Legend has it they killed a witch there, centuries ago. The villagers found her sprawled in the field. She'd just given birth…"

"Twins," Alex said.

Grandma Nurse met her eyes.

"Yes. As the story goes, one was red—with a tail. The villagers beat the woman and the babies to death with shovels, buried them ten feet down in the earth where they found them. Upright, to prevent their spirits from escaping."

Alex shuddered.

"Horrible."

"Those were ignorant times, child," Grandma Nurse said.

"No more than now," Alex said.

The old woman sighed.

"True."

She sipped her tea.

"So. What do you think, Grandma?"

She gripped her tea as a cold shudder worked through her.

"I've never felt such a powerful spirt. Such darkness. Such evil. A soul completely given over to the Dark Lord."

"More than that, child," Grandma Nurse said. "A soul dedicated to bringing the Dark Lord into the world."

Understanding blossomed and Alex gripped the mug more

tightly.

"The twins...one dark, and one light."

Grandma Nurse nodded.

"And now—this family. The man opened the door. The twins..."

"Precisely. The old woman was once a powerful witch. She led a coven centuries ago. As the story goes, they called up the Dark Lord himself to impregnate a virgin they'd lured into the coven. Held her captive for months, but the old woman suffered a heart attack and died. The coven kept the impregnated witch in a cabin, not far from the Witches Clearing, but she escaped just before she was to give birth...'

"And the villagers found her."

"They put an end to it."

"Bloody way to put an end to it. And not all that efficient. Not if..."

"They did their best. What they've done held the old woman's spirit for centuries."

"But how? You said the old woman died of a heart attack."

"She sent her spirit into the young one."

"Two spirits in one body?"

Alex looked down into her empty mug.

"Ah," she said. "The two forces."

"Bound in one body, buried in a deep grave, upright."

"With the two babies."

"Twins."

"So," Alex said. "What can we do?"

The two sat as the sunlight sparkled off the countertops and silver sink and faucets.

Roger fiddled with the amulet, fingering it absently as he stared at his computer monitor.

The words from the document blurred and swam in front of him.

Focus.

He blinked and sat straight, forced himself to read.

"An Inclusive Call for Nonviolent Action to Achieve a Just Peace…"

Wordy.

He sighed, fingertips resting on the keyboard.

Boring.

What had once seemed so vital, so important, were now just words. Swimming on the page.

Not only boring. Useless. How do you reverse centuries of animosity? Deep-rooted hatred and prejudice?

Come on, Roger. You promised you'd have this thing done by the end of the week.

He leaned in and forced himself to focus.

"Dear Friends, Supporters, and Fellow Advocates,

In response to our current situation and adhering to our principles of justice, inclusion, and nonviolence…"

Stupid. Trite. Pedantic. Useless.

How can words change anything?

Action. Action changes things.

His mind wandered, casting him back to Israel, scenes of uproar: mobs rampaging through the Palestinian sector, pulling people from their apartments, beating them…

Light and dark, isn't that what Alex said?

Good and evil.

Simplistic.

Both sides see themselves as light, the other as darkness.

That's the problem. Or part of it, anyway.

He pushed away the violent imagery and tried to focus again.

Tommy off this morning. Quieter than usual. Brooding, almost.

What if…

No.

But, what if? What if the old woman was shifting gears, going after the twins?

The cold center of panic in his soul clenched.

No. Not my kids.

But…

He pushed against the desk, casters on the bottom of his chair straightening and rolling the chair back across the hardwood floor.

He spun in the chair, mind spinning along with the chair.

Sunlight through the window flashed light and dark as he spun.

Light and dark.

The twins.

The old woman.

The other...the witch.

Light and dark.

Action.

But what kind of action?

She's in the basement. Somehow. Something down there a repository of sorts. For her soul. And that of the witch. The other one.

Wait. A witch that called to Mother Mary? How does that make any sense?

God damn it.

Roger stood and paced the office.

Action. I have to do something...

Tommy's uncharacteristically morose face rose in his mind's eye.

Seemed so off this morning. Should have kept him home.

Or at least talked to him about it.

But did you?

No. You just shuffled him off to school with Timmy. Watched them disappear through the doors of that old building and melt into the crowd of children.

Work to do.

Fuck.

I need someone to talk to. To figure this out.

Put this whole business to rest.

He glanced across the room at his computer just as the screen saver kicked to life: a family portrait of them in Jerusalem, at the wailing wall, the old stones rising above them, the crowd of people all around.

The chanting of the Orthodox Jews, bowing and murmuring at the wall.

They believed in light and dark.

Saw themselves as the light. The Palestinians the dark.

Convenient. An excuse to ride roughshod over an entire population. Treat them much as they themselves were treated.... And they don't see the parallels. Astonishing what the mind can do once it settles on a sense of righteousness.

But there is something there, underneath the layers of rationalization and rhetoric. Something spiritual:

Light and dark.

Roger turned his back on the screen, crossed into the hallway, walked to the stairs and rested his hand on the railing.

He gazed down the stairs to the kitchen below, the bottom of the door to the basement just visible.

Dark down there.

Action.

Do something.

Alex. The one with the purple highlights in her hair that matched the unreal luminosity of her eyes.

Such a lovely woman. Her hands so soft and welcoming. A peace there...

Snap out of it, you idiot. You're a married man.

But...she understands. Knows.

Mind made up, he clumped down the stairs, swept through the hallway, lifted his coat from the rack by the door, grabbed his keys from the hook where they hung, and let himself out into the cold, misty morning.

Tommy sat in his place in the story circle at the back of the room.

So tired.

Sleepy.

The room was warm and cozy, the old radiator on the wall ticking out heat, combining with the hot breath and bodies of the other twenty-four kids in the room.

Ms. Eriksson was reading from some book—Harry Potter or

something.

Boring.

She read with passion, doing the voices, making the tale as entertaining as she could, but it left Tommy cold.

His head grew heavy and dipped.

An old woman. At the door. Watching me and Timmy.

Insubstantial, a misty outline with red-rimmed yellow eyes, can see right through her.

But something more solid and real about her than the bed underneath me, the sheets tangled around my body.

Something penetrating, reaching in, passing through my skin and bones as easily as an X-ray, touching me, grasping, scratching, clawing for my center…for me. *Putting images in my head—a dream—a flickering fire in a clearing in the woods, hooded figures singing, no, chanting, a big stone table at the head of the fire, something, no someone, stretched out on it…*

A wad of paper bounced off his temple, stinging him back to the present.

He jerked his head up to see Drago Trunchbill grinning at him, eyes dancing with malice.

Like that old woman, Tommy realized with a start. *Same mean spirit.*

He'd seen Drago at work, tripping kids in the hallway, sending them sprawling. Using the games in PE as an excuse to inflict real pain, making other kids cry. Gathering his gang on the playground, wandering the lunchroom helping himself to tasty tidbits of other's lunches.

And nobody ever does anything.

Drago smirked at him, raised a hand to his forehead, index finger pointed up, thumb perpendicular to create an L for loser.

Drago's eyes flickered, dimmed, became yellow and red rimmed.

Tommy gathered his legs and launched himself across the story circle for Drago.

Drago's eyes flickered again, a niggle of confusion and alarm, and then Tommy was on him. He bowled Drago over onto his back and got his knees on his shoulders.

Ground and pound.

Tommy's fists pummeled the boy. Drago's yellow eyes wheeled in confusion and panic and Tommy did his level best to close them, hammer fists smashing into Drago's nose and eyes.

Smash him. Make his eyes pop. Crack his skull open.

Kill him.

A veil of red black descended on him, coloring his vision, the only thing clear the squirming boy pinned to the floor under his knees. Tommy's whole soul bent on destroying the boy, crushing him, flattening his skull.

A fierce desire to hurt and maim unlike anything he'd ever experienced filled him.

Like a dream. Watching myself from a distance. Something taken control, empowering me.

Kill him.

The classroom erupted, kids leaping to their feet, some circling in to watch, others shrinking away.

Tommy raised a fist and brought it smashing down on Drago's face, raised it again, and then a strong hand seized his wrist and yanked him up and off of Drago, and dragged him, kicking and yelling across the room.

The red black veil snapped away as easily as a gust of wind clears the morning mist from a field.

Ms. Eriksson.

Man. She is stronger than she looks. A lot stronger.

"Tommy Nimanator!" Ms. Eriksson hissed. "What has gotten into you?"

Gotten into me. The old woman. She…

Tommy went limp.

What just happened?

He looked across the room to where Drago was curled into a ball, weakly attempting to sit up, blood pouring from his face.

Good, Tommy thought. *I hope it hurts.*

Fear replaced the deep satisfaction coursing through him.

But what was that?

It was like something just…got into me. A wild force filled with the desire to hurt. To kill.

He allowed Ms. Eriksson to drag him out the door of the room to the hallway.

"You march yourself down to Mr. Schill's office right now, Tommy Nimanator. I'll be along in a minute."

She let go of his wrist and gave him a little shove.

"March, young man. Right now."

Tommy looked up at Ms. Eriksson with wide eyes.

"I'm, sorry, Ms. Eriksson, I…"

The fierce light in Ms. Eriksson's eyes softened and she met his eyes.

"Go along now, Tommy. We'll talk about this later."

He looked at her.

"I don't know what happened," he said. "I just…"

"Go now, Tommy."

She gave him another little shove.

"Scoot."

Tommy trudged down the long hallway, a row of classroom doors with frosted glass on each side, head down.

A cackle sounded behind him and he spun in alarm.

Just empty hallway. Nothing there.

He backed down the hallway, eyes darting from side to side, sweeping up and down the corridor.

Nothing there.

The old woman…followed me here…no, inside of me? Part of me?

Cold dread filled him, sweat popping on his forehead and upper lip. He wiped it away with his forearm, took a last long look down the hallway then turned for Mr. Schill's office.

I am in so much trouble.

Dad's going to freak.

The door to Mr. Schill's office loomed and Tommy reached a hand for the patinated brass of the door handle.

Alex puttered about her shop, distracted.

Forces moving through Allentown. Ancient and implacable.

Reawakening after centuries of sleep.

Why?

Could the man who'd found his way to my doorstep really be the cause? The catalyst? A natural medium, unaware of the power within, intellectualizing all the supernatural events that had sparkled through his life, holding fast to ignorance, allowing the forces that swirled around him ingress through a combination of denial and willful ignorance?

Grandma Nurse thought it possible.

Alex sat at the table in the center of the shop, elbows on the green velvet top, a single white candle burning at its center. She stared into the flame and remembered her conversation with Grandma Nurse.

"He is the key, child," she said. "The forces of darkness have found a new foothold in the land. The culture of the day nurtures petty hatreds, feeds on them, uses them as tools to sway a credulous populace in one direction or another, the city split evenly down the center. There's a spiritual energy coursing through the town like never before.

"Underneath it all, the Dark Lord glories in the malice. The hatred. Feeds it. He's found knots of malevolence in the population, nurtured them, used the blind passion as an open door. Can't you feel the spirit moving through the town?"

"But what can we do?"

"We shine a light in the darkness, child. We bring it all into the light. And then we shut the door."

"How do we do that?"

"This man. Roger Nimanator. He is the key. The old woman is using him. The spirit within him is strong. Stronger than anything she's found in more than two hundred years. It's loosed her. Allowed her ingress to the world."

"So, what do we do? Kill him?"

Grandma Nurse snorted.

"Really? That is what you come up with? You can't destroy darkness with more darkness. You know that, child."

"I was joking, Grandma."

"Not funny. If this man were to die while the spirit is vulnerable…. No. The old woman would collect his soul, turn his power to her ends."

"The amulet…"

"A stopgap. Something to buy us time. If he believes, that is."

"His belief is shaky. Unstable."

"We need to wake him up. Fire up his faith. Only then can we corral the force within him and use its power against the old woman."

"How?"

"To lead us to the old woman's resting place. She needs something physical to tie herself to this plane of existence."

"The gravesite."

"Yes. The house. She is there, somewhere. Most likely buried beneath the foundation."

"Dig her up. Destroy the corpse. Give her spirit nothing to hold fast to."

Grandma Nurse nodded.

"That is part of it, yes. But he must be there. He must see the old woman, confront her."

"Send her back to hell."

"Yes. But we must hurry. She is loose, now. She'll be using his power to travel. To seek out kindred spirits in the town. If she gets into one of those, truly takes over, she may be able to tie herself to this world, take possession so solidly that destroying her resting place will only empower her. With a kindred soul, open to her, she can do great harm."

"You think that's possible?"

"I think she's already working on it. And has found one. At least one."

"But she can only be in one place at a time. Right?"

"Not even Satan himself can be in two places at once. But his army is legion."

Grandma Nurse's shoulders rounded and she cradled the mug of tea in her hand, gazed into its depths.

"I think she is using the man's power to roam the town, seeking out kindred spirits, planting seeds of evil. Empowering the wicked. Driving them."

Grandma Nurse smiled grimly.

"I can feel the forces gathering, child. A reckoning is coming. You've felt it, too, haven't you? The air is filled with dark energy, hatreds burning hot and bright. Ripe for the plucking. There are far too many out there who've allowed the dark spirits in. All the old woman has to do is plant a seed, provide an image, point them in the direction she wishes them to go. Each truly evil act opens the door a bit wider, provides the dark spirits with access to this world."

Alex closed her eyes as a vision gripped her:

Dark energy swirling through the town. Tendrils reaching into the rowhouses and apartments, the cottages on the periphery, finding hearts filled with malice and infecting them with dark power. An orgy of violence and evil ready to take over the town.

The town center in flames, an army of souls filled with darkness rampaging, overturning cars, setting fire to businesses and homes.

A huge, towering figure at the center. More than seven feet tall and growing with each act of violence. A creature with the body of a man: muscular, broad shoulders jutting out over a tapered waist, abdomen rippling with muscle, thick arms the size of trees, huge hands with long, spidery digits ending with fingernails extended and sharp as knives.

And the head of a goat.

The Dark Lord himself.

The creature waved its taloned hand, and black sparks crackled outwards, each spark alighting on a soul in the crowd, filling it with an overwhelming desire to kill and destroy.

An army of dark soldiers, each taken by a demon.

Bringing Satan's will into the world.

A black tornado sprouted, spiraling high into the sky, spread across the land, reached into the surrounding countryside, seeking more souls, finding them, the violence spreading, fires burning across the landscape, thick black smoke rising to pall the heavens above.

Alex blinked.

Grandma Nurse sighed, raised herself to her feet, went to the stove and came back with the teapot, refilled their cups.

"You have seen."

Alex nodded, wordless.

"I've never seen anything like it," she said. "Such power."

"This is the old woman's vision. If she can get the door to the underworld open, it will come to pass."

The bell over the door tinkled and Alex looked up from her reverie, startled.

Him.

The old woman cackled.

Success. The boy cracked open, a vessel to be filled.

Each blow the boy had struck filled her with glee, the smell of the other boy's blood delicious, his terror empowering, but the rage that filled the child was limited, tenuous, her grasp on him wavering.

It is the man I must have, she realized. *He has the real power. The boy a limited source. Use him, but with caution. The man must remain doubtful, uncertain. If he were to discover the boy is open... and I have used him...it might ignite belief. Awaken him to the power he carries.*

And he has already found an ally.

The old woman's spirit rose above the school, traveled down the street toward the center of town.

A woman.

The old woman could feel the man—nearby, walking with resolution, a fixed destination in mind.

The woman. Violet eyes. A shop filled with spells...

A knot of rage flared within the old woman's blackened soul.

Let him lead me to this ally of his. Then, use the dark one, the one who thinks it summoned me. The power within it grows, its tortured soul fertile ground.

The man passed Trout Hall, followed a side street, turned and descended a set of old stone steps to a shop below.

The old woman cackled again.

Found her.

She sent her spirit down the steps, reached for the man.

A bolt of light flared, its touch fire, burning the old woman in a way she had never experienced.

Her spirit recoiled, blasted by the light, scorched and smoldering, pain unbearable.

The pull of the grave was suddenly too much for her and she felt her spirit being reeled in by the hated one, pulled back to the bones under the stone floor of the old rowhouse.

The man was momentarily forgotten as pain overwhelmed her and she found herself back in the grave, the hated one flaring with light, further scorching her.

The old woman withdrew her spirit into a tight knot, pain radiating throughout.

The man's ally more powerful than I had imagined.

The old woman steeled herself, found her center, forced herself to relax.

So.

A momentary setback. The man is a fool, blind to the full reality of his situation. He's scared, uncertain, seeking answers.

A bolt of fear shot through the old woman.

He must be stopped.

The old woman pushed away the fiery pain scorching her, focused.

I know where she is now.

And I have allies of my own.

Powerful ones, filled with the spirit of the Dark Lord.

All I need to do is to use the tortured one. Set it loose upon the ally. Summon the full force of the Dark Lord for an assault the ally cannot withstand.

Possible.

But not now. I need to gather my strength.

Rest.

Recoup.

Tonight, when the man sleeps, I will sup on him. Renew my strength, find the tortured one and empower it. Help it to open the door a bit further.

And use the forces it looses to destroy the ally.

And then...

My time will come.

It is foreseen. Fate. The dark forces will take over this world.

And it will burn. A glorious fire consuming all the light in the world. Leaving only the Dark Lord and his army of souls.

And I will take my place at the left hand of the Dark Lord.

But I must rest.

Tonight...

Zoe climbed the stairs to her attic room, stroking the cat cradled in her arms. She'd lured the stray with a scrap of meat. It'd been hesitant, wary, crouching low, tail flicking, its eyes darting from the meat held out in Zoe's hand to the sidewalk and back.

But hunger had won out.

Like it always did.

The cat nestled into the crook of her arm as she reached the landing at the top of the stairs.

Zoe grasped the faux crystal doorknob with her free hand and pushed the door to her room open.

The cat stiffened and bunched as Zoe stepped into her room.

Smells the blood. Suddenly realizes what is coming.

The cat's claws came out and it scrambled, but Zoe was ready.

The cat's howl cut off as Zoe's hands closed around its neck.

She squeezed with all the strength she had, the cats four paws scrambling wildly as it dangled from her at arm's length.

It arched and bucked wildly, a tiny gagging sound issuing from its open mouth, and its claws found purchase, ripping open a gash in Zoe's left wrist.

She grimaced and squeezed harder.

The cat's struggles lessened, became mere twitches as Zoe's grip tightened around its neck.

Blood trickled down her arm to her elbow and dripped to the floor, the warped and dry wooden floorboards soaking it up instantly.

The cat went completely limp, but Zoe knew better than to release her grip.

Takes a few minutes. Let it go now, and it'll revive.

Zoe sank to the floor in front of the faded pentagram, her arms trembling with the effort of holding her grip.

Wait.

She stared into the flickering flames of the five black candles at each point of the old pentagram and waited.

Blood dripped from her elbow to splat silently onto the wooden floor, the drops landing inside the pentagram, the floor absorbing them greedily.

Enough.

She set the body down in front of her, slid the black ceramic bowl next to the body, and reached for her knife—a kris.

She clutched the hilt of the kris, fashioned into an elaborate demon with tiny red chips for eyes. The blade itself was formed into a serpent, sinuous folds etched with carved scales. Black flecks of blood encrusted the lines.

She placed the cat in her lap, head dangling over the bowl, and with a practiced move cut its throat.

The cat jerked and blood dribbled onto the floor before Zoe repositioned the cat's head so the gurgling blood drained into the bowl.

The coppery, tangy smell of fresh blood filled the air and Zoe smiled.

She upended the cat and squeezed, the last of its blood filling the bowl, then set the carcass to one side.

Time to do something.

Her last experience with the old woman had scared her.

The old woman laughed at me. Then reached inside me as casually as if reaching for a cup of tea and...

The details had dimmed over the intervening days, as had the horror that accompanied them. And as her fear diminished, hatred took its place.

Hatred was comfortable. Familiar. The central fact of her life for as long as she could remember.

I will have my revenge. Tryan will die. Painfully.

And the old woman will be my servant.

She'd convinced herself that this time, the old woman would obey.

Blood not fresh enough, maybe. Or perhaps I allowed doubt to color the incantations.

Fresh blood. Doubt vanquished.

Yet deep down, at her core, the memory of the old woman's touch sent an icy tingle of fear through her.

She pushed it away.

Believe. The demons are wily, filled with deceit. I allowed this one to cast doubt, gave it the upper hand.

Not again.

Zoe dipped her left index finger into the bowl of blood and set to repainting the pentagram, setting aside each candle as she retraced the five points of the pentagram, letting blood pool there, replacing the candle in a tiny puddle of fresh blood.

She didn't notice the dripping wound on her wrist adding her blood to the cat's.

Candles in place, pentagram redrawn, Zoe turned to the open book in front of her.

Spirit Commado Beside the Black Raven.

She hardly needed the text anymore, the incantation burned into her memory, but she liked the tactile feel of the old book, believed it held power from the ones who had yielded it over the years.

As she recited from the sacred text, a coldness crept into her attic lair.

That's it. Come to me.

My demon.

Damia.

The candles guttered in a now-familiar way, thick black smoke rising in clouds to fill the room, darkening its edges, creating an open space for the demons to enter.

The smoke pooled in the center of the pentagram as Zoe chanted, bloody hands open and resting on her knees.

Red-rimmed yellow eyes peered out at her and a thrill ran through her.

"Damia! In the name of our Dark Lord, Satan, I command you to come to me."

A red spark flared deep within the yellow eyes, then dimmed as the smoke thickened and shaped itself.

The old woman sat in the center of the pentagram, mouth closed, just a line of glowing red-orange where its lips met, the eyes fixed on Zoe.

"Yes, child," the old woman said.

"Tryan lives. I saw him on the street yesterday, with his buddies. Laughing."

Tryan at the center of a group of rowdy boys gamboling down the street near Trout Hall. Happy. Filled with happiness, in fact.

Healthy.

A slap in the face.

Rage coursed through Zoe and her open palms closed into fists, the drying blood gluing the skin together.

"I commanded you to curse him! Fill his cock with cancer. Send him pain beyond anything he has ever experienced."

She glared at the old woman.

"And he's fine. Happy."

Her fists tightened on her knees.

"I command you to curse him! To…"

The yellow eyes flared, red dots at their center growing.

"There is one who stands in the way, child."

Zoe's rage cooled as confusion spread through her.

"One who stands in the way? What?"

"There is a woman. A practicer of white magic. A hexmaster with a lineage as old as mine. She has power, child. She threatens us."

Zoe's brow knitted as she tried to grasp what the old woman was saying.

"Can't you curse her? Kill her?"

The yellow eyes swung left and right as the old woman shook her head.

"This one has power. But together, we can defeat her. Then I will be free to send this cancer into your Tryan. Only then."

"But how?"

"You are in the physical world, child."

The old woman gestured at the blood-encrusted kris on the floor at the edge of the pentagram.

"Hand me the knife, child."

Fear shot through Zoe.

Enter the circle? The circle of protection? No.

Zoe shook her head.

"No. I can't do that."

The old woman cackled, the sound reverberating inside Zoe's head, pushing away thought, sending tremors through her.

"Oh, but you can, child. You will."

A jolt of icy pain shot down Zoe's arm and she watched as her hand closed on the handle of the knife and reached out and brought the kris within the circle.

The old woman stretched out a gnarled hand, knuckles huge and distorted, and took hold of the knife.

A thick snap of electricity sounded and a red-black flare of light traveled along the steel blade and elaborate hilt of the knife. Zoe's entire being lit up with an icy pain that drove all thought away.

Zoe found herself in a red-black cavern lit by the glow of... coals? Fire?

A living fire. One that consumed all it touched. Burned away any light or goodness, leaving only pain in its wake.

Her being became inseparable from the pain, her thoughts burned away.

Just when she thought that she would explode into a million tiny pieces of agony, the pain cut off as abruptly as it had begun and Zoe found herself bent double over her knees, the kris laid out in both hands, her lips upon the drying blood on its blade.

The old woman's cackle filled her head again, and Zoe straightened, slowly and painfully, the taste of the cat's blood on her lips.

"That's it, child."

The old woman sat in the center of the circle, yellow eyes alight with mirth.

Zoe's vision blanked out and an image of a woman with purple highlights in her hair filled her mind.

The woman sat in a basement shop down a narrow alleyway off Trout Hall. A white candle burned in front of her on a green felt table.

"This is the one who stands in our way, child."

Zoe nodded.

"Go to her. Slip the knife between her ribs. The knife will show you the way, find her heart, and put an end to her meddling in our affairs."

"Our affairs," Zoe mouthed.

"Kill her, and I will be yours to command. Without interference."

"Kill her…" Zoe repeated.

Tyran writhing in agony on his bed, penis a swollen black mass bubbling with tumors that sent pain through his whole body, the pain taking over his mind, driving him mad.

Yes.

Zoe nodded.

"I will do it. When, though? How?"

"Just go to her!" the old woman snapped. "You will find her in her shop. Go with the rising moon."

Zoe licked her lips, the taste of blood thick and nasty.

She nodded again.

"I understand," she said.

The old woman nodded.

And then she was gone, the thick smoke from the candles dissipating, the stench of her presence fading, leaving only the bare attic room, the twisted and drained body of the cat to one side of the pentagram, the kris in Zoe's lap.

Zoe nodded to herself.

Kill the woman.

Easy.

Violetta stirred, her spirit heavy and confused.

Centuries of pain. Struggle. Stalemate.

And now—after all this time—the old woman's power rising. Overwhelming. Allowing her to slip from my grasp to...

What?

What she has always sought: the Dark Lord. She wishes to bring him into the world.

The cold dirt pressed into her, held her upright, the twins under her feet.

Memories flared: *The circle of villagers closing. John Lewis stepping in, torch held high, peering down at her, face twisting with fear, repulsion, and rage.*

The torch in his hand replaced with a shovel, the glint of torchlight off its dirt-crusted rim as it rose and fell to cut off the wild howling of...the thing that I birthed.

My shame.

The devil's child.

Pain filling every speck of my being. The warm flow gushing from between my legs slowing, cooling, steam rising into the moonlit field, dirt clods glistening with dew, a coming frost, the breath of the villagers misty clouds closing in.

The snick of the shovel blade slicing through the second child, its mewl cutting off.

The full moon above, the stars.

Dark shapes closing in, cutting off sight.

The rounded blades of shovels rising and thumping down, cutting into me, the pain dim and remote, life force already nearly gone, carried away on the blood tide that fell from between my legs to the frosty earth below.

Then darkness.

Slowly, awareness trickled in.

Alone. A dark cavern of sorts, one without boundaries, limits, or walls.

Just black emptiness.

A growing sense of another presence.

The shock of realization it was the old woman.

Still with me.

Our souls entwined for eternity.

The twins at our feet: dark and light.

The old woman raging at the confinement, a caged wild animal thrashing in fury.

The cage…darkness.

Earth.

A grave.

The old woman's ceaseless efforts to break free.

A dim understanding that she must not be let loose.

That she, Violetta, could hold her in the darkness.

Stalemate.

For centuries.

The dim sense of life moving on, above and beyond the dark place where she and the old woman rested, fought, rested, fought…

A seemingly endless cycle.

Limbo. Purgatory. Some kind of liminal spiritual space.

And then—after centuries (?) of this, a door opening far above.

A glimmer of light and darkness like a planet rising above the edge of a dark horizon.

The old woman the first to notice. To seize upon it.

Tearing loose from me for the first time since that horrible night in the field.

Only belatedly understanding that she had found a key. A way out.

Following her to the source.

A man.

One whose thoughts whirled with things incomprehensible to Violetta. Visions of tall gleaming buildings, made of some strange substance that reflected the sun. Vehicles—thousands of them, *moving without any apparent source of power. Steel birds in the sky carrying hundreds of souls.*

And people. Millions of them. Covering the countryside.

The world beyond the grave where she and the old woman tussled unrecognizable.

But the spirit that ran through the throbbing mass of humanity the same as always: light and dark.

But mostly dark.

Hatred. Rage. The desire to inflict pain. For power and domination.

The old woman's soul glowed with the radiated power of the dark.

The light so thin.

Old woman getting the upper hand.

But then...

A flashing crystal of light.

Another.

Good souls.

Ones with power.

The old woman at the door to the world, scrabbling for entry.

Her spirit rising in pursuit.

Following the old woman.

The door a man. Mind open yet confused, a jumble of half-awareness and denial, his spirit a bright flame of power.

The power he held unwielded. Wavering. Irresolute.

His ignorance allowing the old woman ingress.

The old woman sending her spirit to the man, using the open door to allow the dark forces swirling about the man to enter into her.

The old woman slipping away to travel the land. To seek out more power. Allies.

Violetta discovered she too could send her spirit out.

Reaching for the old woman. Finding the trail, reeling her back to the grave.

Only to have consciousness fade as exhaustion overtook her.

The old woman freed again.

And so it went: back and forth, but with each foray into the world above, the old woman's power grew.

Until it met the one. The brightest spark of all. Its light pure and unadulterated by the dark. Scorching the old woman, disempowering her, sending her spirit reeling back to the grave to smolder there in pain.

An ally of my own.

But the dark forces the old woman had stirred growing.

Open channels to the flow of power from the Dark Lord.

Loosing evil into the world.

Violetta focused on the bright light that had scorched the old woman.

It was hard—the light at the far end of Violetta's reach.

I've focused only on the old woman. Fighting her. Holding her here.

But with each trip, the old woman grows stronger. And I weaker.

I need an ally of my own. The light that scorched the old woman too far...

The man above attainable.

The one who has opened the door for the both of us.

The man himself a bright light colored with shades of darkness, an ungoverned and therefore wavering power.

One in need of guidance and training.

The bright one at the periphery of Violetta's reach connected to the man. But the connection tenuous, uncertain, the man's wavering belief disempowering the light, opening the door to the dark.

Movement caught Violetta's awareness.

A dark force. A knot of hatred and rage so absolute it curdled Violetta's spirit.

Moving toward the bright one.

Touched by the old woman's spirit and dark magik.

Empowered and controlled by the old woman.

Unaware of its entanglement with the old woman's power. Thinking itself independent, its soul a rotten garden, there for the old woman to harvest.

As Violetta struggled for understanding and power, for grace, the light came to her.

Her soul breathed it in.

Mother Mary.
Blessed Mary, Mother of God, how can we fight this?
Stem the oncoming tide of darkness?
Violetta saw the bright one in a basement room. A white candle flickering on the table in front of her.
The man at the door.
Is the door.
The woman holds the power.
Together…they can drive the old woman away.
And shut the door.
Trapping us here?
Despair weighed heavy on Violetta's soul.
My fate.
To be trapped here with the old woman for eternity.
Penance and punishment for all I have done.
Can there be no mercy for me?
No respite?
No freedom?

Violetta's soul withered and writhed at the thought of eternity trapped with the old woman.

She pushed the thoughts away.

Your will then, my God.
Mother Mary, show me the way.

Roger's feet hit the cobblestones at the foot of the stairs and he stumbled as a wave of dizziness passed over him. He staggered to the door, hand groping blindly for support and found the doorframe.

He stood there, his hand an anchor as the world swirled around him.

Darkness closed in on him, and he felt himself swaying as forces ripped through him.

A howling wind buffeting me.

His mind scrabbled to make sense of the imagery and sensations running through him.

Flames. Wind. Tornado? Earthquake?

All sense of time and place had faded away, leaving only a bewildered awareness.

Eternity.

The vast chasm of it: space and time intermixed, roiling, twisting upon one another.

And shot through the essence of all being and time two forces: Light and Dark. Woven together like a two-stranded rope.

The DNA of creation, the two strands birthing all that existed. The tension between the two constant.

"Roger?"

The spinning slowed and Roger felt his body returning to him.

Allentown.

The woman's shop. The one with the purple highlights in her hair.

He blinked and found himself looking into violet eyes.

"Alex?"

Alex took Roger's elbow and eased him over the threshold into the shop.

Roger stumbled, but Violetta's firm grasp held him upright.

Stronger than she looks.

She led him to the table and helped him into a chair.

"Sit," she said. "Let me get you some tea."

Alex rounded the glass counter, and slipped through a curtain of beads into the back room.

Roger's head began to clear as he sat, the smell of incense and candlewax driving away the fog.

He looked about the shop as he listened to Alex putter about in the back room, the clink of glass, the click and whoosh of a gas stove igniting.

A full wall of shelves with herbs and spices in big glass jars. The glass cabinets that lined the floor space filled with amulets, jewelry, statues, and trinkets. Another wall filled with candles. The third lined with books. Under the incense and candlewax a mix of scents.

Makes me dizzy.

The beads clacked together as Alex stepped back into the

room, a mug of steaming tea in each hand. She rounded the counter, set the tea in front of Roger, then took her seat.

Worry wrinkled her forehead and her violet eyes looked into Roger's.

"Something has shifted within you," she said. "I sense resolve, determination."

Roger looked over his shoulder at the door.

"What happened?" he said. He tilted his chin at the door. "Out there?"

Alex glanced at the doorway, then back to Roger.

"The old woman" she said. "Followed you here. Attempted to cross the threshold."

"Attempted?"

Alex smiled.

"My shop is a sanctuary," Alex said. "The darkness cannot enter. Whatever has happened with you worries the old woman. She sent her spirt after you."

Roger looked back over his shoulder.

"She's out there? Now?"

Alex shook her head.

"No. She pushed too far. Attempted to cross the threshold."

Alex grinned.

"And was wounded for her efforts. She'll be back in her resting place now, licking her wounds. Plotting."

Alex leaned back and sipped her own tea.

"So," she said. "Tell me. What brought you here this morning?"

Roger looked into her violet eyes, considering.

"I'm not exactly sure."

Tommy not quite right this morning. The sense of unease running deep within me. The panic at the base of my soul rising, anxiety making it impossible to focus. All meaning bleached out of my work. Spinning in my chair, light and dark...

"I need information," Roger said. "Answers. I can feel the forces swirling around me, moving through the house."

Tommy.

The knot of panic at his center flared.

"Your awareness has grown," Alex said. That is good. The old woman's spirit will find you much harder to manipulate now."

Roger fingered the amulet through his shirt.

Alex nodded.

"Yes. The amulet helps to open your awareness. It also protects you, somewhat, from the dark."

"Somewhat?"

Alex shrugged.

"It is only as powerful as your belief."

Roger sighed and looked down into his tea.

"Well," he said. "I believe *something* is happening. Spirits…"

He shook his head.

Listen to me. Spirits. Holy crap. The world has spun away from me.

Alex reached out and gripped Roger's wrist.

"Push all doubt away, Roger."

"It doesn't seem real, Alex. Part of me can't believe I'm even considering this. Spirits? A world unseen?"

Alex smiled.

"Part of you can't believe. But another part of you has always known, hasn't it?"

Korea. Israel. The flittings at the periphery of my awareness. The dreams. The visions…

Roger nodded as certainty pooled in his gut.

"Yes."

Resolution flooded through him.

Going to take care of this, goddamn it. Put an end to all this hocus pocus bullshit. Send the old woman to hell. Where she belongs.

Roger cocked his head and gazed up and left, eyes running across the top shelf of glass bottles as his mind turned over and over, palpating his awakened sense of a world beyond the here and now.

A spiritual domain that enwraps the physical, permeates its every fiber. Each decision, each act furthering the light—or the dark.

But hell? Heaven?

Myths for the ignorant. A narrative to guide the credulous and the unthinking masses.

"Heaven and Hell are mental constructs, Roger," Alex said.

Roger's eyes snapped back to Alex.

"Can you read my mind?"

Alex smiled and shook her head.

"No. But sometimes your thoughts are written on your face. It's not hard to guess what you're thinking."

She set her empty tea mug down and leaned back, studying Roger.

"You're a rational man. You've prided yourself on your intellect. On your open-mindedness. And the idea that heaven and hell are real troubles you. Too black and white. Too medieval. Reeks of mythology and fairy tales, am I right?"

Roger nodded.

"Here's the thing, Roger."

Alex leaned forward, her elbows on the table now, her pretty face close enough for Roger to smell her perfume.

Lilac. No, lavender. Something with a tinge of musk. Blends with the smell of her, her radiance.

"The spiritual world is unlike anything we know, Roger. And so we construct myths, fairy tales, religions, and folklore. All an attempt to put an order to that which we cannot comprehend. The spiritual world is a world of powers and thoughts. Ideas. It permeates every atom of the physical, like a lattice holding it all together, yet apart, separate."

"That doesn't make sense," Roger said.

"Exactly. The history of humanity is a history of attempts to grapple with this reality. From Alchemy and tribal ritual to modern-day Physics. From metaphor to reality. God. The devil. Light and dark. Good and evil. These strands run through all of human history. But no words, no tale can capture the reality adequately. And so most remain in the dark."

Alex sighed and picked up her empty mug, gazed into it.

"Hell is a mental construct. Imagery attempting to capture the essence of the dark powers that run through our lives. A world of pure evil."

She looked up at Roger.

"You believe in evil, don't you?"

Roger's mind spun across a lifetime of learning: philosophy, literature, psychology, social justice, history. He thought of the long line of single-minded men with the power to build empires and rule over them with iron hands, from Genghis Khan to Hitler to the Kims of North Korea. He thought of the unrest in Israel, the mobs dragging innocent Palestinians from their apartments. Serial killers.

Yes. Evil exists. More than a construct. A power that underlies and drives unspeakable acts: The Ted Bundys of the world. Warlords. Human trafficking.

More than mere psychology.

A power that wishes to kill and destroy. To consume the light.

Light?

Goodness.

Love.

Light and dark.

Roger met Alex's eyes, and he pushed all doubt into a tiny corner of his mind. There would always be doubt—the limits of human knowledge demanded that.

But of the light and the dark?

No. Light and dark are real.

Forces contending with one another to control humanity and the physical world. Entropy versus creation.

And somehow: human souls could choose.

To give themselves over to one or the other.

The power of choice.

The ultimate power.

The one thing that no dictator, or serial killer, no demon could usurp.

The final freedom.

Roger sucked in a long, deep breath.

"I believe," he said.

Alex smiled.

"So...what do we do? How do I banish evil from my house? Send this old woman and her spirit away?"

"You've taken the biggest step. With belief, we act. We find the old woman's resting place. Destroy it. Banish her from this world."

"That easy?"

Alex shrugged.

"Nothing in the spiritual world is easy, Roger. Simple, maybe. But easy? No."

She leaned forward and took Roger's hands in hers.

A jolt of pleasure ran through Roger at her touch.

Hands so soft. Warm. Welcoming. Her skin like silk, her eyes...

Alex's eyes narrowed in amusement.

"Focus, Roger."

Amusement turned to dead seriousness.

"The battle is coming. We will find the old woman's resting place. Together. We will dig her up, and set her loose, then banish her from this plane of existence. But she is well aware of the stakes. Familiar with the battlefield. Wily. Practiced in the art of deception. She will use all of her powers to thwart us. To confuse us. To throw doubt upon our every act. It will take an act of will beyond any that you have ever summoned. You will need to stand resolute in the face of swirling darkness and evil, the power of deceit..."

She let go of his hands, leaned back, and crossed her arms under her breasts, a move that lifted them, and swelled the cleavage she was showing.

So lovely. Her skin...

She dropped her arms.

Roger lifted his eyes to hers.

"Resoluteness, Roger. Focus. Let the journey begin."

Roger sucked in a breath, held it, let it out.

"How do we start?"

A huge demolition machine rolled on steel tracks toward the main building of the Allentown State Hospital. A hurricane fence bordered the grounds, a crowd just beyond milling in the street. The machine stopped about ten feet away from the back wall and extended its boom, steel claws opening and reaching for the lip of the roof. The claws descended, smashing through the brick and concrete of the roof and wall, and tore out a huge chunk of material, sending a plume of dust rising into the cold and misty day.

Some in the crowd groaned with dismay as the demolition machine systematically tore the building down, piece by piece, others, eyes alight with the thrill of destruction, smiled with pleasure. The demolition machine raked the fallen detritus into a pile and bulldozers moved in to sweep it away.

Zoe stood at the window of her room, looking across the street, watching as the clouds of dust rose and the crowd milled about below. Shock waves reverberated from the demolition, traveled through the substrate and rattled the flimsy foundation of the old rowhouse where she stood peering out the attic window.

Beneath the physical rumbling, she sensed the tortured souls, long confined to the basement cells of the building, roiling and tumbling in confusion and angst as the walls which had so long confined and sheltered them came down.

Her eyes glazed over as the souls rolled out of the building, lost and confused. Spirits filled with rage and malice tumbled over and through the crowd below, seeking ingress, a place to reside; others, filled with sadness and grief drifted on the currents swirling around the building.

The old woman's cackle sounded in her head and Zoe startled. She spun around in alarm to face…an empty room, dried and blackened blood of the pentagram on the floor empty, black candles at its five points unlit.

Yet the old woman's spirit was unmistakable.

"Damia!" Zoe said. "Show yourself."

Nothing.

Zoe waited a long moment, every nerve in her body tingling with a sense of the old woman's presence, but the old witch refused to reveal herself.

"Fuck you," Zoe murmured, turning her back to the room to lift the gauzy curtain to one side and watch the crowd below.

She could feel the confusion of the released spirits as they scattered on the misty wind, their sense of exposure and isolation, each looking only for refuge, a place to hide. Escape.

Most had lived tortured, unhappy lives, hidden away from the world, stashed inside the clean marble of the hospital, filled with drugs that made it hard to think, that separated mind from body, made the body heavy and cumbersome, difficult to move.

Hidden away in the shadows, souls dimmed and splintered by madness and drugs, they'd wiled away the years on the periphery of life until the shadow of death had overtaken them. Confused and unhappy, their souls had remained trapped by the walls of the institution, caught in the liminal space between this world and the next.

Harmless, most of them.

Zoe felt these spirits drift away from the site, released, yet still stuck in between, each seeking some kind of respite and release, yet unable to find it.

A dark knot of malice concentrated itself and rolled across the grounds with the mist, the rage within palpable all the way across the street.

Zoe perked up, interested.

Who was this?

The old woman's cackle sounded again in her head, but she pushed it away, focused on this new apparition.

Her view of the street dimmed and darkened and she found herself in a basement room—*the hospital?*—a pair of pliers with rubber grips in her hands, a tall candle burning on a wooden table in front of her.

She watched as her hand held the tips of the pliers in the flame, soot blackening the steel edges, the hot smell of steel and something else—*burning flesh?*—acrid and tangible.

Movement off to the periphery of her vision.

She turned her head to see a naked woman, duct taped to a

chair, hands bound behind her, thick wraps of tape holding her ankles and shins tightly to the heavy chair legs, eyes bulging in horror and pain, another generous wrap of tape around her mouth, wisps of cloth sticking out from underneath.

A thrill of intense sexual pleasure ran through her as her hand opened and closed the pliers, her vision of the woman growing as she moved across the room, pliers smoking with heat, reaching for the torn and blackened skin of the woman's breasts, evidence of a prolonged bout of torture.

A muffled moan of protest and horror from the woman only deepened the pleasure running through Zoe, bordering on a full-body orgasm.

Zoe blinked.

What the fuck was that?

On the street below, she saw a small man with dark hair and a narrow face that made her think of a rat stiffen as the black knot of malice found him.

Ah. That one has found a home.

Another black knot appeared, moved across the grounds, descended into the street below, seeking, looking for an open door, a place to reside.

Another.

The old woman cackled inside Zoe's head, and Zoe nodded, understanding.

A small army of souls. Pure evil. Malevolent demons. Loosed upon the world again—free to play out their wildest desires...

Zoe conjured up an image of Tyran Hollenbeck, sent it to the dark knots moving through the crowd.

Find him.

He is the one you want.

Take him.

Roger walked along the smooth concrete blocks forming the sidewalk, row houses rising up on his left with their little basement windows at street level, oriels jutting out here and there overhead, spindly trees waving skeletal arms in the breeze. He passed the long, low structure of a museum to his right, reached an intersection and looked up from his thoughts, watching the little mini-traffic lights governing the crosswalk idly, eyes traveling up to the sky where the spire of a church pierced the mist and reached for the low roiling clouds above.

Church.

The gray stone of the building looked old, the structure predating the architecture that had sprung up around it.

Roger pulled a hand from his pocket and fingered the amulet through his shirt.

Always been those who've believed in a world after this one. I just never really thought about it.

Huh.

The little traffic light blinked green and Roger returned his hand to his pocket, crossed the street, and turned left, headed for West Park and home.

Alex says to follow the old woman. Find her resting place.

Gotta be the basement. Everything starts from there.

A grave under the stones. House built over it.

An old Spielberg movie came to mind, something he'd seen when he was a little kid. A family in a new housing development —built over a cemetery.

Oh, God. How cliché.

He sighed.

Well, I suppose all these stories have to come from somewhere. A grain of truth and all that.

His phone buzzed in his pocket, and Roger pulled it out.

His heart clenched as he read the screen.

The school? What?

Tommy. Oh God, I knew something was off with him this morning. Dammit, Roger. Too self-absorbed to pay attention to your own kids...

"Hello?"

"Mr. Nimanator? This is Geraldine Spurling, administrative assistant to Mr. Schill?"

Voice rising up at the end of each phrase. Thought that was a

California thing.

"Yes. This is Roger Nimanator. What is it, Ms. Spurling? Has something happened? Are the twins OK?"

A pause, and then, "There's been an incident, Mr. Nimanator. We need you to come in."

Roger stopped and looked left and right.

"Incident? What kind of incident? Are my kids OK?"

Ms. Spurling sighed.

"The twins are fine, Mr. Niman. It's Tommy. It seems as though he's been in a fight."

The look on Tommy's face this morning. Grim.

Cold fear pooled in Roger's gut.

The old woman. She's touched him. That was the look on his face this morning.

God damn it, I knew something was off with him this morning, and I just walked him to the school. Ushered him in.

"He's OK?"

"Tommy is fine, Mr. Niman. The other boy has been taken to the hospital to get checked out, though. Tommy…beat him quite badly, I'm afraid."

Damn it.

Roger looked up the street, glanced down at the phone.

"I'm at 5th and Walnut. I'll be there in ten minutes," he said.

"Thank you, Mr. Nimanator. We'll see you soon."

The phone call cut off and Roger stood blinking at the screen for a long moment, then pocketed it and turned up 5th to head for the school.

"The other boy has been taken to the hospital…"

Holy crap, Tommy.

My quiet boy. Thoughtful. Sensitive behind that impassive face he held out to the world. Timmy far more likely to get into a fight.

What the hell is going on?

The old woman.

God damn her to hell.

Roger picked up his pace, feet slapping the concrete sidewalk, buildings to each side of him a blur. He fought against the urge to run, then gave in and jogged down the street, the urgent sense of his children in danger pushing him forward.

Alex pulled the whistling teapot from the stove and poured steaming water into her teacup.

Roger is ready. Finally able to accept what is happening. Willing to confront the spirts that lie beneath his house.

Got to be a gravesite there. The old woman buried. Upright, according to Grandma Nurse, like they did in the old days, hoping to keep the spirit from escaping.

She carried her tea back into the showroom and sat at her table, white candle burning at its center.

Well, this one didn't stay put.

Still, she's been there for centuries. A hundred and forty years or more at least, the old rowhouse where the Nimanators live built in 1885...

But who's to say she hasn't been playing her games all along? Unnoticed?

How many acts of evil has she perpetuated since she's been there? Or is Roger the door she's been waiting for?

And how could he have lived so long without knowing the power that lies within? He must have had hundreds of hints, thousands...

She thought back to the first time she'd seen him, standing at the door of her shop, one foot across the threshold, the other still on the stones outside the door.

Such a powerful aura around him: bright white with flickering shadows. A thick swath of purple. An innocence and openness. Unaware....

Strange. Like having a talent for playing the piano lying dormant, never tested, never developed, a Mozart who never had the opportunity or inclination to put his fingers to a keyboard.

Well...he's aware now. Mostly. Accepted that the spirits are real. And ready to do battle.

I have to prepare him for the coming attack. The old woman will not go easily. He has the power, and once we've dug up the old woman and reinterred her bones in sacred ground, her spirit will be banished from this world forever.

But she will use every tool in her arsenal. Distraction. Confusion. Illusion. Lies. Deceit.

He must be ready.

She sipped her tea, eyes on the candle flame.

And he will be.

A tiny flicker of doubt within.

I hope.

For all of our sakes. The old woman's power is waxing. She's found allies and other sources of strength since Roger has loosed her on the world. Given her the strength she needed to break away from the other presence...the one which has held her in the grave all these years.

Who was she? Who is she? Bound to the old woman, spirits interwoven—somehow. A ritual of some kind?

What is the source of the light one's strength? Roger has seen a figure resembling Mother Mary...so our mystery ally was Catholic, or at least one schooled in the ways of the church.

Should we approach a priest? Someone to help?

A priest would see the white magic I practice as a gateway to evil. Blinded by his own mythology to the full reality of what passes through this world, the liminal spaces that encroach, the trapped spirits, no shades of gray in his vision.

We'll have to go this alone. Grandma Nurse's wisdom and experience as a guide, Roger as a beacon of power, myself as a conduit for the forces of light.

The image of Mother Mary strengthens Roger. Encourage him to nurture this—it might provide the anchor he needs when the full onslaught of the old woman's power hits him...

A rosary.

Give him a rosary, fuel his belief in the power of it.

It just might do the trick.

Enable him to withstand the storm long enough to carry the work to completion.

And if this colors his perception of the afterlife Catholic, no harm done.

It might even provide him the buttress he will need to navigate the rest of his life, now that he is aware.

For the old woman, dangerous as she is, is only the tip of a much deeper pool of darkness out there. Right now she is the point of the spear piercing his world, and ours, but far from the only one.

Alex sighed and looked down into her mug.

Empty. Huh. Didn't even notice.

Well...Holy Spirit, Mother Mary, Father God—come to Roger. Empower him. Fuel his belief.

She cocked her head as a jolt of unease struck her.

Something's up. He's in a near panic. Running.

Along the street?

She closed her eyes, feeling for his spirit, finding only a vague sense of panic and distress.

She opened her eyes to the flickering flame in front of her.

Well. He will return, soon enough.

Nothing to do but wait.

She turned her head to run her eyes over the bookshelves.

Except...a spell of empowerment, perhaps. Tricky, though: for whatever reason, it is the imagery of the church which comforts and fuels him. Have to find something that will work...

Her eyes fell on an old leather-bound edition of The Sixth and Seventh Books of Moses.

Ah.

That'll do.

She rose, strolled to the shelf, pulled the heavy tome down, and carried it to the table.

Her fingers stroked the cover lightly.

Yes. Feels right.

She lifted the cover, turned over the old pages carefully, found the Table of Contents and used her right index finger to trace down the list, spirit open and tingling with anticipation, waiting for...

A tingle of electricity as her finger found the spell.

She read the chapter title and nodded, satisfied.

Chapter XIII: The Chalice of Holiness.

Yes, this one will do.

She rose from the table and moved to the glass case that bordered the register, slid open the rear panel and reached for the ram's horn that lay curled on purple velvet there. She lifted the horn from its place, returned to the table, cleared away the cards and other detritus, centered the big leather-bound tome, turned to face the east, then lifted the ram's horn to her lips and blew three blasts. Three blasts to the north, the west and the south completed the summoning. She set the horn down on the table, seated herself, closed her eyes and calmed her spirit.

OK.

Do this.

She opened her eyes and her lips moved as she quietly read out the incantation.

Her spirit tingled as the forces from the spiritual world came to her, moved through her, and entered the world.

She smiled.

All will be well.

I think.

"You're not mad?" Tommy asked.

Roger shook his head. The worst of the panic had burned itself out, leaving him shaky and tired, his spirit heavy. He'd navigated the elementary school bureaucracy in a daze, head filled with imagery of the old woman and Alex, heart filled with a roiling anxiety as he felt the spirts swirling around.

It's like the scales have fallen from my eyes and now I can see a whole world surrounding this one, touching its every corner, tendrils reaching into the souls that inhabit this one, driving them, pushing them—most without the slightest awareness of the forces goading their every action.

Mr. Schill's secretary, Ms. Spurling, calm, reassuring, yet filled with a red lust that colored everything she saw, her eyes taking me in, measuring me, the red lust beneath pulsing.

Mr. Schill, also calm and reassuring, yet a gray-black spirit of punishment and retribution coloring his views, pulsing as his eyes fell on Tommy.

"Dad?"

Roger shook his head, blinked.

He smiled at Tommy.

"Mad? No, I'm not mad, Tommy."

Tommy a bright white light, dots of darkness there, but his spirit predominately light. Yellows. A touch of violet. His normal calm light broken by shadows that rippled through in waves.

"I just want to understand. What happened? Exactly? Why did you attack that boy?"

Tommy's eyes widened, then narrowed as he tried to remember.

"I don't know, Dad. Ms. Eriksson was reading to us, we were in story circle, and I was tired. I didn't sleep so good last night. Had bad dreams."

He shuddered.

Roger's heartrate picked up.

"Bad dreams? Tell me about them, Tommy."

He leaned forward, elbows on his knees and focused on Tommy.

Tommy's mouth curled in distaste and fear.

"An old woman. Crouched by my bed."

Roger's heartrate doubled.

Calm. Stay calm. Don't frighten the boy.

"Tell me about her," he said.

Tommy shuddered and wrapped his arms around himself.

"She was whispering into my ear, Dad. I could feel her breath. Something about her—she pushed into my head. She was angry."

"She got into your head?"

Tommy's wide eyes met Roger's.

"Yeah," he whispered. "I could feel her. She's mean, Dad. Really mean. She wants to hurt people. Hurt them really bad."

Roger reached out and gathered his boy into his arms.

Been a long time since he's let me do that, Roger thought.

"OK," Roger said. "You had bad dreams. An evil old woman by your bed, whispering into your ear, touching you inside your head. That'd scare me, too."

Tommy looked up to Roger.

"Really?"

Roger nodded.

"Absolutely."

He considered how best to broach the next thing.

"So…you were tired. It was story time. Did you start to fall asleep again?"

Tommy nodded.

"Yeah. Ms. Eriksson was reading, and even though her voice is nice; she reads well, Dad—does all the voices and everything—the story was boring. My head felt heavy, and I was fighting to stay awake, but kind of drifting off, you know?"

Liminal state.

"And then a spitwad binged off my head, waking me up. I jerked around to see who'd thrown it and Drago Trunchbill was sitting there, grinning at me."

"Uh-huh. Then what?"

"He's such an asshole, Dad."

He glanced up again.

"Oops. Sorry."

"It's OK. Then what?"

"Something about his grin—it was like the old woman was there. His eyes changed…went kind of yellow, with red edges…"

Roger felt a tremor run through Tommy and he hugged him more tightly.

"And then?"

"I don't know, Dad. It was weird. All of a sudden, it was like I was watching myself. I was filled with anger. Like I've never felt. I wanted to smash him. Crush him. And I…"

Tommy paused, mind ticking it over.

"I…just leapt across the circle and landed on him. I got my knees on his chest and started pounding him. His eyes were all yellow with red around them, like the old woman, and I wanted…I wanted…"

His chest heaved as he fought for words. Roger could feel his little heart pounding, Tommy's whole body throbbing.

He patted Tommy's back.

"It's OK, Tommy. I understand."

Tommy looked up at Roger, his eyes welling with tears.

"I wanted to kill him, Dad. If Ms. Eriksson hadn't yanked me off of him…"

Tears rolled down his cheeks.

"What's wrong with me, Dad? What happened?"

Roger tucked the boy in close, his head under his chin, hair redolent of Head and Shoulders.

"Nothing's wrong with you, son. You were just tired, and the boy goaded you."

The old woman.

Rage ran through him and he felt his arms tremble with it.

"Dad?"

He took a deep breath and forced himself to calm.

"Shh. It's OK."

"Is it?"

Roger nodded and cradled the boy to his chest.

"It is. Don't worry about it. You just need a good night's sleep. You'll see."

They sat for a long while, quiet, taking comfort in one another.

Roger's mind spun with the implications.

That old bitch touched my boy.

She'll die for that.

But how do you kill a spirit?

Alex's calm face appeared in his mind.

Follow her. Dig her up. Reinter her somewhere sacred. Drive her spirt from this world back to hell.

Where she belongs.

Spell completed, a sense of peace descended upon Alex, filling her with a resolute calm that lay on a foundation of strength in the face of the onslaught of the darkness.

The eternal Angel summoned.

Here to protect.

Its presence was so comforting, so pleasant, that Alex lingered with the Angel for a long time, savoring the peace and power of its spirit.

Something to the old text, after all. The Christian mythology, steeped in the ways of Moses and the patriarchs, powerful. No wonder it ruled the world for so long.

An intuitive sense of rightness, of certainty raised Alex's spirit.

Time for you to go, Alex thought.

She conjured an image of Roger, of the rowhouse in West Park.

Go to him. Give him the comfort and strength you have brought me. Protect him. And his children. Together, we will put an end to the evil he has inadvertently loosed upon the world, send that old hag back through the gates of hell.

The angel's spirit filled her from the tips of her toes to the crown of her head, her body electric, humming with a love like none she had ever experienced.

And then it was gone.

The angel's sudden absence left Alex feeling tender and exposed.

Don't be silly. The power of the light is still strong within me.

She ran the tips of her fingers over the thick pages of the old book, feeling the power there, a renewed sense of wonder running through her.

She turned the pages and read on, scanning the old pictographs depicting the tale of Moses versus Pharaoh. Her spirit leapt as she turned the page to find CHAPTER VI. GENERAL CITATION OF MOSES ON ALL SPIRITS with a pictograph of the spell:

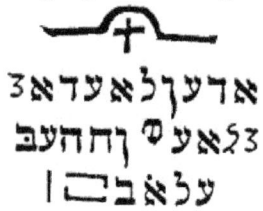

אדעןאלעד א3
בחחן סעא53
עלאב‏‎‏‎ו

Yes. This is the way through to victory over the powers of darkness the old woman has harnessed.

Yet there was no transliteration, no words to inform her of the spell. Just the pictograph.

Perhaps Grandma Nurse will know. Looks like Hebrew. Can't be that hard.

She turned the page: THE PENTAGON:

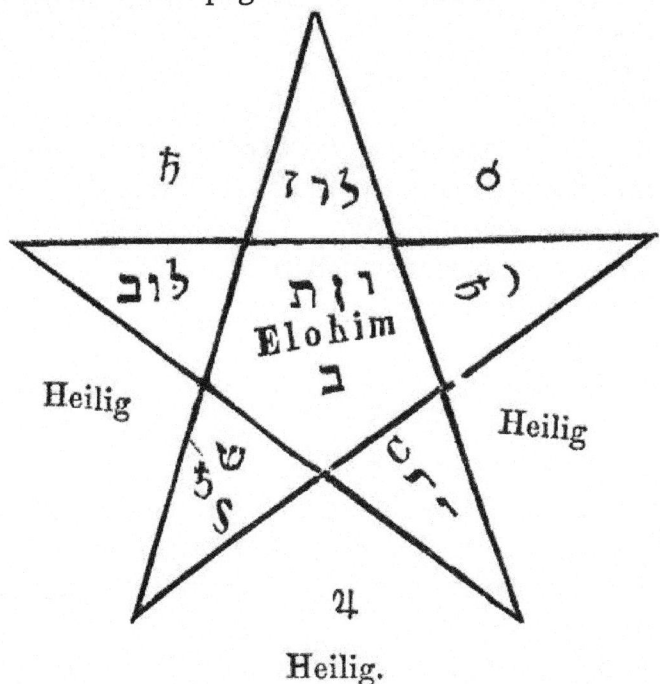

Heilig.

The room around her dimmed, the candle in front of her a flickering light in the haze as a vision overtook her:

A basement. Rough stones for a floor. Uneven, some of the stones pushing up from the dirt. The earth beneath glowing red, outlining the stones, growing brighter, filing the room with an orange-red glow.

The spirit of the old woman.

The red glow brightened, lit the old wooden stairs leading up to the kitchen above. The glow seeped under the door into the house, a red mist now, taking shape, climbing the stairs for the souls that rested above.

A cold breeze sighed through the room, and Alex felt her skin bunch, goosebumps rising.

Alex pushed back against the rising darkness around her, and the Pentagon was suddenly there, filled with a white light that drove the darkness away.

Alex blinked and found herself at the table in her shop, the smell of herbs, incense and candles comforting.

So. The Pentagon and the General Citation of Moses are the tools to put this old bitch to rest.

For all eternity.

She nodded to herself.

Another visit to Grandma Nurse. Pack the necessary tools: the ram's horn, an engraving tool to carve the Pentagon. A pick and shovel. A bag for the remains.

Alex closed her eyes and envisioned it:

Blowing the ram's horn to the four corners.

The Chalice of Holiness.

Carving the Pentagon into the wall above the old woman's remains.

The General Citation of Moses on All Spirits.

Pulling up the stones over the old woman's remains. The scritch of the spade digging into the earth underneath the old rowhouse. The dull thump of the shovel hitting bone. Digging up the bones, filling the sack with remains.

Spiriting the bones away to a sacred spot. More digging. Dumping the sack at the bottom of a hole. Covering it with six feet of earth. Smoothing out the ground, and then, the final touch: The Pentagon engraved into the earth above her.

Alex smiled.

It will work.

Alex sighed with the relief that comes with the solving of a vexing puzzle, picked up her tea mug, stood and made her way into the back room to brew another cup.

A final, celebratory tea before the work begins.

Zoe stood on the sidewalk, hands thrust into the big pockets of her old black trench coat as the misty rain beaded on her face.

She clutched the hilt of the kris, thumb caressing the elaborately sculpted little demon with tiny red chips for eyes. Black flecks of blood encrusted the lines of the blade, darkening the sinuous folds etched into carved scales.

A powerful weapon—imbued with a curse designed to cause its victims unbelievable pain, an agonizing death, with the power to pierce spirit as well as flesh, to wound the essence of the victim, separate them from the path, send their souls to hell.

Or at least so claimed the old man in the shop in New York.

New York.

Zoe sighed as she remembered the trip to the city—a rare outing financed by a windfall gift from her grandmother's estate.

I could live there. Dozens of covens, a community of like-minded souls.

Like the old man in the shop.

Evil had imbued the man's spirit so thoroughly that it poured off him in waves, an aura that raised the hair all along Zoe's body.

Then and there, Zoe had decided she wanted what he had: power. The power to send thrills of terror into anyone who dared approach her.

She'd already made forays into the dark arts, had minor successes with her spells and divinations.

But her power was a tiny, flickering spark in the face of this man's roaring inferno of evil.

The hilt pulsed in her hand and the old woman's face pushed into her reverie.

"*The knife will show you the way,*" she had said.

Light flickered inside the shop below.

Just go in and kill her.

"She is the one who stands in our way…"

No. Better to find a hiding spot, watch the street. Follow the white witch to ambush her, slip the sinuous blade between the ribs of her back and penetrate her heart, separate her soul from her body and path, send her to hell.

As she stood, irresolute, at the head of the stairs, the lights in the shop winked out.

Now!

The old woman's spirit pulsed at the center of Zoe's core and something tore inside her head, pushed her out of her body to rise above, and Zoe found herself looking down at the scene below.

She saw herself on the lip of the stairs, in the black trench coat, hand gripping the demon hilt of the kris, her face flickering, wavering, the old woman's red-rimmed yellow eyes looking out from her face.

What?

No!

She reached for her body, tried to reassert control, but the old woman was too strong.

You bitch!

The old woman's cackle sounded in her mind, and Zoe watched helplessly as her feet found the stairs and descended.

A woman in a black cloak exited the shop, the hood up, its peak hiding her face.

The woman turned and inserted a key into the deadbolt, turned it to snick into place.

Zoe's body hit the landing, and the woman stiffened.

Now!

Zoe watched from her vantage point a few feet above as her hand pulled the kris from its place in her trench coat, black blade glistening in silvery light from the streetlights.

The woman half-turned just as Zoe's arm shot out, driving the blade of the kris into her side.

Light exploded in a deafening snap! that blinded Zoe and set every nerve in her body alive with an agony like none she had ever experienced.

It's like I'm being blasted apart. Atom by atom.

The pain crested, driving all thought and sense away, her world electric white light that was pure misery.

The light destroys the dark.

Zoe felt herself slipping away, the light obliterating her being, scattering her force.

A dim awareness of the old woman screeching, an image of flames licking at her body as she burned, the burning crackle echoing the pulse of pain running through both Zoe and the old woman, their spirits entwined.

At the last instant, just before both she and the old woman were about to be shattered into nothingness, the pain and light clicked off.

Zoe found herself at the foot of the stairs, on the landing, bloody kris gripped tightly in her left hand, the woman in the cloak crumpled at her feet, hood pooled on the cobblestones, a tinge of purple hair splayed out in front of the door.

Zoe gasped as breath returned and the pain abated.

Every atom in her being resonated with the agony she had endured, but she was alive.

Whole.

And the bitch was at her feet.

Zoe looked down at the witch, a dark pool spreading out to cover the cobblestones, seeping between the cracks to the earth beneath.

She felt for the old woman's spirit, but she was gone.

Good.

The figure at her feet groaned, and rage ran through Zoe.

"You bitch," she said. "You dare to stand in our way?"

Her foot lashed out and her boot caught the witch in the side.

The woman moaned and a thrill ran through Zoe.

"Hah! Don't like that?"

She put the boot to the woman again.

And again.

Each strike was a sexual thrill like and Zoe found herself trembling, pleasure replacing the pain, bringing her to something like orgasm.

She spasmed, the carnal delight so great she thought it might tear her apart.

And then the pleasure snicked off, gone.

The figure at her feet was motionless now. Quiet.

"Die, you bitch," Zoe said.

She looked down at the defeated enemy at her feet and giggled.

"I hope it hurt. I hope you died in agony."

She giggled again and put the boot to the figure a final time.

Nothing. Just the feel of the hard toes of her boot denting flesh.

She must be dead.

Zoe sighed, satisfaction oozing through her pores.

She hawked up a big wad of phlegm and spat it onto the figure, then thrust the dripping, bloody kris back into its place, turned on her heel and climbed the stone steps up to the street above, joy singing in her heart and soul.

The spirits loosed with the destruction of the old hospital swirled through the night. The stones and concrete that had housed them shattered, their cages broken, they were exposed, vulnerable. Like animals flushed from their dens, they sought shelter.

The openness frightened most of them into something like panic, and they milled about in confusion, seeking a place to hide.

The bulldozers and demolition machine sat idle, their operators gone. The stones and concrete of the basement ripped from the earth and dozed into a pile of detritus had been mostly carried away by trucks and dumped in a landfill miles away, the basement itself filled with earth, smoothed over.

The timid, frightened ones hovered over the grounds as confused and miserable in their liminal state as they had been in life, helpless victims doomed to an eternal misery of hollow melancholy and unending despair.

The more powerful ones, the vicious killers fueled by the demons they had allowed to possess them in life spread out, their newfound freedom electric, empowering. These spirits throbbed with a malevolence that resonated through the town in waves. Their demons nosed about the city seeking new souls to inhabit, spirits to provide them with flesh and the agency to renew the bloody work they had dedicated their existence to.

Like-minded souls, knots of dark desires fueled by hatred and rage, their auras black, all light shut out, met the prowling demons with open arms, welcomed them in.

Violetta stirred: a new presence wafted through the house, a spirit of light and love.

The Eternal Angel!

The old woman was back in the grave with her again, her spirit scorched and blackened, something out there having wounded her, weakened her.

And now: a deliverer?

Could it be?

After all this time, locked in limbo with the evil old woman, twins at my feet, could I be delivered from this?

Hope surged within her, a tiny flickering light where none had existed for centuries.

Please, God. Please let it be.

Mother Mary, free me from this state of damnation.

I am so sorry for what I have helped to bring into this world. The evil I have birthed.

I was bored. Angry at the taunts and petty cruelties of the others. Allowed my anger to grow into something evil.

And the coven promised something so much more interesting than the dull day-to-day life of the farm. I didn't believe in all their stuff. Not completely.

Not until it was too late.

And I tried.

I tried so hard to get away, but...

A warm glow touched her at the very center of her soul.

Violetta's spirit leapt at its touch, hungry for its warmth, the unfamiliar pulse of love an ache that resonated sweetly through her spirit.

The old woman responded to its touch as well: a rippling agony that fueled an ancient hatred, a hatred that stretched back to the beginning of time.

Violetta felt the Angel withdraw.

No!

But the old woman's hatred was gaining power, resonance.

How? How could she rally?

Now?

With the Angel in the house?

Something outside the confines of the grave, outside the house, fueling her.

For the first time since her broken and dead body had been gathered up by the villagers who had murdered her, buried upright in a deep pit with the twins at her feet, bound to the soul of the old woman, Violetta rebelled.

No! I will not be bound! I will be free!

She sent her spirit in search of the Angel.

It will show me the way.

To freedom.

The man who had opened the door to this world, awakened both her and the old woman from their stony sleep, lay in his bed above.

His bedroom was the furthest she had been able to travel since the cold dirt covered her body.

He can provide me with the power to meet the Angel.

He can free me.

She found her way up the stairs to the kitchen, her spirit passing easily through the thick wooden door.

She felt for the Angel.

It was here.

It touched me.

Where has it gone?

Why come, then leave so suddenly?

The old woman's spirit was reviving, its wounds healing, its power growing.

Something happened.

It was as if, just when the Angel had found this place—sent here? By whom? To what purpose? An ally?—something had pulled it away...

Violetta focused her energies. Tried to suss the threads of the spirits now running rampant through the house.

The man has found an ally.

A white witch?

A priest?

The ally had summoned the Eternal Angel, sent it to the house.

But then...something cut the ally down. And in doing so, cut the string which had pulled the Angel here.

No.

I will find her, lend her what little power I possess.

Together, we will loose the Angel upon this house.

We will send the old woman back through the gates of hell.

The tiny flicker of hope the Angel had awakened within guttered, then began to burn more brightly.

A chance.

Perhaps, the good Lord is allowing me a final chance to be free from this limbo—this antechamber to heaven and hell—freedom from the old woman, in death as much her pawn as I was in life.

Perhaps, the Lord has sent the Eternal Angel with the key to free me and the power to banish the old woman from this realm forever.

The Angel's passage left a faint glowing trail.

Violetta summoned her strength, fueled by something she thought never to experience again: *hope.*

The old woman seethed and writhed as her spirit bubbled and suppurated from its contact with the white witch.

More power there than I had thought. The light within blinding, anathema to the dark.

Hurt me more than I thought possible.

And yet the child, the tortured one, had done it! Driven the cursed blade into the white witch's side. Inflicted a grievous wound, an almost mortal one.

Almost.

Rage redoubled, hatred kindled: *the accursed light.*

The white witch must die. She has found her way to a path that threatens everything, managed to send the Eternal Angel after me.

A bolt of fear shot through the old woman's spirit.

After all this time? To be banished? Sent to the Dark Lord's throne a failure?

There would be no sitting at Satan's left hand, no participation in ruling his expanded dominion. Instead, an eternity of agony and punishment, just another failed acolyte.

No.

Hail Satan. Praise the Dark Lord for empowering me to inhabit the young creature and wield the cursed blade and drive it into the white witch.

But the bitch had turned, warned at the last moment, the tip of the blade falling short of the heart, scraping past ribs, severing flesh, but missing everything vital. The curse still strong, though, nearly driving the bitch's spirit away.

Enough to pull the Eternal Angel away.

Enough to gain a moment's respite.

But not enough.

The bitch alive.

Rallying.

The Angel at her side, nurturing her, touching her with its accursed light.

Healing.

The old woman would've spat, had she a body.

As the power of the Dark Lord once again pulsed within her spirt, fueled by the fathomless hatred and rage of the old woman, she sensed something at once encouraging and alarming:

The bitch who was to birth the Dark Lord has left the grave.

I am free of her.

Up to this point, she has only left to follow me, to suck me back to the grave, hold us both in limbo, her awareness of the deeper realities limited, her spirit stuck here, thoughts dimmed.

The coming of the one upstairs has empowered her as well, but dimly. Just enough for her to continue to hold on to me, to do what she can to keep me from fulfilling my destiny.

And now she has left?

On her own?

The Angel touched her. Its touch awakened something within the obstinate bitch.

But where would she go?

To what purpose?

The old woman flexed the wings of her spirit, tested the parameters of her power.

I am free.

Dark mirth filled her.

Free of the stupid bitch.

The pain from the light of the white witch and the touch of the Eternal Angel had nearly passed, and the old woman's spirit soared free of the grave.

She passed up the stairs to the kitchen, drifted up the stairs.

The man.

Dangerous to me now. His power ascendant, but no longer there for the taking.

He is aware of the battle.

Broken through the veil of confusion and ignorance.

No longer a tool, but a weapon pointed against me.

If he is able to harness the power of the Eternal Angel...no.

And the white witch, wounded as she is, spirit hovering on the brink of departure, is not yet dead.

Her power rekindling.

She cannot be allowed to rejoin the man. To bring the Eternal Angel here.

The man must die.

Tonight.

She sent her spirit up the stairs to the landing above.

The man's aura glowed behind the door to his room.

Curse him. With his newfound awareness and power, he has slipped from my grasp.

The old woman turned her attention to the other door, at the opposite end of the hallway.

The boy.

The dark one.
Asleep. Vulnerable.
A tested and proven tool.

The old woman's spirit drifted down the hallway, passed through the door, and entered the room.

Pain rippled through the darkness.
Cold.

Alex shivered and blinked awake to find herself curled on the cobblestones at the door of her shop.

Locking up.
Something behind me, an overwhelming sense of evil.
Turning, a sudden stab of pain in my side, the pain radiating through my spirit.
Like I'd been stabbed in the soul.
A figure in a dark trench coat, knife in hand.
That face…elongated with red-rimmed yellow eyes flashing with malevolent glee.
Spirit dimming, strength abandoning me. The light within dimming…
Falling.
Falling.
A dark pit swallowing me, my spirit cut loose from my body, claimed by the pit. Caged by the dark.
Someone kicking my body, a dim sense of pain, my spirit hovering on the brink of existence.
The old woman's cackle echoing.
Darkness.
So dark.
Empty. The absence of light absolute.
Alone.
So alone.
No spirits. No light. Just darkness.
Feeling my spirit withdraw, sucked deeper into the cold, beginning to disintegrate.
A jolt of pain rejoining my spirit to my body.

Alex pushed a hand into the cold cobblestones and tried to rise.

Pain shot through her and she gasped and lay panting, her breath misting in front of her face.

I can do this.

She pushed again, gritting her teeth against the pain, and lifted her head.

At the foot of the stairwell. The door to the shop above, keys still in the lock glinting from the streetlight above.

Alex raised herself into a sitting position, the pain in her side sharpening as if the knife were still there, between her ribs, grating against bone and flesh with every move.

She panted, her breath visible, gathered herself and reached for the door.

Slowly, inch, by inch, using the door for support, she rose to her feet and got a hand on the key, turned the lock to unbolt it, grasped the door handle and let herself back into the shop.

The smell of candlewax and herbs mixed with incense comforted her, and she staggered across the threshold and leaned back against the door, shutting it, then her trembling legs lost all strength and she collapsed to the floor.

A fresh jolt of pain, and warm blood ran down her side, soaking her panties.

Attacked.

The old woman has found a willing vessel, one who glorifies in causing others pain, whose spirit delights in the suffering of others.

Why?

Roger! His little boys.

Of course. She's been burned by the light twice now, is feeling the sting. So she's decided to take me out. Shift the balance of power in her favor.

And with the power Roger yields...

The old woman cannot be allowed to have him. Or his boys.

Not only would the spirits of this little family be forfeit, tools of the Dark Lord, but the power within Roger...

Enough to usher in an age of darkness like...

No. Not possible.
But maybe...
She sat up in alarm.
Pain spiked, radiating through her side. Her spirit pulsed and throbbed in agony, a dark loneliness at her center like nothing she had never experienced.
I've got to get up.
Do something.
But I'm so tired.
Weak.
Her sight dimmed, the dark outlines of the shop fading.

A foul smell filled the bedroom and Tommy writhed in his bed, the sheets cocooning him, holding him tight.
His nose wrinkled, and he pulled the sheets tighter around him.
Knees on Drago's chest.
Those yellow eyes looking out at me.
Smashing them. Blood flowing.
The warm wet feel of blood, the smell...
Wonderful.
The thrill of smashing his face, the look of stupid bewilderment and pain giving way to fear.
Delicious.
Smashing.
Kill him.
Kill...
Tommy opened his eyes.
My room.
A dream.
Something noisome and dark moved at the periphery of his vision.
Tommy gagged, the smell like road kill on a hot day mixed with a touch of something burning—like fireworks in a nightmarish fourth of July.
Something is wrong.

Someone bad here.
Tommy struggled to sit up in bed.
Why am I so heavy?
Can't move.
Panic filled him and he put all his strength into an attempt to sit up.
Nothing.
The panic filling his mind grew, driving away all rational thought.
I'm suffocating!
The dark shape at the periphery of his vision moved closer, a shadowy mist pooling in the room, rising into a column beside his bed, taking shape.
A woman?
The woman's presence radiated a dark, malevolent glee and something inside Tommy clicked in recognition.
That is exactly what I felt when I was smashing Drago's ugly face...
No!
The presence next to his bed solidified, grew more substantial.
Got to wake up.
Get out of bed.
The figure reached out a spectral hand and placed it on his forehead.
The world went dark, the outlines of his room gone. The horrible smell waxed and Tommy fought down the urge to vomit.
What's happening to me?
The spectral hand pushed down, pressure on Tommy's head growing, pain building.
He gasped as the pain crested and something in his head gave way, split open. He felt the dark presence of the woman pushing at him, reaching deep for something inside him.
The dark thing.
It's inside me.

Wants...
The darkness took him, and Tommy's awareness blinked out.

The rat-faced man squirmed in delight at the images playing across his screen.

An open window on the screen showed a naked woman in a wooden box. She was lit by bright lights, speakers blaring mariachi music.

The rat-faced man nosed the cursor to the bottom of the screen and checked the time.

3:00AM.

Almost time.

The volume of the mariachi raised, the lights blared more brightly, and the naked woman scrabbled into the corner of her tiny box, drawing herself into a ball, thin arms wrapped around scabbed and bony knees.

The rat-faced man leaned in.

This is it.

They said that today was the day.

Six months in a box. Tortured daily. Fed a diet of thin soup with a chicken's head in it one day, a cat's arm the next, a mouse the day after that.

And she'd eaten it! Even the beak of the chicken!

The rat-face man studied the woman.

She'd been beautiful, in the beginning.

Now a skinny and filthy hag, inflamed wounds crisscrossing her body, arms lumpy and swollen where they'd injected her with blood. And other things.

She'd been raped.

Often.

Sometimes, just the one guy, a giant in a leather hood.

He was brutal.

My favorite.

No. My favorite the gang rapes. Five men taking their turn, holding her down, burning her with red-hot irons, twisting her flesh with heated pliers.

Can't believe she's still alive after all that.
And today...
Today she dies.
And I get to watch.

The mariachi music cut off abruptly and the woman lowered her head to her knees and curled more tightly into a ball.

The clacking sound of the padlocks holding the wooden box shut opening, a beam of light, and a gloved hand reached in and grabbed the woman by her hair, and yanked her out of the box.

The scene changed, switched to the cam that showed the dark little room with its paraphernalia of torture.

The rat-faced man reached down and unzipped himself, his penis pushing at his pants.

So hard.
Make it last.
Time it to her death.
This is going to be awesome.

The old woman's spirt flexed, gathering strength.
The others. The ones from the asylum. Out there, seeking vessels.
Finding them.
I feel it. Their strength feeds mine.
My army!
At last! After all this time, the gates of hell opening, loosing spirits into this world.
Now to use the little one, claim the spirit within the man.

Her spirit took hold of the boy's body and she sat up, swung his little feet over the side of the bed and put them on the floor. Stood.

The boy's body swayed, overbalanced, and she took a clumsy step.

So small. Take some getting used to.
Oh—to feel living flesh again! After all these years!

She stood for a moment, feeling the breath, the beating heart, the blood flowing through the little boy's veins, the feel of bare skin on hardwood floor, cool air on his skin. She raised his arms and stretched, testing the confines of the flesh that was the boy.

She turned and looked at the other bed where the other little one slept.

A thrill ran through her.

To feel hot blood on my hands again! To smell it! To watch death overtake a victim while my own heart beats in victory and joy...

The little one thrashed and then lay still.

That one filled only with light. No darkness in him at all.

She took a step toward the bed.

A good place to start. Reap this one's soul.

She held the hands of the boy she'd taken out, looked at them.

Wrap them around the other one's throat. Get a good grip and rip his throat out. Bleed the soul out of him.

The spirit of the boy she had possessed flared, and the old woman's vision dimmed as her grasp on him loosened.

Rage ran through her.

He's fighting me, the little shit.

I need to strengthen my grasp.

She turned from the bed and moved to the door.

The boy's spirit subsided, and she pushed it down further.

Get the little one later. Save him for a dessert. After I've reaped the man's soul—and his power.

She made her way down the hallway, descended the stairs and walked into the kitchen.

A rack of knives hunkered by the stove, and she selected the biggest knife and withdrew it from the rack.

Yes. This blade will do the work.

The boy's spirit flared again and the old woman felt her grip on him loosening.

No! You little turd! You will not defy me!

She stood for a long moment in the dim light of the kitchen, struggling against the boy's spirit.

A dream. Nothing more than a dream. Go with it, boy.

She felt the boy's doubt sharpen, and his grip on her loosened.

That's it. Sleep. Rest. Only a dream.

Her vision cleared and she tested the little body, raised the knife, made a few slashing motions.

No resistance.

Doubt the key.

She moved up the stairs, the boy's little body supple and quick, heart beating rapidly.

That's it, little one. Sleep.

She made her way to the door of the man's room and eased it open.

Light through the window cast a beam on the man's sleeping face.

Perfect.

She padded over to the bed on the boy's little feet and stood, got both hands on the handle of the knife and raised it.

Drive it straight into his chest, just a little off-center to your right. Through the ribs, into his heart.

The boy's spirit flared again, and the old woman froze, unable to bring the blade down.

No! Sleep! All but a dream.

Her arms trembled as she fought the boy.

Too much resistance.

Another tack.

She conjured the face of the boy's tormentor, the bully at his school.

This is your chance, boy. Kill your enemy.

You're confused—this is a dream, after all, and dreams are confusing.

Not your father there in the bed, but the evil one—Drago.

Look!

See?

The boy's spirit wavered, confused, and the old woman smiled and brought the blade down.

Alex fought her way up from the sucking darkness pulling at her and opened her eyes.

Incense. Herbs.

My shop.

A jolt of panic ran through her as she remembered.

Something bad is going down. And I'm hurt. Really hurt.

A warm glow filled the center of the shop, a ghostly luminescence that floated in the air, pulsing with white light.

The Eternal Angel!

Relief filled her, quickly replaced with anxiety.

But…I sent you to Roger. How?

The luminesce floated over and surrounded her.

The warm glow of the light suffused her body and spirit, drove away her pain and confusion. Her wound burned with radiant heat, an itchy but good feeling as her flesh knitted itself together.

Strength filled her and she stood.

Peace, tempered by a rising anxiety.

Roger lying in bed, an evil presence at his side.

Something sharp, pointed, poised to…

No!

Quickly, a spell of protection.

A cornucopia of possibilities spilled through her mind, and she sifted through them.

He said he's seen Mother Mary, his spirit open to the Christian mythology.

Something with Mary, something he can believe in.

Belief the most central and important aspect of any spell.

An old charm rose in her mind, a Christian-based one.

Yet Jesus at the center of this one.

Couple it with a spell that draws the spirit of Mary.

The glow of the Angel's spirit brightened.

Confirmation. Cast the spell to gain time, then go: go to Roger, perform the ceremony, banish the old woman back to hell and shut the door on her forever.

Her lips began to move, almost on their own, and the words flowed out of her:

By Mary's milk and Christ's blood.

Banished be all evil.

I stand with Christ, who commanded evil spirits out of pigs,

causing them to be dashed against the rocks below.
As Christ commanded Satan, so do I, calling upon Jesus' name.
In the name of Jesus Christ, who came to save us from Eve's sin,
Do I release thee of all foulness
That has encompassed this child of God's glory.
In the name of the four apostles,
Do I surround you with angels who shall protect you.
Matthew, Mark, Luke, and John stand by you.
Go forth now free of all evil,
And be sure of your salvation through Jesus' blood.
Amen. Amen. Amen.

The warmth that had knitted her flesh together, healed her, grew to a hot fire that was almost uncomfortable, but something wondrous about it empowered her, and she felt her spirit soaring.

A bright snap of white light filled the room, gathered itself into a ball and shot through the room, out the door, and zipped up the stairs to the street above and rocketed into the sky, bound for West Park.

Hope filled Alex and she smiled grimly.

Fuck you, you old bitch. Your time has come.

She stood for a moment in the warm glow of the Angel's spirit, then moved quickly about the shop, gathering the paraphernalia for the rite of banishing: the ram's horn, a book of spells, various herbs, oils and candles.

All went into a felt bag that she slung over her shoulder.

Alex moved to the door and took a last look around the shop.

Got everything?

Her mind moved ahead to the coming rite, and she pictured herself in the basement of Roger's rowhouse.

Chalk!

She hurried over to the glass case by the register and lifted a box of charmed chalk from the case, stuffed it into her bag, then dashed across the room, out the door, up the stairs and onto the street above.

The streetlights lining the street pulsed and brightened,

pointing the way up the road toward West Park.

The spirits are with me.

And we shall prevail.

Alex's boots echoed off the walls of the buildings lining the streets as she hurried up the sidewalk, through the misty night, bound for her rendezvous with the old woman.

You are going down, you bitch.

You and all of your miserable acolytes.

For all eternity.

The old woman brought the knife down, its point directed at Roger's heart.

As the blade descended, a light flared in the room.

The knife stopped short, millimeters from Roger's skin, skidding off an invisible barrier, and plunged deeply into the mattress at his side.

The old woman screeched with rage, but already she felt her grasp on the boy slipping, the pull of the grave insistent, her power waning.

No! Not now! Not when I was so close.

But try as she might, the bitch in the grave had awakened, and her spirit had somehow gained a power that the old woman could not resist.

Her spirit was sucked across the room, down the stairs, through the kitchen, back to the cold earth under the stones of the basement.

Violetta had awakened to the absence of the old woman. After centuries with her spirit twined through the old woman's like twin strands of DNA, her departure felt like she'd been ripped in half.

She could feel the old woman close by, her spirit mixing with another's.

Here.

Just above.

She's after the man. His spirit, the power within.

No.

She gathered her essence, sent her spirit up through the cold earth, the stones above, the stairs to the kitchen.

A black trail led up the stairs to the bedrooms on the floor above.

Like the slime of a slug.

Violetta followed the trail, saw where it had passed down the hallway to the room at the end of the hallway, doubled back, descended the stairs, returned, and made its way to other bedroom, at the other end of the hallway.

The man.

She drifted down the hallway to the man's room.

The door stood open.

One of the twins at his bedside, knife raised above his head glinting in the light, trembling.

She's possessed the boy.

But he is fighting.

Keep up the fight, little one. Help is coming.

As Violetta crossed the threshold a ball of bright light white snapped through the wall from the street with a sizzling, popping sound.

The light flared, its brightness illuminating every nook and cranny of the room.

The boy's face rippled, elongated, yellow eyes rimmed with red rage bugging.

The old woman.

The light flared more brightly, impossibly so, like a small sun had blinked into existence.

The boy's face relaxed as the old woman's grip lessened, then rippled again, yellow eyes glowing with an unearthly light, and his little hands tightened on the knife handle and he brought it down.

A sizzling snap and the blade deflected, millimeters from the man's chest and buried itself in the mattress.

The old woman's howl filled the room and Violetta reached for her.

Weakened. The light overwhelming her.

Violetta seized the old woman's spirt, felt it rejoin hers, and focused on the grave underneath the stones of the basement, willed herself back to place.

Darkness descended as the grave closed over them, the old woman's spirit firmly entwined with hers.

Roger bolted awake.

That smell. The smell of death—like when a rat has been crushed under the steel hinge of a trap, its body decaying...

Silver light from the descending moon outside the window lit the room.

A figure by his bed, shaking, trembling.

Small.

The smell diminished and Roger felt something leaving the room, dragged unwilling away.

The figure by his bed whimpered.

"Tommy?"

Roger reached for the boy, but something hard between them pressed itself into his side.

He scooted onto his side and saw the handle of a kitchen knife sticking out of the mattress, its blade buried in the mattress.

Cold sweat burst out of every pore and horror filled him.

He pulled the knife from the mattress and flung it across the room.

"Tommy?"

Tommy stood, hands at his side, face blank.

He whimpered again.

"Tommy!"

Roger reached for the boy and pulled him into the bed, held him close.

"Daddy?"

The boy looked around the room, eyes rolling.

"How did I get here?"

He struggled in Roger's arms.

"What's happening?"

Roger held him close, felt the boy's heart hammering in his chest so hard his ribs vibrated.

Holy crap. The old woman. Somehow...

"I was having a horrible dream..."

Tommy began to cry, sobs wracking his little body.

"An old woman. With yellow eyes. Came into my room..."

Roger put a hand to the back of the boy's head and sucked him in closer, the smell of Head and Shoulders somehow deepening the dawning horror of the situation.

Tommy sobbed.

"Came right to my bed, reached for me, Dad, reached *into* me..."

"Shh," Roger murmured, burying his nose in the boy's hair. "It's OK. Daddy's got you now."

"She's evil, Dad. Pure evil! She wanted..."

More sobs wracked his little body, each tearing at Roger's heart.

"Shh," he said again.

He stroked the boy's hair, looked above his head to the open door and down the hallway to the stairs.

The old bitch.

Somehow got a hold of my boy.

Horror gave way to a rage that filled every atom of his soul.

No.

That fucking bitch dies.

Tonight.

Roger sat up, cradling the boy, murmuring to him.

For the first time, he noticed the room was brighter than it should be.

Glowing.

Something new here now.

Roger cocked his head, felt for his center, let his spirit inform him.

A new force. Light. Power.

Here.

Alex. She's done something. Sent help.

Hope fueled the rage inside.

Roger sat up.

"Just a dream, Tommy. Everything's going to be OK, I promise."

Tommy's sobs subsided and he sniffled.

"No, Dad. Not a dream. There's something here. In this house. Something evil."

An image of the uneven stone floor of the basement raised itself in Roger's mind.

"Shh. Nothing Daddy can't handle."

He sat up, swung his legs over the side of bed, and stood, Tommy cradled in his arms.

"Let's get you back to bed, son."

Tommy buried his face in Roger's chest, his little arms shot around his neck, and he held tight.

"No! I can't go back there! The old woman."

Roger carried the boy out of the room, bent his head to nuzzle the boy's head with his cheek and nose.

"Don't worry. I'm awake now. She can't get you."

Tommy stiffened.

"You believe me?"

Roger nodded.

"I believe. And I am going to take care of it. You'll see."

He carried Tommy down the hall, through the open door of the twin's bedroom, and set him down in the bed.

"I'm going to take care of it."

He set the boy down in the bed.

Tommy's arms shot around Roger's neck and tightened.

"No, dad! No! Don't leave me."

Timmy thrashed in his bed, then lay still again.

That boy could sleep through an earthquake, Roger thought.

He gently loosened Tommy's grip, a hand on each of the boy's and tucked them under the covers.

"You stay here. Don't come out until I come to get you, got it?"

"No, Dad. Don't…"

Roger kissed the boy's sweaty little forehead.

"Shh. I told you. I've got this. I know exactly what to do."

He stood and looked down on the boy.

Tommy's frightened, tear-stained face gazed up at him.

The terror and misery on the boy's face ripped Roger's heart apart.

You old bitch. Time to send you to hell. For good.

"Shh. Trust me, OK, buddy?"

Doubt rippled through Tommy's face, but he nodded.

"Good. Now stay here until I come to get you."

He crossed the room to the threshold and looked back.

"I love you son. With all my heart."

"I love you, Dad."

"Now. Stay put."

Roger stepped into the hallway and closed the door.

He turned and looked down the stairs.

The basement. Alex said the old woman must have a place.

Everything started in the basement.

Got to be there.

He made his ways to the stairs, mind spinning.

Gardening tools in the corner of the basement: shovels, rakes, pruners, a trowel...

The old bitch is down there.

Just got to dig her up, then scatter her bones.

Something like that.

I think.

Doubt filled him.

That easy? Just dig her up?

The white glow from his room had followed him and he paused.

But now...something new. Something Alex has done, shifting the balance of power.

No idea what this is, but I can feel its strength.

But is it enough?

He smiled grimly as his feet carried him to the kitchen.

He reached for the door to the basement, gripped the door handle, then paused.

Boots.

He retreated to the hallway and snagged his boots from their place on the mat by the front door, slipped his feet into them, laced them quickly, then returned to the door to the basement.

This ends now.

He yanked the door open, reached for the light switch and turned it on.

The dim glow of the hanging bulb in the center of the basement filled the room and Roger looked to the far corner and spotted the gardening tools.

His feet found their way down the rickety old stairs, across the uneven stones and then the solid wood handle of the shovel was in his hands.

He looked about the room, mind spinning, vaguely aware the glow that had accompanied him to the basement had dimmed.

Where to start?

In the center. Dig down, and then out, if there's nothing there.

Six feet deep at least.

He carried the shovel to the center of the basement, slipped the blade between two of the stones, and pried one up on its edge.

He set the shovel aside, reached down and got his hands on the stone. His fingers scrabbled for purchase, and he pulled.

The stone didn't budge.

Anger filled him.

You old bitch! You're down there, aren't you? Fighting me. Fighting this.

He adjusted his grip, got his fingertips under the bottom edge of the stone, braced himself, and pulled.

The ground around the stone crumbled and released its grasp, and Roger lifted it from the ground and heaved it to the far corner.

Take that, you bitch.

He reached for the stone next to it, now loose, plucked it from the earth and heaved it over to the corner to join its fellow.

Come for my family, have you?

Fuck you.

The white glow that had followed him into the basement faded some more, but Roger scarcely noticed. He focused on the next stone. Then the next.

Going to send you back to hell, you bitch.

Tonight.

Zoe hustled along the sidewalk, her hand gripping the demon hilt of the kris in her pocket, her spirit soaring.

That was amazing.

She fondled the hilt of the kris.

Power.

The power to not only take a life, but a soul…the ultimate prize.

But the old woman had come. Taken over. She was the one who'd ultimately driven in the blade, pushed my spirit to one side, a mere onlooker to the action.

Gone now.

I need to do something. Something on my own, without the old woman. Something that will give me the power I need to force the old woman to bend to my will.

Not the other way around.

She's been using me, the bitch.

Zoe gripped the knife.

Plunging it into the white witch was glorious. The burst of power as her spirit left her body. Filling me. Before the old woman snatched it away.

I need to kill someone.

On my own.

And then…the old woman will be mine.

The rage and confusion of a lifetime of abuse filled her.

Been different my whole life.

The old man never let up on me. Never let me forget. Always driving at me, sneering, calling me a girly boy. Ridiculing me.

Not my fault I was born different.

But he made it my fault.

Told me my mother had taken one look at my deformed body,

found it too disgusting to bear, just up and left.
But I know.
He killed her.
He's the one. The miserable old bastard, sitting on the couch downstairs, a pile of empty beer cans at his feet, fat, disgusting stomach hanging over his belt.
Dear old dad.
Dear old dad needs to die.
The idea electrified her.
Why didn't I think of this before?
He's the one.
Zoe turned and headed for Rittersville.
My neighborhood. Home.
She could see him, slouched on the couch in front of the TV, beer can in one hand, cigarette in the other, the room a musty miasma of cigarette smoke, beer breath, farts, and sour sweat.
Let myself in. Walk up behind him, get a hand on that greasy hair of his, pull his head back, and slit his throat.
Yes.
That is the way.
His blood will pave the way.
Human blood much more powerful than the pathetic little kitties I've been using.
Understanding filled her.
That's why the old woman has the upper hand.
Reenact the rite with the blood of dear old dad. Do it right this time.
Spilling the blood of your father has to count for something, right?
Then the old woman will be at my mercy.
Her power mine.
And then...then, I will have my revenge.
On all of them.
Including the old woman.

Alex stood in front of the rowhouse.
Something happening inside.

The two windows set at street level glowed with an unearthly light, backlighting the spindly stalks of the flowers planted there.

He's in the basement.

Alarm shot through her.

He can't do this alone. Has no idea what he's into.

Roger, you fool.

The basement glow dimmed, pulsed with a dark aura that sent chills down Alex's spine.

No, no, no.

She hustled up the steps to the front door.

Got to get in. Get down there.

Before it's too late.

She reached for the handle, but the door was locked.

She rattled the handle and pounded on the door.

"Roger! It's me, Alex! Let me in!"

She put an ear to the door and listened.

Nothing.

She tried the door again.

Locked.

She could feel the dark power growing, its aura spreading, gaining power.

He's down in the basement, digging her up.

Oh, Roger. You poor fool. She will consume you, body and soul.

She gave a last, desperate hammering on the door.

Nothing.

She retreated to the street, looked right.

Rowhouses, built so tightly together they appeared to share walls, stretched down a long block.

Too far.

She looked left.

Just two houses to the corner, a little alleyway leading back.

She shouldered her bag, hustled down the street to the alley, turned the corner and raced to the rear of the building on the corner.

An old wooden fence guarded the back yard of the rowhouse

on the corner lot.

Alex adjusted the bag on her shoulder and got a toe of her boot into the bottom support rail of the fence, gripped the top of a wooden slat and pulled herself up and over.

The rickety fence swayed under her weight and she overbalanced and tumbled into the yard, thin, leafless winter vines snarling around her legs so that she landed heavily on her side, her feet tangled.

She ripped her feet clear and stood, then pushed through the brush to the open space of the back yard.

Another rickety wooden fence bordered the far side and she climbed up and over. This time, she was careful to clear her feet of the vines winding their way through the slats and landed on cat's feet in the second yard.

A light flared, blinding her.

Motion sensor?

A dog barked with a deep bass rumble from within the house.

A light went on in an upstairs window.

Alex hustled across the yard, shoving lawn furniture out of the way.

The dog inside was going crazy.

Another light flicked on in the house.

Hurry.

An impending sense of doom landed on her and her movements grew heavy.

What?

Body suddenly so heavy. Hard to move.

She reached the far side of the yard, every step more difficult than the last.

The old woman.

She senses my approach. Trying to stop me.

The fence on the far side was of a different sort, a tall iron thing with sharp points atop each iron rail, a thick hedge from the neighboring yard crowding up against it.

Got to get up and over.

She gripped an iron rail and pulled herself up.

So damn heavy.

She recalled the spell she'd cast to protect Roger.

Mother Mary...

The weight lessened, and she braced a foot against a separate rail and levered her way up.

Got to get a toe on the cross rail. Up and over. Can't slip, those spikes...

The dog inside the house was frantic.

Got to get over before the neighbors come out to investigate.

She put everything she had into a final surge and managed to get a leg up and over the spikes. She pushed off her foot to vault over the iron spikes and hedge to fall to the other side.

Almost.

A spike pierced the edge of her cloak and snagged, spreading the cloak across the thick hedge and pulling her up short.

Her full weight came down and the neck of her cloak shot up to catch her under the chin. Her weight tightened its grip and the neckline of her cloak cinched tight at the base of her throat.

She hung there, vision dimming as she writhed and scrambled, hands reaching for the cloak.

No. I can't die here. Not like this.

Roger.

The twins.

Need.

Me.

She got the tips of her fingers under the hem of the neckline and pulled, twisted her head as tiny white lights flared at the edge of her vision.

Her head popped through and she fell hard to the ground below.

She lay there gasping, as her reddened vision cleared.

My bag.

Her cloak trailed halfway down the hedge, bag hanging from a branch at the top.

She jumped, got a hand on the handle of her bag and managed to whip the strap up and over the branch.

She gripped the bag in both hands and made her way to the back of the Nimanator rowhouse.

Back door.

A dark aura pulsed from the house, and Alex could feel the open door the old woman had punched through the world to the world beyond, spirits milling about excitedly.

Got to get in there. Stop this.

She marched up the brick patio to the back door.

She pulled on the handle of the screen door and it slid grittily in its rails to one side. She gripped the handle of the sliding glass door and pulled.

Locked.

Damn it!

She bit back a scream of frustration and yanked up and left with all her strength. The glass in the door groaned and a long white crack appeared and spread. She yanked again and the glass buckled and gave way, shattering.

She kicked the jagged shards of glass out of the way and stumbled into a back room of the house.

I'm in.

Please, God, Mother Mary, Holy Spirit, the power of light…let me not be too late.

The rat-faced man tossed the come-soaked paper towel onto the floor, tucked himself back in his pants and zipped up.

Not as satisfying as I'd hoped.

It was good, but not enough.

Time to do this myself.

That little bitch from the library. The one who lives on the corner of North Freemont and Roosevelt. In the white brick house. Got that little red fire escape right up to her bedroom window in back. The one who thinks she so damn hot. Too good for me. Always giving me that look.

The look they all give me. All them bitches. Always looking at me like that.

Like I was some kind of garbage.

He'd had his eye on her for some time. When she first started working there, she'd been kind of nice. Almost friendly.

The library had a great section of true crime. The kind of books that rendered the lives and crimes of serial killers, rapists, thrill killers in vivid 3D detail.

Guys who took what they wanted.

The kind of men that take life into their own hands. Shows them bitches who's boss.

The rat-faced man had worked his way through the whole collection: Bundy. Dahmer. Gacy. The Toybox Killer. Others more obscure. The more brutal and sadistic the better.

And that bitch with her perky little breasts and blond ponytail got to where she wouldn't even make eye contact with me.

So he'd followed her home. Traced her through the streets to the white brick house on the corner. Waited.

Out in the dark like some kind of dog.

He grinned, showing his crooked little yellowed teeth.

Only this dog is a wolf.

The red stairs that led to the platform outside her bedroom window were wood. Solid. Didn't creak.

Got them wispy little curtains you can see right through, if you're close enough.

And he'd been close enough.

Many times.

Watched her prepare for bed, sitting in that sexy little nightgown of hers in front of the mirror, brushing her hair.

100 strokes. Some kind of nightly ritual.

Well, he thought, *I'll give you 100 strokes. You bitch.*

He glanced at the clock in the lower right-corner of the monitor.

3:00AM.

Perfect.

Excitement shot through him.

Really going to do this.

He stood and paced back and forth in front of the monitor, thinking.

Got to do this right. Take my time.
Need tools. A kill kit.
He patted the bulge in his front pocket.
Got my knife. Need some duct tape. Something to hold her down. A gag. Something to keep her quiet enough the neighbors don't hear, but not too quiet.
Got to hear her scream.
Beg.
Got to take enough time that she understands.
Who's boss.
Who's in control.
Me. That's who.
The rat-faced man opened the bottom right drawer of his desk and rummaged through it.
Duct tape. Pliers. They might be fun.
He picked up his black backpack from where he'd dropped it by the door, came back and began filling it with the tools he needed.
A dim part of his mind wondered at his newfound confidence.
I feel strong. Unstoppable. A power running through me.
But it was strange. It was like the weak part of him, the part that all those bitches sneered at, had been pushed off into a corner. Like something had taken him over. Filled him with a dark power he'd never had.
Well. What the fuck.
I like it.
And it's finally time.
Time for me to play.
Time for me to show them bitches who's boss.
He watched himself as he piled the tools into the backpack, found a pair of black leather gloves, slipped on his coat, walked down the hallway to his door, locked up, hustled down the stairs and out into the street.
The cold night air hit him and he paused for a minute, sucked it in.
Tendrils of mist filling the street, wafting around the

streetlights, swirling, a thick gray aura.

This is what it means to be alive.

Finally.

He pointed himself in the direction of the librarian's apartment and hustled down the sidewalk, into the mist, his black Converses making almost no sound.

A creature of the night.

On the prowl.

He chuckled to himself, his mind alight with all the things he was going to try, a song of evil in his heart.

The old woman felt the ground above her head coming away.

The fool thinks by digging us up he will destroy us.

No. You release us.

She guided the man toward the prison that had held her for fast for nearly two centuries.

That's it, dearie. Keep coming.

Each shovelful of dirt and stone lessened the weight of confinement, allowed the spirits swirling throughout the room and town closer.

She felt her power growing.

The power of the dark army, rising up beyond the walls of the rowhouse: the rat-faced man on the street, soft shoes making no noise on the sidewalk, the little teen witch wannabe who'd opened itself so fully to the dark powers that the old woman had claimed her effortlessly, the stupid tool—a new spring in its step as it made its way back to its den, spirt pulsing with thoughts of patricide.

And there were others: the spirits loosed by the destruction of the old asylum had found homes, dark pockets of bitter souls filled with anger and hatred, open to the Dark Lord.

And now the man was pulling away the dirt and stone that kept her bound, bringing the open door within him closer.

My army awaits.

Together, we will usher in a new era.

The reign of the Dark Lord, Beelzebub, Lord of the Flies, Satan himself come to claim his place, the power of the dark finally strong enough to banish the light.

Or at least torture it into a dim glow.

She felt the spirit of the violet-eyed bitch to whom she was chained flare in alarm, look to the light.

A problem. The little bitch holding back the onrushing tide of darkness, holding me fast to the grave. Willing to sacrifice her own soul just to spite me. To hold the door closed against the Dark Lord. Found herself Mother Mary moments before her death.

The bitch.

But now—with the power of my growing army, the weight of the earth above lessening with each thrust of the spade wielded by the man above—I will claim her spirit.

The old woman renewed her vows to the Dark Lord, Latin phrases mixing with the imagery of the sacrifices to come, the sacrifices already made, and the ultimate weapon—the dark twin at her feet, the vessel brought into this world solely to allow the Dark Lord in, a child conceived on the black altar by Abaddon himself, archangel of the underworld.

Satan's entry delayed by the villagers who'd caught the purple-eyed bitch in the field. The child's life cut short by the blade of a shovel—much like the one scritching its way down to her now.

But the spirit of the twins lived on—trapped. The weight of the trap lessening with each spadeful of dirt removed, an open vessel nearby, ready for possession.

The old woman summoned all of her powers, called upon the Dark Lord and the demons below, and turned it all on the purple-eyed bitch.

The scritch of a shovel cutting through hard dirt and stone echoed through the limbo that was Violetta's world.

For most of the centuries she'd been trapped, she slept. A dreamless nothingness that etched at the soul like acid.

Eternal pain.

Eternal torment.

The absolute absence of light.

The old woman's spirit nestled within hers, spiraling around her essence, eating away at it—a cancerous tumor that threatened to consume her.

But they'd reached an equilibrium that had held them in stasis.

For two hundred years.

Until the coming of the man above.

The one that had opened the door to the spirit world.

Cracked the darkness with just a sliver of an opening to the world above.

Enough for the old woman, who had never ceased striving, never given up, to seize and claw and climb her way out.

Violetta had only realized what was happening after the old woman had made her way up, out of the dark limbo into the world of light above, cracking open the door that separated the worlds, allowing others in, her power growing.

But the door opened to more than the dark.

The light was there, too.

Mother Mary.

Up to now, Violetta had been in the thick of it. The old woman would gain ground, her power ascendant, and then Violetta would find the light, rise up, and reel the old woman back.

She set herself to call on the light again, to go after the old bitch and suck her back to the grave.

I just need to...

To...

Confusion settled on her, the sound of the shovel echoing through her spirit, a jumble of words filling her ears, echoing, Latin and other lost languages, voices whispering, murmuring, shouting, screaming, all the words jumbling together.

I...

Roger dug with a grim mindlessness, thrusting the shovel into the ground, lifting it to toss the dirt out of the hole to the growing pile of dirt above.

He'd started with rage and determination to destroy the old

bitch, but the routine of the work had dulled his mind and purpose.

The rage was still there, though, and growing with each thrust of the shovel blade.

But the purpose, the reason behind the work driving him forward, had dimmed.

As had the glow that had followed him, now just a flickering light, about to go out.

How long have I been digging?

His body continued the work: thrust the cutting edge of the spade into the earth, step down to drive the blade all the way in to the curled ridge of metal at its step, lever it up, heave the dirt, repeat.

Mindless, monotonous work.

He could feel a force guiding him, knew in the center of his being that he was on track.

On track to what?

No matter.

Dig.

The force guiding him drove him forward.

Follow the force. Allow it to guide me.

The shovel his something hard, and Roger lifted it and thrust it back down.

Not a stone this time. Something different.

He scraped the earth away from the object impeding the blade and revealed a gray-white bone, wisps of raven-black hair still attached.

The top of a skull.

A skull?

What?

He dimly recalled that he'd wanted this. To find the bones he'd been certain were there. Dig them up. Scatter them.

Why?

He shrugged.

Just know I need to do this.

He drove the shovel into the ground again. And again.

Light above receding. Drawing farther away.
How deep am I?
He glanced up, body still moving, shovel still pulling earth away, exposing more pale gray bone.
Must be ten feet now.
Huh.
He dug.

Alex stepped across the floor of the back room, shards of glass crunching under her boots.
The tiny hairs on the back of her neck rose.
Something evil here.
She spun around, certain an evil presence was right there, ready to claim her.
Nothing.
Behind me.
She spun again.
Nothing.
Something.
The power of the presence sucked at her, drained her energy, muddled her mind.
Evil.
Presence.
Behind me, but not behind me. Above, but not above. All around, but not...
She stopped, confused.
What?
How does that make any sense?
The presence settled on her, a heaviness that slowed reality down, made her feel as if she were trying to push her way through some thick, viscous liquid.
Her mind was a jumble of imagery and thought; nothing coherent, nothing complete.
Tired.
Heavy.
Dreaming...

Just a dream...

She stood on the hard tile flooring, tiny shards of glass gritty underfoot, frozen in mid-step, senses overwhelmed by a lethargy and weight that trapped her in the moment, a fly caught in amber.

From deep within, a tiny voice cried in alarm.

The voice was like the drone of a buzzing mosquito, just enough to interfere with the onset of sleep.

She brushed the voice away.

Sleep. A dream...

The tiny voice grew more strident, alarmed.

Problem?

What?

Fatigue weighed her down, pinned her in place.

The voice resonated with an alarm that began to penetrate the thick world pressing in on her, slowing her thoughts, the heavy confusion that had taken hold.

Sleep...just for a minute...dreaming...

The voice grew in volume as if approaching from afar.

Through the thick veil of confusion and heaviness, the tenor of the voice sent waves of alarm that awakened her deadened nerves, sparked the lethargic synapses of her brain into assembling a coherent thought.

Danger.

Awareness began to return to her, and Alex felt as if she were coming awake to find herself underwater, the surface too distant to see.

Breathe. I've got to breathe.

She looked up and found a faint glimmer of light, far above.

Move into the light.

Her being struggled against the heavy viscosity holding it back like a living liquid, fighting against her with a growing sense of rage, desire to hurt her, destroy the very essence within.

Alex focused all her energy into swimming toward the light, a tiny dot on the horizon, like the meager glow of a lighthouse on a far-distant shore.

The light banishes the darkness.

Black mist wafted through the limbo in which she found herself, obscuring the light.

No.

Focus. On. The. Light.

Everything else had fallen away: there was no physical world. There was only spirit. Light and darkness.

The light.

The tiny glow flickered, then brightened.

Light and dark: no thoughts of Roger, of the twins, of the danger, of the old woman, or the Eternal Angel.

Alex put the full force of her spirit into willing the light into being.

The light grew larger, brighter. Began to push back the dark mist swirling all around.

As the light grew, so did her awareness.

In a house.

Night.

Something happening.

Something bad.

But who?

What?

She pushed the confusion away, focused her spirit on fueling the light, bringing it into the world.

As the light grew, the weight of the dark mist began to fall away, her mind to clear.

The heaviness and confusion were losing their grasp, falling away with the sound of a thousand murmuring voices filled with hatred and bitterness.

The light filled her vision, brighter and brighter, and she blinked…

To find herself in the back room of Roger's house, the Presence nowhere and everywhere, but somehow diminished, pushed back.

Tiny voices yammered and howled and growled and rumbled and squealed and whimpered at the very edge of her awareness,

pushing for her, clamoring, clawing.
The dark powers are here, a door open, letting them in.
I've got to...
What?
Roger.
Oh my God.
What have you done?

Zoe stood in the parking lot in front of the long row of dilapidated rowhouses that stretched down the hill.
Rittersville.
Home.
Home. What do they say? 'Home is where the heart is?' something like that.
She could feel the old man in there, his crabbed, miserable, squalid little spirit of pettiness and cruelty throbbing as he doused himself in beer and nicotine.
Going to drive a blade into your miserable black heart, you fuck.
She looked up the hill to her left.
So strange. The hospital gone now, its brick and mortar hauled away, chain link fence nearly invisible in the mist surrounding the site.
Something deep within her stirred, resonated with the remnants of the spirits that had been housed there.
Weak souls. As forgotten in death as they had been in life. The walls and grounds that had housed them for years torn away, exposing them to the world.
Zoe's eyes flared, a dark pulsing visible to her now, disparate dots of the lost souls drifting aimlessly, lost.
She closed her eyes and reached deep within her to the place that resonated with the aimless souls.
Suicide. Overdose. Disease. Old age. Madness.
And victims: souls of those who'd suffered horrible, prolonged torture.
The old hospital had housed what they used to call the criminally insane.

And someone there had allowed at least one of them free rein. Provided them with the space, the tools, and the victims.

Zoe smiled.

Of course they did.

Humanity a blot in the universe. A mistake. A cancer that ate away all it touched.

But where did they go?

The killers?

She plumbed the depths of her awareness, sent it as far and wide as she could.

Gone.

Released into the world with the destruction of the hospital, the killers had a sense of purpose. They had gone hunting. Hunting for souls. For those who'd opened themselves to the dark powers, made space in their souls for...

She cocked her head, thinking.

Why did they pass over me?

Because I am aware.

I know.

And the old woman.

The thought of the old woman snapped Zoe back to the here and now and she turned her attention to the front door of her own home, the rowhouse at the top of the hill, paint peeling of off the white siding, moss growing on the shingles of the roof, gutter dangling at an angle where it had pulled away from the roof.

Her eyes went to the peak of the roof.

She envisioned her little attic den, blood-soaked pentagram on the floor, angled roof pressing down.

Go ahead, Zoe. Go in, drive a blade into the old man's wizened little heart, collect his blood and redo the spells.

Get the upper hand on that bitch.

She's not going to use me again.

No.

She will be mine. Mine to command.

And then...finally, Tryan's time will come.

If I can't make the cancer within his soul spread and overtake him, I will use the knife on him.

One way or another, I'm going to look into his eyes and watch the life drain from them. I'm going to capture his soul and make it mine.

And I will torture him for all eternity.

All I have to do is kill the old man.

And everything will fall into place.

Zoe put her chin down, gripped the demon-head of the kris tightly, and marched to the door.

The rat-faced man stood in the alley behind the librarian's white brick rowhouse.

So easy. Not even a gate there to get through. Three concrete steps up from the sidewalk. Ten feet of concrete to the red wood of the fire escape. Eleven steps to the platform outside her window.

He pictured himself at the window, slipping the crowbar under its lip, prying it up, raising it and slipping in before the little bitch came fully awake. Climbing on top of her, one hand on her mouth to hold in her screams, the other with the gag ready, stuffing it into her mouth, pulling out the duct tape…

Got to get this right.

No fuck ups.

Think it through.

Be quick.

But his mind kept jumping ahead to the reward: the librarian gagged and spread-eagled on her bed, four limbs roped to the four corners of her bed, eyes wide and rolling in her head, following him as he paced the room, reaching down with his knife to cut away her nightgown, watching the panic in her eyes grow.

At my mercy.

My control.

The bitch.

Going to take your life from you.

Own you completely.

But going to do it slow.

Watch those big eyes of yours, the ones that wouldn't look at me before.
Going to make you look at me this time, you bitch.
Oh yes.
You will acknowledge me.
Understand.
Who's boss.

Heart hammering in his chest, the thud of his pulse loud in his ears, the rat-faced man climbed the three steps from the sidewalk and moved to the red wood stairs of the fire escape.

Silent as a ghost.

Roger pulled the last of the bones from the grave, adjusted them on the floor of the basement.

He worked mindlessly, his body distant and foreign to him, something within driving him forward.

Faint bells of alarm rang through his soul, but they pealed from an unbridgeable distance, dim clangs on a foreign shore.

Back down.
Something more to unearth.
Something important.

He climbed back into the hole and picked up the shovel, drove it deeper into the earth.

The shovel snagged on some kind of rotting old cloth.

Roger cocked his head, spun the blade around, began scraping away earth from the edges of the bag.

This is it.
This needs to come up.

Alex stood in the darkness of the back room.

The Presence pushed in on her, but she had regained her footing. Fully aware of the danger, she was not helpless.

The Eternal Angel. Where has it gone? I watched it flash across the night sky...

She closed her eyes and focused.

Her voice, calm and sure, filled the room.

"Arise, thou Eternal Angel. Arise, thou Eternal Angel. Arise! Thou Eternal Angel! Thou that art, wast, and wilt be in the old and new covenant…"

The view behind her eyelids reddened as a glow filled the room.

She kept her eyes closed until she had completed the spell, then opened them.

A pulsing column of light at the center of the room drove away the darkness.

Alex sighed. Released from the pressure of the Presence, she realized for the first time the depth of its power.

This is far more than just the old woman. This is legion—an army of demons and sprits.

The old bitch has opened the door, somehow, and they are coming.

Satan's army.

Roger doesn't stand a chance.

The thought of Roger and the mortal peril he was in got her moving.

The Angel followed.

Alex rushed through the room, her boots loud on the tile-covered concrete floor, found her way to the kitchen.

As she entered the kitchen, the door at the far end opened, and Roger stepped in.

His hair was matted with dirt, smears of it across his face where he had wiped away sweat. Mud caked the boots on his feet, and smeared his pajama bottoms, the weight of it making them sag on his hips. A trail of sodden dirt led up the stairs to where he stood.

Something about his movement wrong.

The tiny hairs on the back of Alex's neck stood up.

The Presence was back, pushing in on her.

She looked for the Eternal Angel and was alarmed to see its glow diminished, fading.

No!

Roger cocked his head, his brow furrowed, then his face smoothed out.

Like a mask. A mask of flesh. A thing that looks like Roger. But isn't...

"Alex?" Roger said. "What are you doing here?"

Fear shot through Alex.

The old woman. She has him.

"Roger," she said. "Wake up! You have to fight this! I know you're in there!"

Roger began to speak, his voice calm, sibilant, words running together. Each word echoed in Alex's head, and she frowned and tried to focus.

"Pilot light went out, that's all," Roger said.

Heaviness filled Alex and she blinked.

So tired.

"Everything's OK," Roger said.

The words echoed and rippled in Alex's mind, each echo carrying a weight that sent waves of fatigue through her.

"Nothing to worry about," Roger said.

He took a step toward her.

Alex blinked, her eyelids suddenly heavy.

Too heavy.

Impossible to keep open.

Rest a moment. Just a minute or two. Gather my strength.

A jolt of alarm shot through her.

A prayer came to her, fully formed in her mind.

"Oh, Mary, mother of God..."

She opened her eyes to find Roger upon her, shovel raised, blade angled.

He stood there, frozen, ripples running through him.

He's in there, but barely—the old woman, or one of the demons she commands...

Got to speak to him in a way that penetrates.

Mother Mary.

She is the answer—from the beginning, that is how he's seen the light.

So...

"Hail Mary! Full of Grace! The Lord is with you. Blessed are you among women."

The rippling tension running through Roger increased. The blade of the shovel, cocked over his shoulder like a baseball bat, vibrated visibly, shaking.

"And blessed is the fruit of your womb. Jesus."

Roger's face contorted in snarl of rage.

A voice issued from him, thick and guttural, filled with loathing.

"How dare you," he said, mouth a slit, barely moving, the voice seeming to come from all directions at once. "You goodie-goodie bitch! You dabble in matters beyond your ken."

"Holy Mary, Mother of God!"

A sneer worked its way into the Voice, a current of repulsion and disgust mixed with a sense of triumph tinged with fear.

"You have no belief, you cunt. All is one to you."

Roger's whole body was shaking, his dirt-smeared knuckles whitening on the handle of the shovel.

"Pray for us sinners, now and at the hour of our death."

Roger swung the shovel, putting the full force of his body behind it.

Alex ducked and the blade whistled over her head.

This is not working, Alex thought. *Roger is in there, but buried too deep. The force controlling him—forces?—too strong.*

Roger raised the shovel in both hands over his head like an ax.

Can't let him hurt me. Not now.

Alex straightened from her crouch, brought both of her hands up and used the strength of her full body—legs thrusting, glutes tensing, abs tightening, shoulders bunching and pushing, arms thrust forward—to catch Roger on the underside of his ribs, striking him at an angle that lifted him up and pushed him back.

The move caught the Roger thing off guard, and he stumbled back, teetered on the edge of the stairs, shovel clanging to the floor as his arms windmilled for balance, and then he slipped and tumbled down the stairs back to the basement floor below.

Ah shit, Alex thought. *I hope that didn't kill him.*

She stood for a moment, gauging the air, feeling for the

Presence and the legion of souls it carried.

The Presence throbbed. Dimly.

The glow of the Eternal Angel renewed behind Alex, casting a silvery-white glow on the empty black space at the top of the stairs.

Lot of help you were, Alex thought.

Could what that thing said be true? Do I lack belief? Is that the problem?

She pushed the thought away.

No. More lies. The dark powers are filled with lies. Clever lies built on the foundation of a supernatural knowledge of the spirit of the victim: insight into all of our sins and doubts and uncertainties. The lies we tell ourselves. Lies, lies, lies.

She walked to the head of the stairs and looked down.

Roger lay sprawled at the foot of the stairs, arms splayed, legs contorted.

Shit. He looks dead.

Tommy lay in bed, heart pounding.

Dad's doing something. In the basement.

He'd lain there, sheets pulled up to his chin, eyes wide, heart pounding as he'd listened to his dad pad down the stairs, slippers almost silent, only the creak of the third and sixth steps giving Roger's passage away, straining his ears and his heart to stay connected, to feel the protection Dad offered.

Each footstep took that farther away.

What's he doing?

Doubt and fear gripped him, spiking his blood pressure and heartrate.

What if she gets him?

Like she got me?

What if she gets him, and he comes up here...

He sat up and looked over at Timmy.

"Psst. Timmy!" he said. "Wake up."

Timmy groaned and rolled over, cocooning himself in the sheets.

"Timmy!"

Nothing.

How can he sleep like that?

It's not normal.

Terror pulsed through his body with every heartbeat.

Maybe she got him! Maybe Timmy's...

He sat up and scooted back against the wall, bunched the sheets up to cover himself.

As the terror crested and drove away rational thought, Tommy felt a heaviness descending on him, pushing his head down, weighting his eyelids, filling him with a fatigue that dimmed the panic clamoring within.

He welcomed it. A respite from the terror that threatened to tear him apart.

So tired.

It's late.

Had a big day.

Sleepy.

His eyelids closed, his head drooped, and he surrendered consciousness.

Gratefully.

Violetta struggled for thought.

Confusion rippled through her as her spirit groped in the thick darkness that surrounded her.

I need...

What?

Something happening...

Something big.

Something new.

Something I need to stop...

But her thoughts remained fragmented, her spirit confused.

The spark of defiance and anger, the thing that had kept her after the old woman for more than two hundred years still pulsed within, but it had lost its direction and purpose, become muddled and confused.

Unable to form a complete thought, she grappled with the confusion, more lost and alone than she'd ever been.

The rat-faced man crouched on the wooden platform of the fire escape outside the librarian's window.

A light behind him cast his shadow across the hardwood floor of the librarian's bedroom, caught her sleeping face and lit it with a silvery glow.

You're going to be mine, you bitch.
Body and soul.

A newfound power and certainty ran through him.

I feel strong.
Untouchable.

The power was odd, though, made him feel as if he were outside his body, watching himself as he watched the librarian. Dreamlike.

Going to be the best fucking dream of my life.

He set his backpack down, unzipped it, and pulled the crowbar out, nestled its tip under the lip of the window frame.

Got to move quick. Pop the fucking window and get in on top of her before she comes fully awake. Get her under control.

He levered the crowbar fully into position and then put all his weight onto it.

The sturdy wooden frame of the window buckled, glass shattering, then the latch above gave way and it popped up.

The rat-faced man dropped the crowbar, grabbed his backpack, and slithered into the room as the librarian bolted upright in bed, eyes wide, head swiveling left and right as she tried to make sense of what was happening.

The rat-faced man watched himself move smoothly through the room, a black-gloved hand rising to cover the librarian's mouth as it opened, his arm shoving her back on the bed as he jumped up and got a knee on her belly and pushed her back onto the mattress.

This is going to be good.

Zoe stepped into the house, the smell of the old man's sour sweat and cigarette smoke wrinkling her nose.

Well, not for much longer, you old bastard.

The old man's head was canted down, nodding off as the TV droned in front of him, long ash of his cigarette straight, like the ghost of a cigarette poised over the big ashtray at his side.

Zoe gripped the head of the kris and closed the door behind her.

Time to say goodbye, you old bastard.

Can't believe I never thought of this before.

Alex straightened Roger out and felt for a pulse in his neck.

There. Strong. Thank the light.

Got to move quickly, before he awakens. Before it awakens.

She stood and oriented herself.

A pile of paving stones lay scattered around a deep hole, dirt heaped in piles beside and over the stones.

Alex walked to the edge of the hole and peered over the side.

That's got to be ten feet deep. How on earth did he...

Her eyes landed on a heap of gray sticks laid to one side of the hole, a roundish object with bits of dirt—*hair?*—stuck to it at the head of the pile of—*bones?*

Oh, goddess of light, he's found the one.

The witch.

The source.

Something lay at the foot of the pile of bones, a sack—burlap or some other rough cloth.

Oh...no...

The twins. Where are the twins? Upstairs?

Safe?

Fear crested in her, and she faltered for a moment, swaying on the lip of the precipice, her hands gripping the strap of the bag slung over her shoulder.

Darkness colored the edge of her vision, bringing her back to the moment. Even as panic flared, she pushed it away, focused on the light.

Just do it.

Don't let any of this nonsense get to you.

Focus.

She looked across the pit Roger had dug to the far wall.

Get started.

An inaudible hiss sparked in the dim recesses of her consciousness, not sound, exactly, but not not sound. The hiss came with a feeling of mortal peril, something entering into the most holy parts of her, scrabbling at them with filthy crusted talons, bent on destroying all that was light within.

Begone, she thought. *You cannot fool me.*

I know.

The hiss lessened, and she took a step.

The hiss roared—inaudibly—something between sound and presence, surreal. The more she attempted to focus on it, the more it fragmented her ability to string together logical thought.

She forced herself to take another step.

Like trying to move through butter. Rancid, putrid, butter.

The foul stench registered through her ears, her eyes heard the far wall shifting in place, writhing like the skin of a snake, her nose tasted the bile that suddenly filled her consciousness.

Everything off. Like something has scrambled…

What?

Got to…

Her leg sounded like thunder as she lifted it to take another step.

As her foot found its place and she moved forward, the taste of bile in her nose doubled and her stomach clenched.

She turned and vomited a mix of black and red fluid into the hole.

Focus.

The wall writhed and buckled, something she felt rather than saw. Like sandpaper scratching a groove down her spine.

The wall.

An image came clearly to mind:

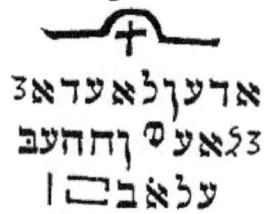

אדעלאעדא 3
עא℘ וחחעב 53
עלאב⬜ |

The General Citation of Moses on All Spirits.

The confusion of her senses lessened for a moment, and she saw her path to the far wall.

She smelt rather than felt each step, like a burst of sulphur that burned the olfactory centers in her brain.

The imagery swirling in her head deafened the occipital lobe in her brain.

Focus.

She held the image tightly, and stumbled the rest of the way to the wall.

She dug into her bag, a burst of colors blinding her, each finger raising a different hue of darkness, confusing her further.

Focus.

Her fingers found the stick of chalk and she pulled it out and began to draw the markings of the General Citation on the bricks.

Each letter brought a touch of order to the sensory confusion plaguing her, and her lips moved with the syllables of the spell as they should.

Something rustled behind her.

Black stars flared in her vision as something inhuman growled behind her.

Not a growl, exactly. More like the voice of a beast trying to speak —an ox, maybe. Or a goat.

The growl lengthened, stuttered, began to form words that sounded within her brain.

"Bitch. Stupid bitch."

The words felt like blows to the head—from within. Her skull ached at the building pressure within, the words of the spell faltered, and she bobbled the chalk in her hand.

"*Playing. With forces. You have no idea...*"

She smelled more than heard the words, the sensory confusion that had attacked her redoubling, her body distant and alien to her, the fingers gripping the chalk deafening to the point she wanted to drop it, anything to find relief from this assault.

The Voice gurgled, a liquid laughter that burbled like a brook of lead running through her head.

"*Your little scribbles mean nothing. The finger painting of an ignorant child. Nothing.*"

Alex tried to close her ears to the Voice, but it was impossible, easier to stop pulsing of the blood through her veins.

Focus.

On...?

The Voice laughed again, the laughter echoing in endless ripples that reverberated through her spirit, throwing her into further confusion.

She tasted the chalk in her hand, the laughter in her head the smell of smoldering sulphur, her mind and body under a tremendous assault.

The laughter grew and grew in volume, deepening in pitch, its echoes physical, tearing at the fabric of her body and soul.

The Light.

Darkness had overtaken her, the basement a distant memory, her purpose here obscure, unfathomable, but the thought of the light sparked a dim glow at the far edge of her vision, and she groped for it, a lifeline out of the depths of the pit in which she found herself.

The Voice fragmented into a hundred, a thousand voices, all speaking at once in varied pitches and timbres at varying speeds, a babble that pulled at her, threatened to break her, to suck her into insanity, leave her a babbling, incoherent mess, broken and vulnerable.

All sense and understanding had left her.

There was only will.

Naked, vulnerable will.

A thousand tiny claws scrabbling at the only remnant of the being she once was.

She directed her will to the light.

The babble increased in intensity, an onslaught of sound and sight and feeling and smell, everything unutterably *wrong*.

The sense of wrongness threatened to pull her off track as the babble and cacophony and smell and sight and feeling all whirled around her, pulled at her, tugged at the threads of her being, an army attacking her from all sides and within.

The light pulsed, and Alex held tight to it.

Alarm rang through the babble, the voices growing frantic, a sense of panic infecting them.

The light grew.

Inch by inch, Alex pulled herself up out of the darkness and confusion.

The babble diminished in intensity, the relief of it nearly overwhelming her, causing her to lose focus, but at the last minute, even as she felt herself giving in to the relief, alarm shot through her.

A trap. The battle far from over.

Focus.

The light.

The babble screeched in rage and pain, and the Voice returned.

"Stupid bitch. *The light cannot save you. And you cannot save him. He belongs to us. He is of the kingdom now. Our day is here. We are coming...*"

Understanding flooded through Alex and she pushed through the confusion of her senses, brought the Light into being, and slowly, ever so slowly, the wall in front of her took shape, the half-completed Citation in front of her.

She leaned into the wall, chalk in hand, lips once again moving with the words of the spell and completed the etching.

A long, drawn out howl sounded inside her head, the smell of it beyond endurance, putrid, intolerable.

She turned her head and vomited into the pit, then straightened and looked across the gaping hole in the basement floor to the foot of the steps beyond.

Roger stood, swaying on the edge of the pit.

His eyes glowed with a red light, his face an expressionless mask.

Something was wrong.

The rat-faced man watched himself overpower the librarian, black-gloved hand mashing her face as he pushed her head back into her pillow, her eyes wide and rolling with terror as she struggled underneath him.

He was outside himself, that was the problem. As if something had taken over, pushed him to one side, taken control of his body.

No! he thought. *Not fair!*

He watched as his knees pinned the librarian's arms to the bed, his hands duct taped her wrists to the bedposts with double wraps of tape, pausing once to punch her in the forehead when she began to scream, then ripped off her panties and shoved them into her mouth, lay another strip of duct tape over her lips.

Like watching one of those videos on the dark web.

No. Worse than that. Less sharp and clear. Dimmer.

No feeling at all.

Disappointment filled him as his consciousness dimmed further, and he felt himself crammed into a smaller and smaller corner of his mind, the events of his body now distant and dim as if happening across a field obscured by a strange and dark mist.

No...

This is my moment...

Mine...

Alex stood facing Roger across the pit.

The Presence was there, filling him, his face a mask, his eyes glowing with a tiny red dot at their center.

She felt the Presence coil, ready itself for an attack.

The flow of the Eternal Angel bobbed gently over the pit, between them.

Alex recast the spell, murmuring it, willing power into the light of the Angel.

A howl filled the room, starting at a pitch just below hearing, rising, up, higher and higher, climbing into tones beyond the other end of the range of hearing, yet still palpable, filling her with pain.

Protection.

The Pentagon.

The glow of the Angel throbbed with the howl, brightening, then dimming, a sense of the clash of two mighty forces reverberating through the basement.

Alex spun, found the chalk still in hand, walked to the brick wall and drew the Pentagon in quick, thick strokes, then filled it in with the symbols and letters as she remembered them:

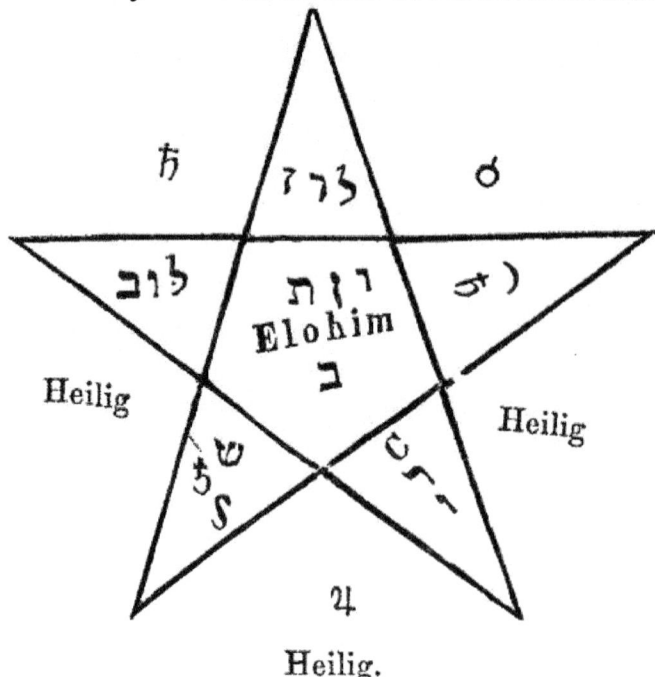

Pentagon complete, she turned to face Roger and the thing

that had taken hold of him.

The confusion in her mind dimmed, she felt herself coming back into possession of her faculties and a wave of relief coursed through her.

Attack.

"What is your name?" she said.

Roger's face rippled, the mask falling.

A laugh, thick and evil, barked from his mouth.

"You? You ask our name? By whose authority?"

Waves of doubt assailed Alex, the light cast by the Eternal Angel dimmed, but she held fast under the assault, remained focused on the light.

"By the power of the Light, I command you to tell me your name!"

Roger's face twisted into an ugly caricature of hatred and rage.

"What do you know of light? Bitch? Dabbling with your candles and incense, oblivious to the kingdom, the true kingdom, the kingdom that will inherit this world."

"Your name!"

Roger's body began to shake and convulse, dried mud on his pajamas falling off to plop the ground beside him.

"We are many. We prepare the way."

"The way?"

The laugh returned, the pressure of it immense. Alex's skull felt like it was about to burst. Each syllable of the ugly sound throbbed through the lines of her skull as if the eight bones were about to pull apart from one another.

"He is coming, you stupid bitch. We open the door. And He comes to take his place on the throne. To rule this world."

Alex fought against the pressure, her hands pressing into her head, a futile attempt to stop the pain.

"By the power of the Light I command you to…"

The laughter grew louder and Alex fell to her knees, her move only increasing the evil mirth.

"You? You command nothing. You are a pile of shit and blood.

A stinking, useless worm. A blot on the fabric of the universe with your clumsy and disgusting body. A bag of shit water. Nothing more."

Alex looked across the pit, hands still holding her head.

"Roger! Roger! I know you're in there! You have to find the light! Move to the light!"

Roger's face rippled again, the red glow of his eyes dimmed.

"Alex?"

The pressure in Alex's head let off.

"Yes! Roger! Find your way to the light! We will…"

The skin on Roger's face twisted horribly, betraying the anguish within, then smoothed out.

"Nice try, bitch," said the Voice.

The pressure was back and Alex gasped in pain.

Roger moved stiffly round the lip of the pit toward her.

"Time for you to die."

Rage filled Zoe from head to toe, stood her short hair straight up, raised the hackles of the back of her neck, bunched her hands into fists, the left hand tight over the demon head of the kris.

Him. He is the real source of all my misery.

Fat, drunken piece of shit.

Time to die, Daddy.

She leaned back against the door and heard it click.

Elation ran through her, and her step was light as she crossed the filthy floor to the back of the couch.

An old movie droned on the TV.

Zoe's father's head was down, his chin on his fat chest.

His fingers holding the cigarette twitched and the long column of ash fell into the overflowing ashtray beneath, the acrid odor of the burning filter dying as the cigarette died.

Grab him by the hair. Pull his head back. Cut him from ear to ear.

Be sure to get the carotid arteries on each side.

Zoe pictured the splash of blood crossing the room to spatter against the TV screen.

She smiled and reached for his hair.

Darkness surrounded Tommy.

Terrifying, yet somehow comforting. A part of him welcomed it, embraced it—its thick embrace shielding him from... something.

A tiny spark of awareness registered movement.

Moving?

How can I be here, in the dark, comfortable, and yet—moving?

He felt for the familiar contours of his body, where his skin met the world, and found...

Nothing.

The tiny spark, wrapped in layers of darkness, was sounding a warning, like a shout from someone just beyond the horizon in the dark of the night.

The alarm was approaching the horizon of his awareness, like the first crest of light before the sunrise.

Dimly, he felt the movement more clearly now.

But he could not find his skin. His body.

A jolt of alarm ran through him as he realized:

No heartbeat. Just...silence.

The alarm breached the horizon.

The dark no longer comfortable, too thick—suffocating, claustrophobic.

A voice whispered to him: "*a dream. All but a dream. Relax. Sleep. Rest. Be calm.*"

Alarm pinged the center of his consciousness.

Heard that voice before.

Got to...

The voice whispered, more forcefully, its words carrying a wave of fatigue and forgetfulness: "*Sleep. Rest...*"

A wave of exhaustion carried the sense of alarm back over the horizon, its voice fading.

But not completely.

Tommy struggled with the two voices, the largest part of him welcoming the dark, but a growing part beginning to panic.

Something is not right.

Wake up.
"Sleep."
No.
"Sleep. You are so tired. More tired than you've ever been before."
Yes. I...am...tired.
A flare of fear.
No!
There was only absence. No breath. No heartbeat. Only darkness. Absence.

The fear grew and came closer.

Tommy reached for himself, growing desperate.

The voice was a thunderous, murmuring, babbling presence now, buffeting his sense of self, overpowering it, driving him further back into the cloying darkness, the darkness thickening somehow, holding him, keeping him from...

What?

Violetta felt the darkness breaking loose. The sense of entrapment and confusion lifting.

The old woman was gone.

She felt her spirit rising, spiraling up toward a growing light.

The light melted the centuries of grim determination, of combat and struggle.

A new kind of pain shot through her, from her innermost center. The pain of birth.

Of...hope.

Could I really be free?

Her rise continued, the light growing, its penumbra touching her essence now, a strange combination of pain and release, of freedom.

From all of it.

Freedom from pain. From worry. From the constant combat of the old woman's schemes and attempts to...

The old determination returned in a flash:

She's up to something.

If I am free...so is she.

Her rise to the light slowed, stopped, the outer edges of the light just touching her, sending waves of healing and love through her.

A face appeared at the center of the light.

A loving, glowing face.

Hands reached for her.

Mother Mary.

Violetta reached back, spirit filling with joy. Mary was a being of light: glowing, human, yet not, a spirit. Violetta embraced the light, but not fully, a part of her still focused on the old woman and the danger she represented.

Mary's face glowed with understanding and love. An eyebrow dipped: concern. A warning.

Violetta longed for the full embrace Mother Mary offered, the release and safety of it, but her sense of mission, her determination not to let the old woman win returned.

Come with me, she thought.

Help me.

Mary smiled, but the light dimmed, and she receded into the distance, and Violetta felt herself falling away, back, back to…

Dirt.

Stones.

Bones.

A sharp jab of realization:

The grave uncovered. My bones freed.

The twins…

Darkness and malevolence swirled around her, something new, a power beyond anything the old woman had ever conjured.

She's opened the door.

Satan's army approaches.

The first soldiers already through.

A battle waging here…

The man…overtaken, but not yet lost.

A new power: an angel…

Another soul—human, alive, embattled, but fighting, aware of

the forces swirling through the room.
  Two mortal souls, each tormented and fighting.
  Another approaching.
  Soul bright, fresh and innocent, yet almost completely overtaken by the dark—a child.
  The old determination flared anew.
  No!
  She will not have these souls.
  The darkness will not.

The rat-faced man watched from across a chasm of darkness as his body straddled the librarian, a knee denting the mattress to either side of her slender hips.

It'd been a struggle, she'd put up a bit of a fight, stronger than she looked, managed to sink her perfect little teeth into his wrist just above his glove.

He'd felt nothing. Not even a tug.

Not fair. This is my moment. Mine.

But the presence which he now realized had been with him for a long time had completely taken him over. No longer just a whisper in the corner of his mind, a flash of imagery sparking a full-bodied lust to rape and kill, the presence had full control.

From the minute I crossed over from thought to action, he thought. *Growing with each step I took on the way here, my mind filled with the imagery of what I was going to do to her, excitement growing, filling me, and yet somehow—pushing me out of myself.*

Never noticed the world fading away as I closed in on the librarian's corner rowhouse apartment.

And by the time I had her down, strapped to the four corners of her bed—all feeling gone. Just a dark heaviness, vision dim, barely able to see, watching my body take control of her, numb, no feeling at all, not even when she sank her teeth into my wrist.

A wave of loss and grief rolled through him.

He noted blood dripping from his wrist to dot the fitted sheet of the librarian's bed.

Blood evidence.

DNA.
Got to burn the whole place down once I'm done.
But as he watched his gloved hand flick open the knife, wave it in front of the rolling eyes of the librarian, he realized he no longer had any control at all.
None.
Just along for the ride. That's all.
What the fuck.
The spirit within him turned its attention briefly to him, and the rat-faced man felt cold horror wash over him.
A voice, a thick and phlegmy sounding bass, sloppy and nearly unintelligible, exactly like what the rat-faced man figured a corpse would sound like if it could talk, echoed in the dark recesses of his soul:
A twofer. I claim two souls: hers and yours.
The rat-faced man watched as the thing within him raised his left arm and squeezed a black-gloved hand into a fist, causing the blood from the bite mark to drip onto the squirming librarian's face.
She dies tonight—mine.
And you will follow.
Also mine.
But not before I've used you up.
The entity paused, and the rat-faced man could feel the spirit soaking up his despair and fear, growing stronger with each pulse of the growing realization spreading through his spirit.
Damned. Cursed.
Doomed.
The spirit laughed, the sound like bits of rotting meat falling off a carcass to the floor below, and the rat-faced man felt his spirit shoved violently further into a dark recess of consciousness as the thing within renewed its attention on the bucking, struggling body of the librarian beneath him.

A shuffle at the top of the stairs drew Alex's eyes.
A small boy, bare-footed, clean blue pajamas with patterns of

red and yellow cars on them, stood there, eyes glazed.

A butcher knife in his hand.

A dream.

A dreadful, horrible dream.

Darkness all around. Voices closing in, a babbling army of them.

What is happening?

I was doing something. Something important.

Digging. I was digging.

Why?

Rage and fear driving me.

Hatred.

The feel of the shovel in my hands. The smell of the dirt. The hatred growing.

Nudging at me. Like a living thing. Whispering to me.

The rage pointing the way.

A flash of understanding—the rage and hatred the key. The answer. A living spirit to guide me. To help me achieve…

Something.

The decision, barely acknowledged, to give the rage its head, allow it to take over, guide me to a glorious victory. Victory over…

The babble increased inside his head. A thousand voices of all pitches and timbres, some too fast to follow, high squeaky whines, others too low and slow, like an old-fashioned tape recording eating itself, the onslaught generating a tremendous confusion.

A new voice penetrated the darkness, cut through it like a knife of light.

"Roger!"

A word. Bereft of meaning. It echoed through the darkness, warping and morphing into a cacophony of syllables to join the ongoing babble that surrounded him, pushed in at him, crowded him, fractured his consciousness into disconnected fragments.

"Roger!"

Meaning behind the word, embedded in it—somehow.

Something central.

Roger. Roger. Ro-ger. Rrr-o-gerrr.

The syllables bounced around the babble, losing any glimmer of meaning as the joined the cacophony that surrounded him.

He puzzled over them.

Ro-ger?

Not two things. One.

Roger.

The babble raised in a crescendo, dimmed, raised, dimmed.

Hard. To. Think.

Roger...

A response? An affirmative?

Yes. No.

A name.

Name?

Who?

Wait.

The new voice cut through the babble.

"Roger! Your son! Help!"

Roger.

Son.

The new word reverberated through the noise, echoed, grew in resonance—a sharp, ringing syllable that sounded again and again, began to drive the babble back.

Son.

The core of his soul reverberated with the word.

A light blinked into existence in the dark that surrounded him.

Son.

Roger.

Realization flashed through him, and with it a resurgence of the babble, the cacophony climbing to new heights, its shattering power crashing against his consciousness.

But he had a focus now, sight and sound: the light and the word, "son."

He felt himself climbing out of the babble, the sensation like that of walking out of a thick sea, feet planted on the ground of meaning, the babble falling away with each step like sand sucking at his legs as he trudged toward the shore, toward the light, and the word: Son.

The light grew, shapes around him took form, and he felt himself rising now, consciousness of his surroundings and situation clearing, growing sharper.

Roger's face rippled again, he blinked, and looked confusedly across the pit to Alex.

"Alex?" he said. "What?"

His face rippled anew, and he struggled against the force invading him.

"Roger!"

His face cleared. He blinked and Alex could see the light of understanding flicker and brighten.

"Oh, my God. What's happening?"

"It's OK, Roger. Embrace the light. Look to it."

A glowing pillar of light rose from the pit in the floor, expanding as Roger focused on it.

A figure moved within.

Violetta settled back into the space she had occupied for so long.

My bones.

Freed, after all this time.

Buried upright by the villagers to prevent being able to dig out of the grave, their belief in the efficacy of this as powerful as the actual practice.

And now, my bones are unearthed.

My spirit free.

The man. The one upstairs. He has done this.

The old woman separate from me, now—gone?

A pillar of light filled the pit the man had dug to free her bones.

Something moving within...shiny.

A rare happy memory intruded on the scene:

Father and I working the field. Turned over something shiny. Quartz, he called it. Like a rainbow in his hand as he held it up to the sunlight...

But the brilliance here beggared the glimmering quartz of memory. This glimmering was alive—intelligence and love oozed from it.

And power.

Violetta looked more closely.

An angel moved about within the pillar of light.

Gabriel!

If she had had corporeal existence, Violetta would have fallen to her knees.

As she focused her attention on Gabriel, he brightened and grew, his eyes bolts of lightning, his mouth fire.

Relief coursed through Violetta.

Not too late.

God is here. With us.

The angel spread his wings, the light from within growing, filling the dark corners of the basement.

For the first time, Violetta noticed the other souls: three of them.

Souls still embodied.

Struggling with the dark forces, the door to hell open now, a stream of demons and lesser spirits swirling through its passage into this world.

The small boy at the top of the stairs frozen in thrall, his terror rendering him defenseless against the spirit that held him in its grip.

The man from upstairs, also in thrall, but fighting—a spirit of rage and hatred having meshed with his own, the man struggling now as the confusion the demons brought lessened with the presence of Gabriel and as the light of understanding washed over him.

The woman. Her spirit the cleanest of the three.

But weak.

The belief in her strong, but her focus on the light, the manifestation of the spirit, not the source of the light. Creation rather than Creator.

Just enough to keep her from being completely overrun.

Not enough to free herself, let alone the two other souls locked in combat.

Peace filled Violetta. A peace she had never known in life. A peace that surpassed all understanding.

For a moment, she rested with it, bemused as a deeper understanding flowed through her: *the peace always there for the taking.*

Available to all.

And yet—so few take it.

So many choose the opposite: unrest, outrage, fear, a thousand lesser states of being, when this, this peace we were made to live in and with is right there for the taking.

As the peace spread through her, the glow of Gabriel brightened.

Surely the mortals will see this now.

Call upon the power of the angel. Of the Lord himself. Of Mother Mary.

Mother Mary!

The man had been open to her.

A niggle of belief.

Enough to save him before.

Enough now?

Violetta faced Gabriel.

The very creature who had broken the news of the coming messiah to Mary herself.

"Mother Mary, come to us," Violetta murmured.

"Remember, O most gracious Virgin Mary, that never was it known that anyone who fled to your protection, implored your help or sought your intercession, was left unaided. Inspired by this confidence, we fly unto you, O Virgin of virgins, our Mother. To you we come, before you we stand, sinful and sorrowful. O Mother of the Word incarnate, despise not our petitions, but, in your mercy, hear and answer us. Amen."

A figure shimmered into existence.

Surely enough for the living to see.

The figure sparked with a bright light, began to take shape. First, the robe, brilliant, shining, bright, then Mary's eyes from within, filled with love and compassion. Bit by bit, she manifested between the angel and Violetta, her face turned to the man who had worked his way around the pit toward the woman on her knees in front of a large pentagon she had inscribed on the brick wall, the chalk still gripped in her hand.

The man stood over the woman, his body in rictus as the forces within fought for control.

Movement on the stairs caught Violetta's attention.

The little one. The son. His spirit smothered by the darkness, welcoming it—using it like a blanket pulled up over his head to keep the evil forces at bay. Too young, too naïve, too innocent to know that turning away from the darkness only encourages it.

Mary called.

"Roger."

The man began to tremble.

"*Roger,*" Mary called again.

Slowly, his head turning on his neck as if made of stone, body twisting along with it, the man turned his head.

As the light from Mary fell on his face, he blinked, a hand came up to shield his eyes, and Violetta felt the understanding fill him.

Instantly the power of the dark lessened.

The little feet moved more quickly down the stairs now, a sense of urgency upon the child.

No! He cannot.

But the child had reached the basement floor now, the knife gripped in its hand, and it scrabbled with a sideways crab-like movement that would've raised the hair on the back of Violetta's neck if she'd had any.

It moved quickly, the light of Gabriel flashing silver on the blade in its hand as it slid behind the man and raised the knife to strike.

Roger stood and faced the light, a hand raised against its

brilliance.

Mother Mary.

Real.

Here, now.

Wonder sparked in the deep recesses of his being, the little spot of panicked awareness that had been his core for so long calming, relaxing for the first time in memory.

Peace.

The light of…God?

His mind began to play with the light, to tease it into shapes, to question…

It dimmed.

And the panicked spot in his soul grew, a sharp stab of alarm running through him.

Something behind me.

He spun, raising a hand defensively.

Something flashed silver and a sharp pain stabbed through the palm of his left hand and he jerked it away to find a kitchen knife had pierced his hand, entering between the tendons in his palm, burying itself to the hilt, six inches of red-stained steel poking out the other side.

Tommy stood before him, blinking in the light and gloom of the basement.

"Dad?"

The pain was intense, but the sight of Tommy's confused and frightened face, tears pouring down his cheeks superseded it.

Roger grimaced and reached out his good hand to pull Tommy close.

"Shh," he said. "It's going to be all right."

He turned back to face the pit, his good hand holding Tommy tight up against his back.

Alex rose to her feet and tossed the chalk she'd been gripping into the now empty grave.

Her lips moved as prayer and spell filled the room.

The pillar of light grew, flashing brighter and brighter, illuminating Mother Mary, enhancing the radiance within her as a third presence joined them.

A young woman with flashing violet eyes.

The spitting image of Alex.

Roger turned to look at Alex, but she was tightly focused on her work, hands making motions now, pulling herbs from her sack, casting them over the bones at her feet.

The light kept growing, blinding now, and the cacophony that had filled the room began to recede as if moving down an invisible passageway, back to where it had come.

The sound now filled with anguish and despair, the demons and spirits sucked back to hell.

Three figures danced together over the pit. Mother Mary and the Angel reached out for the woman with the violet eyes, each of the three glowing so brightly now their outlines blurred, merged, and became one.

The three spun, faster and faster, a smell like ozone in the air, a sound like a ringing bell of glass filling the room, rising, growing, reaching a pitch that passed beyond the ability of the human ear but resonating even more sharply within, and the sound and light built and built to a level that drove Roger, Alex, and Tommy to their knees, the light overtaking every inch of dark in the room, and then, with a zipping sound like closing of a great rift in time and space, the light—and the dark—snapped out of existence and the three were left on their knees, staring at one another in wonder under the dim glow of the bulb above.

The old woman bucked in agony as a great black talon pierced her essence, yanked her from the bloody work at hand, driving away all thoughts of the coming of the kingdom, leaving only pain, an agony that obliterated everything but itself—the essence of all suffering filling her spirit.

She felt herself being sucked down a black tunnel, away from the world, the sensation of the demon head of the kris in her palm fading, the sight and smell of the blood distant, the unspeakable agony paralyzing her spirt, a dim understanding growing...

I failed.
The kingdom...
Her passage through the dark tunnel swiftened, the agony redoubling—impossibly—as a demonic face flashed in front of her.
My lord—Satan.
The twisted face in front of her radiated the purest hatred and rage the old woman had ever encountered.
Her soul barely had time to register what was happening before the awful agony, the impossible torture of it redoubled yet again, fracturing her soul and her thought into a permanent state of the ultimate suffering and all thought ceased. Forever. Only the awareness of the pain remaining.
For all eternity.

Zoe drew the knife across the old man's throat with her left hand, his greasy hair bunched in her right as she pulled his head back to expose the tender underside of his neck, his floppy jowls parting as the kris cut its way across.

As the blood spurted over her hand, she felt a ripping inside her, something leaving...

The old woman.

Gone.

Color and meaning left the world, leaving only the gray and bloody reality of the dismal little room, TV droning, layer of yellow nicotine coating the greasy walls, the thick oil of the old man's hair smearing her palm, the warm, coppery scent of blood, the vibration of the couch as the old man went into convulsions, a deep gurgle from the cut pipes of the old man's anatomy sounding off the walls, the absolute pedestrian ordinariness of the world overtaking all the gloss she had imbued it with with her incantations and sacrifices.

Just a room.
Just a dying greaseball of a man. A maggot.
Nothing left.
No meaning.

Despair swept through her in a mighty wind and she brought the dripping wavy blade of the kris to her own throat, felt its bite as she pressed, hard, against the left carotid and in one swift movement, drew the blade across her throat to the other carotid.

She fell onto her back, blade still in hand, blood spurting up to obscure her view of the ceiling, then lessening, the ceiling and the world fading as a black tunnel took hold of her, and she felt herself whizzing down a black passage, a growing sense of anguish overtaking her, the sense of a pool of fire and agony awaiting her...

And then she was gone.

The rat-faced man found himself crouching over the body of the librarian, a pounding at the door.

The librarian lay splayed out on the bed, her lifeless eyes wide, an expression of horror carved into the rictus of her face.

What happened?

I was on top of her...and then...

He raised the knife in wonder, blood dripping from its blade. He gripped the hilt with a double-handed grip, the vague idea of plunging it into the librarian's gaping chest taking him.

The door burst open, heavy footsteps thumped across the wooden floor, and the rat-faced man's head exploded as a 110 grain 9mm bullet entered just above the spine and exited between his eyes, taking a solid inch of bone and flesh with it.

The rat-faced man toppled to the floor.

As he fell, a black tunnel claimed him, and the fall continued and continued and continued...

Alex and Roger sat together in Roger's car, the bag containing Viioletta and the twins' bones in the back, next to the shovels, incense, candles, chalk and herbs.

Together, they watched as the moon neared its peak.

Roger glanced at the clock on the dash.

"Nearly 3:00."

Alex nodded.

"About time," she said.

The two looked at one another, the kind of deep gaze through which unspoken understanding communicates.

Alex smiled, the moonlight catching her nearly perfect teeth, touching the purple highlights in her hair, bringing the violet of her eyes momentarily visible.

So pretty, Roger thought.

Alex drove an elbow into Roger's ribs, then popped open the door and climbed out.

"Come on," she said.

Roger reached down and popped the trunk release, then climbed out after her.

They met at the rear of the car, the fog of their breath joining in the cold air.

Moonlight glistened off the frost forming on the lumpy ground at the edge of the woods.

Alex nodded at a thin trail leading through the roadside brush to the field.

"Cemetery is right there," she said. "Consecrated in 1822 with the death of the town founder's wife. Once coal was discovered and the mines opened, the influx of new people meant they needed more space than was available here, so they relocated."

Roger reached into the trunk and grabbed the shovel with his right hand.

"You going to be OK?" Alex asked.

She gestured at his still bandaged left hand.

Roger shouldered the shovel as Alex reached in and grabbed the burlap sack containing Violetta and the twins' bones, then reached up and closed the trunk.

"I'll be fine," Roger said. "The blade missed everything vital—all the tendons and arteries. Mostly just meat."

He flexed the hand carefully, testing it.

"Just aches," he said. "But it's the ache of healing."

Alex nodded and led the two made up the narrow path, Roger close behind her.

"Holly gets home tomorrow?" she asked.

Roger nodded, then said, "Yeah. Just about twelve hours from now."

"What are you going to tell her?"

Roger shrugged.

"I can't see you shrug, Roger."

Roger smiled.

"Got it anyway, though, didn't you?"

"So?"

Roger sighed.

"I can't tell her everything. She'll have me on meds."

The path petered out as they reached the field.

Alex looked up at the moon, then turned her eyes to the lumpy field. She held out both hands, closed her eyes, and murmured something.

The hair stood up on the back of Roger's neck, but he kept his mouth shut, just gripped the handle of the shovel over his shoulder more tightly.

Alex's hands moved, palms down, in a searching motion, and she turned to the right a little, waved her hands a little more, then opened her eyes and pointed to a flat patch of earth at the foot of a large pine.

"There," she said.

Roger followed her, then swung the shovel down and stepped on the curling lip of metal at the blade's edge and drove it into the earth.

Alex sighed.

"Yes. This is it. The spot."

She moved to one side and squatted, black cloak spreading out to hide her boots.

Roger's breath puffed out in little clouds as he dug, and the ache in his hand grew sharper.

"You want me to dig a little?" Alex asked.

Roger shook his head.

"Nope. I've got this."

"Men," Alex said. She looked across the field to the moon.

"So," she said. "What are you going to tell her?"

Roger leaned into the shovel, pulled up another spadeful of rocky earth and tossed it onto the growing pile next to the hole.

"Pet cemetery," he said.

Alex snorted.

"Ten feet deep? In the basement?"

"It's filled back in. Stones back in place. Going to tell her the smell was what set Tommy off. Some primal part of him aware of the smell of death. Set off nightmares."

Alex shook her head.

"She'll have him in counseling."

Roger paused and looked at her.

"Is that such a bad thing?" he said? "The boy's been through a lot."

"Just another way of burying the truth," Alex said. "Rationalizing it. Intellectualizing it."

She raised an eyebrow at Roger meaningfully.

"Oh, shut up," Roger said.

He started digging again.

"Roger, you can't hide the truth. That's where the real danger lies. You now that now, right?"

Roger sighed.

"What is truth?" he asked.

The moon moved across the clearing as they finished the work.

Alex lay the bones carefully in the grave, arranging them in order as best she could, careful not to let the few strands of hair detach as she placed the skull at the head of the grave.

She reached under her cloak and removed a bag of herbs, chalk dust, and other items she'd prepared, then poured the contents out, a thick dust trail to outline the bones completely, like a crime scene outline of a body.

Roger stood to one side as Alex completed her ritual, Latin mixing with another language he didn't recognize.

Truth, he thought.

An image of Mother Mary flashed in his mind's eye, and he

pushed it aside.

Myth.

Already the whole experience felt surreal, even as he stood there watching Alex go through her incantations.

She believes.

In some sort of fuzzy concept of the light. Of goodness. And darkness. Evil. Not even Satan as a real being is clear to her, he's more of a conceptual thing.

We hang narratives on the outlines of truths beyond our understanding, he thought. *Maybe one narrative serves as well as another.*

Maybe there is no such thing as truth.

Maybe...

Alex stepped back from the grave and nodded at Roger.

Filling in the grave went much more quickly than the digging of it, and the two of them were working their way down the narrow path back to the car well before the first light of dawn.

They drove silently through the night, each lost in their own thoughts, in the easy companionship of friends.

The lost souls of the Allentown State Hospital swirled through the town, looking for vessels in which to come to rest. They joined a shimmering mass of dark entities that swept through the night, dark little knots of hatred and rage.

Plenty of available vessels to begin the work anew.

For the door never really shuts.

The liminal places between this world and the next are as integral to our reality as the more comfortable solidity of the physical world.

The work never stops.

If you are open.

LIMITED BIBLIOGRAPHY

I used the usual barrage of websites and books researching this. What follows is a list of sources I cut and paste and kept at the end of the work. I read all of these, used bits here and there, and generally made the material my own. I also dug into the history of Allentown, primarily through the web resources provided by the town itself.

--The Red Church, or The Art of Pennsylvania German Braucherei, by C.R. Bilardi, 2009. (I did not get to this one. Just ordered it after I finished editing this.)

Davies, Owen. "The Nightmare Experience, Sleep Paralysis, and Witchcraft Accusations." Folklore 114, no. 2 (2003): 181–203.

Herr, Karl. Hex and Spellwork: The Magical Practices of the Pennsylvania Dutch. Red Wheel/Weiser, 2002.

Lanham, MD. Satan in America: The Devil We Know: Rowman & Littlefield Publishers, Inc., 2009.

New Castle News. "Grill Youth in Death of Girl." March 19, 1929.

Poole, W. Scott. Monsters in America: Our Historical Obsession with the Hideous and the Haunting. Waco, TX: Baylor University Press, 2011.

Rhone, George. "The Swamp Angel." Keystone Folklore

Quarterly 10, no. 2 (1965): 86–91.

Scheibel, Johann. The Sixth And Seventh Books Of Moses (Illustrated) . Global Grey. Kindle Edition. . Global Grey. , 2013.

Tinsley, M. Ferguson. "This Time, Zombie Land Tale is True." Pittsburgh Post-Gazette, October 31, 2003.

Tucker, Elizabeth. "Ghosts in Mirrors: Reflections of the Self." Journal of American Folklore, 118 (2005): 186–203.

MUSICAL SUGGESTIONS:

I listened to a few main soundtracks while working on this:

Andrews, Michael. *Donnie Darko* (Original Motion Picture Soundtrack)

Bensi, Danny, and Juriaans, Saunder. *Ozark* Seasons 1 & 2 (Original Soundtrack)

Blair, Brooke; and Blair, Will. *Blood On Her Name* (Original Motion Picture Soundtrack)

Blair, Brooke; and Blair, Will. *Nightstalker* (Original Motion Picture Soundtrack)

Blair, Brooke; and Blair, Will. *The Silencing* (Original Motion Picture Soundtrack)

Carpenter, John. *Lost Themes III: Alive After Death*

Carpenter, John; Carpenter Cody; & Davies, Daniel *Halloween Kills* (Original Motion Picture Soundtrack), 2021.

I returned to a few of these for the final edit/revision, but mainly listened to soundtracks from *Stranger Things*. In particular, I listened to the following over and over (from the song "Rats" onward, also skipping over "Tammie")

Dixon, Kyle and Stein, Michael. *Stranger Things 3* (Original Score from The Netflix Original Series)

I hope you enjoyed reading this as much as I enjoyed creating it.

I am eternally grateful for your friendship.

AFTERWORD

I hope you like this book. A combination of real-life events inspired the story and the character. Visit my website to read about them at:
https://peterjwhite.weebly.com/the-hollow-men.html

If you liked the book, please leave a reivew on Amazon. We indies rely on people like you to get the word out. Thank you!

Sign up for the Ghost Hunter Newsletter at
https://peterjwhite.weebly.com/news.html
to get the second book in the Ghost Hunter series: *Slouching Towards Tenancingo* for **FREE.** (And to be apprised of approaching publication dates, character info, interesting links and stories related to the series as well as free short stories and other bonuses. It's a win-win situation here. And how often do those come along? Go for it!)

To learn more about the five books in the Ghost Hunter series (number six is in progress) and other titles by the author, go to PeterJWhite.Weebly.com.

Other Books in the Ghost Hunter Series:

Ghost Hunter: The Hollow Men

Ghost Hunter: Slouching Toward Tenancingo

Ghost Hunter: Bangkok Redemption

Ghost Hunter: The Bad Beginning (prequel)

Ghost Hunter: What Lies Beneath

Horror

Ghosts of a Coven Past: A Tale of Witchcraft, Spirits, Satanism, and Possession

ABOUT THE AUTHOR

Peter J. White

Peter J. White was born in Colorado and raised in SE Alaska. He has degrees in Education, French, and an MFA in Creative Writing. He taught ELL in Bangkok, Thailand for six years, and currently teaches high school English in Washington State. Hobbies, past and present, include writing, bicycling, mountain climbing, kickboxing, MMA, and yoga.

BOOKS BY THIS AUTHOR

Ghost Hunter The Hollow Men: A Paranormal Vigilante Thriller

When the ghostly victims of a small-town crime lord find him, ex-special forces soldier Max Sinclair realizes the only road to peace is to serve them the justice they crave.

But the Bannister clan has tentacles that reach from Eastern Washington into Mexico, trafficking women across the border and into their brothels. Haunted by visions of the dead, Max burns a swath through the Bannister empire, doing his best to set the dead free, but odds are he'll be joining them before he's done.

The Hollow Men is the first novel in the Ghost Hunter series about a vigilante who sees the dead—Max Sinclair. Haunted by visions and longing for justice and redemption, Max hunts down evil incarnate—his soul hanging in the balance as he walks the line between the dark and the light.

"Jack Reacher meets The Sixth Sense. In Hostel."

"Peter J. White and his Ghost Hunter: The Hollow Men should be at the top of that list and profiled on library book recommendation lists as a standout." —D. Donovan, Senior Reviewer, Midwest Book Review/Editor, Donovan's Literary Services.

★ ★ ★ ★ ★ "Gripping and Timely Page Turner: From the first line, this tale grabs you and draws you in. Human trafficking is the dark side of our civilization, the modern, brutal form of slavery. Mr. White takes this subject on with a hard punch and a supernatural twist that keeps you on the edge of your seat."—Amazon Reader

★ ★ ★ ★ ★ "Exciting Read: Non-stop action in this thriller! Great character development in this book that is hard to put down. I am a big fan of Peter J. White!"—Amazon Reader

Ghost Hunter Slouching Toward Tenancingo: A Paranormal Vigilante Thriller

Max Sinclair is heading straight into the heart of evil: Tenancingo—center of the Mexican human trafficking industry. There's a man down there that's done someone he loves wrong, and Max aims at setting things straight.

On the way, he's accumulated some powerful enemies—of the cartel variety—and attracted the attention of the Black Queen: Mexico's most prominent priestess to Santa Muerte.

Hunted by the Queen, haunted by the dead, fueled by a fierce desire for justice, Max wages war against the evil that blackens the land. But with the Barrera cartel's five million dollar bounty on his head, odds are he won't make it to his final reckoning.

Slouching Toward Tenancingo is the second novel in the Ghost Hunter series about a vigilante who sees the dead—Max Sinclair. Haunted by visions and longing for justice and redemption, Max hunts down evil incarnate—his soul hanging in the balance as he walks the line between the dark and the light.

"Jack Reacher meets The Sixth Sense. In Hostel."

"Peter J. White and his Ghost Hunter: The Hollow Men should be at the top of that list and profiled on library book recommendation lists as a standout." —D. Donovan, Senior Reviewer, Midwest Book Review/Editor, Donovan's Literary Services.

★ ★ ★ ★ ★ "Gripping and Timely Page Turner: From the first line, this tale grabs you and draws you in. Human trafficking is the dark side of our civilization, the modern, brutal form of slavery. Mr. White takes this subject on with a hard punch and a supernatural twist that keeps you on the edge of your seat."—Amazon Reader

★ ★ ★ ★ ★ "Exciting Read: Non-stop action in this thriller! Great character development in this book that is hard to put down. I am a big fan of Peter J. White!"—Amazon Reader

Ghost Hunter Bangkok Redemption: A Paranormal Vigilante Thriller

Back in Thailand, Max Sinclair is hot on the trail of a Thai gangster who killed the one he loved. But when a street child he's befriended is snatched up by a ring of pedophiles, Max diverts his mission of vengeance to save her.

Max is thrust into a world of Black Magic, Spirit Doctors, human sacrifice, and The Ancient Ones: forces older than mankind who work to extinguish the light.

Meanwhile, he's stepped right in the middle of a power struggle between a Thai Mafia kingpin and his counterpart in the Russian Mafia.

Caught in the middle of a triangle of powers seeking to dominate

the land, Max doesn't stand a chance of surviving.
But he will not be denied, no matter the cost.

And maybe, along the way, he'll find the balance he seeks, and ultimately, redemption.

"Jack Reacher meets The Sixth Sense. In Hostel."

"Max is a completely compelling protagonist whose concerns and strengths are constantly tested by forces both human and supernatural, beyond his control, and the story's tension is nicely paced and developed.
The result will prove of special appeal to occult fiction readers who normally don't choose mysteries, as well as mystery readers who have been appreciating the budding new genre of paranormal mystery writing"—D. Donovan, Senior Reviewer, Midwest Book Review/Editor, Donovan's Literary Services.

★ ★ ★ ★ ★ "Gripping and Timely Page Turner: From the first line, this tale grabs you and draws you in. Human trafficking is the dark side of our civilization, the modern, brutal form of slavery. Mr. White takes this subject on with a hard punch and a supernatural twist that keeps you on the edge of your seat."—Amazon Reader

★ ★ ★ ★ ★ "Exciting Read: Non-stop action in this thriller! Great character development in this book that is hard to put down. I am a big fan of Peter J. White!"—Amazon Reader

The Ghost Of Ekamai Towers: The Door Opens

"The Ghost of Ekamai Towers" is a standalone short story fashioned from a segment in the upcoming novel: Ghost Hunter: The Bad Beginning, part of the Ghost Hunter series available December 2022 on Amazon, in time for Christmas!

In "The Ghost of Ekamai Towers," (and The Ghost Hunter series) Max Sinclair is a former special-forces soldier who resigned his commission to study Muay Thai in Pattaya City, Thailand. His trainer, Ong, puts him through a rigorous Yok Khru initiation supervised by a legendary Thai Buddhist monk, Phra Saksith. The training opens a door to the spirit world around us, nearly overwhelming Max.

"Jack Reacher meets The Sixth Sense. In Hostel."

"Peter J. White and his Ghost Hunter: The Hollow Men should be at the top of that list and profiled on library book recommendation lists as a standout." —D. Donovan, Senior Reviewer, Midwest Book Review/Editor, Donovan's Literary Services.

★ ★ ★ ★ ★ "Gripping and Timely Page Turner: From the first line, this tale grabs you and draws you in. Human trafficking is the dark side of our civilization, the modern, brutal form of slavery. Mr. White takes this subject on with a hard punch and a supernatural twist that keeps you on the edge of your seat."— Amazon Reader

★ ★ ★ ★ ★ "Exciting Read: Non-stop action in this thriller! Great character development in this book that is hard to put down. I am a big fan of Peter J. White!"—Amazon Reader

"Ghost" tells the story of Max's first encounter with this spirit world.
Follow Max's journey with the Ghost Hunter Series, available on Amazon.

"Jack Reacher meets The Sixth Sense. In Hostel."

"Peter J. White and his Ghost Hunter: The Hollow Men should

be at the top of that list and profiled on library book recommendation lists as a standout." —D. Donovan, Senior Reviewer, Midwest Book Review/Editor, Donovan's Literary Services.

★ ★ ★ ★ ★ "Gripping and Timely Page Turner: From the first line, this tale grabs you and draws you in. Human trafficking is the dark side of our civilization, the modern, brutal form of slavery. Mr. White takes this subject on with a hard punch and a supernatural twist that keeps you on the edge of your seat."—Amazon Reader

★ ★ ★ ★ ★ "Exciting Read: Non-stop action in this thriller! Great character development in this book that is hard to put down. I am a big fan of Peter J. White!"—Amazon Reader

READ ON FOR AN INTRODUCTION TO THE GHOST HUNTER SERIES

Ghost Hunter: The Hollow Men

Peter J. White

Between the essence
And the descent
Falls the Shadow
"The Hollow Men"
T.S. Eliot

Chapter One

Max killed the big Kawasaki Ninja.

A hot wind whistled, blowing sand and dust cross-wise. A tumbleweed the size of a large dog scratched its way across the road and into the desert.

He stepped up onto the old fashioned boardwalk, his boots clomping on the weathered wood, and made his way into Riker's Bar.

Inside, the room was dim and smoky, despite laws to the contrary.

A few scattered cowpoke-looking men sat at tables with varying amounts of empty beer bottles in front of them, three men at the bar.

No one looked.

Max strode to the bar and threw a leg over a stool.

"Bushmill's. Beer back," he said.

The bartender gave him a long look, nodded, and turned to serve up the drinks.

Max put his elbows on the bar and used the mirror to scope out the room.

Just as he thought.

He'd counted eight men at the assorted tables on his way in.

Now there were nine. And a woman in a red dress.

"A goddamn red dress," Max said. "Shit."

What the hell is it with dead women and red? Do women attracted to danger and bad men like red? Did their men dress them before they killed them?

"Excuse me?" said the bartender.

Max looked away from the mirror.

"Nothing," he said. "Thinking out loud."

The bartender gave him another look.

"I seen you before?" he asked.

"Doubt it," Max said. "Never been here."

"Huh," said the bartender, "I would've sworn...."

"I get that a lot," Max said. "Common type: Bald guy, goatee."

"Huh," said the bartender again.

Max looked around the bar: booths against the wall, tables scattered at the periphery of a dance floor, some pool tables and actual pinball machines in the back. Standard. He didn't imagine there was much need for anything to draw in customers: those who drank would come.

"Bar's been here a while?" Max said.

The bartender leaned back and crossed his arms.

"Yup. Big times here in the old days."

"It goes back that far? Oil boom days?"

"Yup. Black Callahan's place, originally."

Max frowned.

"Black Callahan. He the one that got himself hanged?"

Max scrutinized the man next to the woman in the red dress in the mirror.

Big fellow. Old-fashioned fancy, shirt with a string tie, black leather vest, cowboy hat. Jet black hair, beady eyes, five o-clock shadow like sandpaper on his face.

The man's gaze stayed fixed, riveted. Unnatural. He didn't move. Didn't blink.

Neither did the woman beside him.

She was a beauty. The red dress complimented her red hair. Fair skin, with a dusting of freckles. Bright eyes that never moved or blinked.

The couple looked as if they'd been captured in amber, a static holographic image.

The bartender stepped forward.

"You know the history?"

Max nodded.

"Heard of it."

The men in the room worked their drinks, their talk low.

The couple at the table shifted.

The big man's face colored and contorted, a mixture of rage and pain rippling across his features, bending them into the mask of a devil.

The woman's bright eyes bulged, and the top of her head dented in, blood and brain matter running down her pretty face.

"Killed her right here in this bar," the bartender said.

"Figured," said Max.

"Bashed her head in, that table over there." The bartender gestured at an empty table in the back. "With a hammer."

"Hmm," said Max. "Looks more like the butt of a pistol, to me."

"What?" said the bartender.

Max shook his head, looked away.

"Heard different. That's all."

Max picked up the shot of Bushmill's.

"Bottoms up."

He threw the shot back in a fluid motion, grimaced, picked up the short glass of beer and tossed that down on top of the whisky.

"Better," he said, wiping his lips with the back of his hand.

"You sure I ain't see ya before?" the bartender asked.

Max shook his head.

"I told you. I'm a common type, that's all."

The bartender's eyes didn't waver, "Nope. Something tells me there ain't nothing common about you at all. Not a thing."

Max's smile never touched his eyes.

"So I've been told," he said. "What do I owe you?"

He reached back to pull the wallet from his pocket, and the bartender jumped a little.

"Easy," said Max. "Just getting my wallet."

"Sorry," the bartender said. "Just feeling a little spooked, I guess. Been feeling that way since you come in."

Max met the bartender's gaze until the bartender turned to polish the glass in his hand.

"Yup," Max said. "Get that a lot."

He slipped a ten dollar bill out of his wallet and laid it on the bar.

"Keep the change," he said.

The bartender offered him a nervous smile in return. "Thanks," he said.

Max nodded, took a last look at the tableau in the mirror—the demonically twisted face on the big guy, the bulged eyes and brain matter on the face of the redhead—then turned to go.

Just eight men in the room.

"Right," Max said.

He eased the door closed behind him on the way out, pulled it shut.

Boots on the boardwalk and back to his motorcycle.

"Shit," he said. "Cannot get a break."

He threw a leg over the bike, kicked it off its stand and started it up.

"Seriously."

The bartender picked up Max's shot and beer glasses, carried them to the sink as the rumble of Max's motorcycle faded.

He spun quickly, shot a look at the room, relaxed a little, and turned back to the sink.

Chapter Two

Max read the sign as he flashed by.

Aston: Food. Gas. Rest.

Looked to be a town of a couple of hundred at best. Just another farm town slowly dying in the 21st century.

The sun was low against the rolling green hills, and Max figured this was his best bet for the night. He kicked the bike down into fifth, the 998cc engine howling, slowing the bike, fourth, third, then eased the bike off the main road into the town.

Simple but surprisingly wide Main Street for such a small town.

One with an active city council: lots of potted plants and floral arrangements hanging from hooks with well-kept wooden signs welcoming one to town.

In the dusk, the flowers looked black, the words on the sign a ghostly white glow.

Just off Main Street, a motel. Classic sixties model: two story, doors painted different colors, white with blue trim.

Max wheeled his bike into the spot in front of the office, dismounted, stuck his helmet on the mirror and clomped in.

An old farmer type was sitting in a chair behind the desk watching some reality show, hands clasped on his big belly. He raised an eyebrow at Max.

"Room?" said Max.

The old guy laughed.

"You got your pick," he said. "Got a trucker in 207, back corner there. That's it."

Max nodded.

"How about the other top corner, then?"

"That'd put you right on Main Street," the old guy said.

Max looked out the window at the empty street.

"Wouldn't say traffic was a problem," Max said.

The old guy laughed again.

"Well, I suppose you got that right," he said. "Name's Slim."

Max's lips turned up a bit.

The old guy laughed.

"One of those opposite things. Never was. Slim, that is."

"How much for the room?"

"Thirty bucks a night'll do."

Max took another look around.

"You have a busy season around here?"

"No, not hardly," said Slim. "Got the Onion Fest in April. Fourth of July. Labor Day. Occasionally a group of farm workers come into town for a big night. Like that."

Max pulled out $30 in cash and laid it on the counter.

The old guy groaned and hoisted himself out of his chair to shuffle down the counter and grab a form.

"Fill this out," he said.

"That room got any history?"

"History?"

"History. As in suicide, murder, any kind of unpleasant death. Like that."

Slim gave Max a long look.

"No, I don't believe it does. That matter to you?"
Max nodded.
"It does. I'm...sensitive that way."
Slim's face lit up.
"You like, one of them whatchamacall'ems? Mediums?"
Max did not smile.
"Just sensitive. Key?"
Slim sighed and reached under the counter and came up with a key with a room tag labeled 201.
"Not much of a talker, are ya?" Slim asked.
Max shook his head.
"Don't generally have a lot to say. Thanks for the room."
Max palmed the key and slid out of the office.

Slim watched Max fire up his motorcycle and move it to the space under his room. He was a little pissed the guy didn't want to talk. A medium, or whatever. That was interesting. Come morning, he'd bet the traveler would have something to say.

Max climbed the stairs, stuck his key in the door, and disappeared inside.

Chapter Three

The room smelled like mold. Musty, unused. Queen-sized bed, little TV mounted in the corner across from the bed. Tiny bathroom.

A sense of the surreal settled on Max, the objects and walls of the room taking on a dull shine. His olfactory sense clicked up a few notches, something ephemeral and unreal awakening atavistic survival mechanisms.

Max sniffed.

Dirt. Freshly turned earth. The smell blossomed and turned putrid. Like a rendering truck passing by on a broiling summer day.

Ah, God, Max thought. I asked him, too.

Max looked in the mirror over the bureau and sure enough—there she was in the bed. Wasn't a lot to look at in life, Max figured, and death hadn't improved anything.

Bruises discolored her cheek bones. She had one split eyebrow, a broken nose, a fat lip, and her jaw hung loose. And that was what Max could see without trying.

Her neck was canted at an unnatural angle. Cause of death, Max decided.

"God damn it."

Back in the office, Slim protested.

"I"m telling ya, mister. Never heard of anything like that."

There was a glint of malice and delight in his eye that Max didn't like at all.

"Give me a ground floor room. Right in the middle." Max surveyed the motel, opening himself a tiny bit.

He regretted it instantly. Misery echoed through the courtyard, reached all the way into the office. A lot of unpleasantness had gone down in this motel.

Max considered getting his money back and heading up the road a piece, but figured it'd take him a couple more hours to come to a place with a decent motel, and he didn't want to sleep out in the open. He wanted a bed. Untroubled sleep.

That seemed out of the question here, though. He might get some sleep, but it was certain to be troubled.

"Ah, the hell with it," Max said. "That one."

The room with the purple door, dead center on the ground floor, felt the least troubled.

Slim reached back under the counter, came up with a key.

The setting sun glinted off the key, and just for a flash—reflected red in Slim's pupils.

Room 113 had a similar musty smell to 207. Max braced himself and waited, but nothing else came…just a musty room. With mold.

Max stood with his back to the door and took in the room in the reddening light of sunset. Same as 207. Through the darkening gloam, Max checked the mirror. It reflected the same view his eyes saw.

"OK, then," Max said.

He stepped away from the door, turned and closed the curtains, then turned on the overhead light.

So far, so good.

Bathroom. A surprising number of deaths occur in the bathroom.

The bathroom was pleasantly clean. A touch of mildew spoke through the smell of bleach, but nothing else. The mirror reflected the whole room, and both were empty of visions, ghosts, or views into the world of the dead.

Max reached over and slid the shower curtain back. Sparkling clean tub and fixtures. Looked over his shoulder at the mirror. All sparkle and clean.

"Thank God," Max sighed.

He went back to the bedroom, and started unpacking his saddlebags.

Lying in bed, fingers interlaced behind his head, Max stared at the ceiling.
Thailand, he thought. That's what kicked it all off. Fresh off the teams, there to train Muay Thai. The place was steeped in spirit lore, animism, dark practices, open debauchery, institutional corruption—absolutely chock a block with dark and dangerous entities.

And yet…there was a sweetness and docility to the people, a nobility and a grace that counter-balanced all the negative.

The Muay Thai camp he'd gone there for was superlative. Run by an old Thai boxer, Ong, who'd been a legend—one of the first to open his camp to foreigners—it taught the discipline with no frills, just a strict adherence to time-honored methods that produced some of the best fighters in the world.

It'd started so well…

Max shook his head at himself.
Nostalgia. Bullshit.

Yeah, the first year was solid, and the second started well. By then he was taking on fights against real Thai fighters and holding his own. Even had a girlfriend—a spectacular beauty with a mean left hook.

Max fingered the ropy scar tissue bristling through his eyebrows.

He'd been cut by elbows, pounded by kicks, dropped by flying knees, but he'd stood his ground and earned respect.

The gym owner, Ong, had taken him on. For real. Old school stuff—as serious about the spiritual aspect as the physical. Meditation and morning prayers at the temple.

And then....

The dark side had opened up.

Hookers a dime a dozen.

And...the night that cracked it all wide open.

Max blinked, remembering.

A door had opened in his head. A door there was no shutting, or at least, no shutting all the way.

Since then, Max was constantly leaning against that door, leaning hard, but it always stayed a crack open. He could step back and let it swing wide at any time, but that was never good.

Too much misery behind that door. Too much death.

The bed was surprisingly comfortable, and Max's eyes grew heavy. He let sleep take him.

The slap of flesh on flesh startled Max awake.

The hell?

He sat upright, his whole body tense, listening with his nerve endings and his ears.

Slap. A thump of something hitting the wall.

The room next door.

Max got up and padded to the window, cracked open the curtains, and peeked out into the parking lot.

Empty. Just the trucker's rig off to the side, his motorcycle in front of his room and a lot of empty space.

The light in the manager's office was on, but no one occupied the chair behind the desk.

Moaning. A scream cut off...

Max opened himself a tiny, tiny bit...

Red blossomed inside his head: blood on walls, blood on the bed, blood on the mirror, blood on the floor. Blood. The room next door drowning in it.

What the hell is this place?

Max slid to the door, opened it carefully, slipped through and over to the window of the room next door.

The curtains were open, the same bloody tableau he'd had splashed inside his head on view.

Max backed away from the window and let the door in his head open a notch—that shimmery sense of the unreal silvering his view.

He spun a quiet 360, arms out.

Waves of misery and pain radiated from every room of the hotel.

Women had died here. Lots of them. All of them nasty, brutal deaths. Images of brutish sex flooded Max's mind. Men using their fists and their sex as weapons. An ugly, savage current of emotion swept through him, almost carried him away.

Max leaned back against the door in his head and held it as shut as he could.